THE SPACE BETWEEN

JP RODRIGUEZ

darkstar fiction

Cover design by Emma Dolan

We acknowledge the support of the Canada Council for the Arts
for our publishing program. We acknowledge the financial support
of the Government of Canada through the Book Publishing Industry
Development Program (BPIDP) for our publishing activities.

Darkstar Fiction
an imprint of Napoleon & Company
Toronto, Ontario, Canada
www.napoleonandcompany.com

13 12 11 10 09   5 4 3 2 1

Library and Archives Canada Cataloguing in Publication

Rodriguez, J. P., 1973-
        The space between / J.P. Rodriguez.

ISBN 978-1-894917-88-9

        I. Title.

PS8635.O3745S63 2009   C813'.6   C2009-904808-6

For Kirsti

Obviously

"It's not what you see that is art. Art is the gap."
-Marcel Duchamp

LAND

FOG

Left to stare out the window long enough, all human minds inevitably drift toward their own demise. And I've certainly been staring out the window long enough. My gaze hangs heavy like the pendulum of a stopped clock, but my mind is unsettled as the thoughts in my head flutter and spin like the tumult of blowing snow on the other side of the glass. I sit here warm in the eye of the storm though, and in my head's tempest there's also a calm centre now, a sphere of stillness. I sense its influence spreading as each turbulent stream of thought that flows into it is allayed and subsumed. A blizzard like this is a call to arms for the human psyche, a sanity inspection. I've nothing to fear.

But it makes you wonder—what could there be behind these walls around and within us? Forcing my mind beyond all its constraints of words and images, I end up in absurd dreams and wishful thinking, but never anywhere I can call home. Though I may ultimately fail in answering this question in a manner acceptable to myself, I have come up with some frightfully disturbing ideas.

Such as: Imagine our minds, released from their bodily anchors, continuing to exist, free at last to float through the ether of forever—but don't get too comfortable, for this is no pleasure float—our minds retain their impressions of pain. In fact, they're stuck on a repeat cycle whereby they perpetuate for eternity the last sensation registered before leaving their bodies.

Imagine your newly liberated mind, an immutable sounding board for the echoes of pain from the bones that shattered upon impact with the tractor-trailer that crushed your body and your car…or the knife that sliced your jugular just before the rapist discarded you…or the electricity that gorged on your organs as the chair attempted to make two wrongs equal a right.

What if our minds continue on in an everlasting state of pain? Far-fetched, sure, but prove me wrong. It's a theory that's ultimately as possible as any other concept of life after death, and it's a sobering thought, one that could keep you awake at night, if the subject of death itself doesn't already.

As I said, I've been staring out the window awhile. Forgive me.

This bus and us passengers, we're stuck, stranded in the middle of the frozen windswept wasteland that is the Saskatchewan prairie, and other than the millions of miles a minute at which we hurtle through space, we're going nowhere. The snow's been whipping around relentlessly for well on eight hours now, and I feel like we're being blended up for flavouring in a colossal metallic milkshake—for whom is anyone's guess. At times during the Canadian winter, human will and perseverance must take a back seat while old mother nature drives all over the road, drunk. I for one appreciate and cherish this aspect of my country's climate. Like a touch of insanity in a person, it spawns intrigue and impetus. And I'm always happy to oblige any circumstance that puts us human beings in our rightful place.

The snow has taken with it all traces of the world without and left us little choice other than to focus on what's within. Travel companions have expanded beyond their pairings, and complete strangers who would normally turn their eyes from each other on the street are becoming fast friends. Perhaps this is what the world needs: to be locked for an indeterminate

amount of time in a steel and plush metal tube going nowhere fast
and rancid faster. There's probably a statute of limitations on how
long the camaraderie will last though. Your opinion on this will
depend on the colour of your armband in the battle of the good
versus evil natural state of man, but it really doesn't concern me. I
know I'll be able to hold out—time is beyond me now.

The only immediate problem to speak of really is that we
can't get off the bus for a cigarette. No one is allowed off—for
insurance purposes, the driver tells us. Maybe I should have
gone with my original plan and taken the train, but there's no
guarantee that it would have been able to make it through this
storm either. I must give credit where it's due and state that this is
one prize-fighting, top of the charts, no-holds-barred Canadian
winter blizzard—one for the books. Even the proverbial black
eyes of the polar bear are shut. It's pretending to hibernate.

"Hey, *Maple Leafs*," I hear from close behind. I tense up.
I happen to be wearing a Toronto Maple Leafs hockey cap, a
calculated attempt to hide my eyes and blend in at the same
time (I won it at a pub quiz night and have never worn it
before). So, assuming it's something to do with me, I look back
and see a tall, ruddy blond, full beard brewing, standing half-up
in his chair and trying to catch my attention. Low-slung black
bags prop up deep-set eyes that require no such help expressing
their weariness.

"The Canucks are good too," I try, and the guy laughs.

"Wanna drink?" he mouths.

Is it that obvious? I furrow my brows in an exaggerated
expression of gravity and nod decisively—for a drink, I'll risk a
conversation.

He motions to the empty seat beside him, and I waste no
time in following the directions. A polished flask is thrust at me,
the sort you see in airport gift shops the world over but never
actually see anyone using. I take it and shake his hand, thanking
him gratefully.

"I'm Iain," he tells me, and I take a small sip of what turns out to be decent Scotch.

"Thanks, Iain. You're a mind reader." I offer the Scotch back to him, but he motions for me to pass it to the woman sitting directly across the aisle. She accepts it as graciously as I did.

"This is pretty crazy, eh?" he says. I agree with him, and he asks me where I'm going. I tell him Vancouver. "Me too," he says. "I just got back from Japan."

Thankful that he wants to talk about himself, I egg him on. "Really?"

"Took the long way home, the longest way really. The Trans-Siberian train then a freighter from Liverpool to Boston." He keeps his eyes steady on me while he speaks, as though I'm a fish on the line. And I guess I am.

"Wow," I offer, along with raised eyebrows and a sideways glance at the flask in the woman's lap. She's staring at it, her finger caressing the chrome, a carnal trance. She notices me looking and smiles.

"You wouldn't believe it if I told you how many carbon emissions this frees me from the guilt of," Iain continues. "I could drive a Hummer for the rest of my life and still be in the black. And it's always nice to check out the prairies, make sure they're still flat."

"Hard to tell at the moment."

"Got that right. This is insane!"

"Teaching English over there?"

The woman hands back the Scotch, and I pass it over to Iain. He little more than wets his lips with it then returns it to me.

"Three years," he says, shifting in his seat so that he's now sitting closer to me.

In turn I resettle myself, restoring the original distance between us. "All finished?"

"For now, anyway. I was going to stay longer, but I got bored. Needed a change, you know?"

"Yep." And I do. That feeling tends to show up at my door faster than for most people. I also taught in Japan. Two and a half years. Longer than I've lived anywhere since. I tell him this, and he looks happy to hear it.

"Small world, eh? Where were you?"

"Tokyo...well, Yokohama really, but it's all one city."

"I was in Aomori."

I hesitate, wanting to go back to my seat, but wanting another pull of Scotch even more. And this conversation's innocuous enough. Maybe it won't hurt to give an inch. "I wanted a small town too. Messed up my application though."

"What do you mean?"

"Well, they had all the prefectures listed on the application, and all I knew was I wanted a reasonably small town near the ocean or mountains. A friend had lived there for four years, and he told me he'd been in Kanazawa, and it would be perfect for me. When I looked on the application, I saw Kanagawa and just assumed they must pronounce their Gs like Zs."

Iain laughs. "No!"

This feels surreal. It's been two weeks since I've shared half as many words with anyone. He's still laughing, nodding in knowing appreciation, and I can almost fool myself into believing I miss this. "Instead of lonely hikes to misty mountain temples, I ended up in the busiest place on earth."

He laughs some more, looks at the blank out the window, and it seems to give him an idea. "So what now?" he says.

Suddenly my brain catches up to my gut, and I realize this was a mistake. Better never than late. "Well, if you have more booze..."

"No, I mean what does your future hold."

He's staring at me intently, and I get the oddest sensation somehow that he's on to me. I know he can't be. Not possible. But now my heart's speeding up in the way it tends to lately, and I fight to control the tremors, reign in my breathing. "Well I—" I try but

am blank. Damn it! Where are the answers I rehearsed? Where?
All I can do is start coughing, pretending to have caught
on my words. Holding my throat, I get up and motion to the
bathroom, head toward it. I look at the woman, and she opens
her narrow mouth as if to say something finally, but the white
out the window pulls her words away, and she turns to see
where they went.

~~~~~

I've never met anyone else who can remember the moment
they were born. I can: It's hazy and distant, indescribable, but I
remember seeing light for the first time. I suppose the memory
of the power of that event has left me searching for something
that will equal it, demystify it. Or, maybe, *re*-mystify it. Perhaps
only the end of the story will.

Something, maybe, to do with truth, moments of it,
moments of cold hard reality, of connection, of definition and
delineation in something other than sand.

The way I see it, we westernised (modern?) humans are
overfed and under-stimulated, overworked and under-joyed,
manoeuvring our characters in an attempt to rack up points
in a game few of us understand, and even fewer of us want to
be playing, let alone selling our souls to win. The majority of
our emotions are second hand, and most things that affect our
lives on a daily basis do so on nothing more than an illusory
level. At the end of most days we've come no closer to knowing
ourselves. We watch the hero in the movie getting tortured
and beaten, the bad guys trying to get some answer out of
him, and we cheer as he refuses to give in and takes death over
dishonour, but would or will you act this way? Do any of us
really know how we'll react when the gun is pointed at our
heads for real?

Maybe the point is that we don't want to know the

answer, regardless of what it is. Is this why so many behave so inexplicably, so selfishly, humming to block out the song? We stare enthralled at the face in the mirror, loathe to face the unknown behind it.

Or maybe there is no answer.

~~~~~

I try to know you, but you won't let it happen.
I try to know myself, but I'm full of surprises.

~~~~~

The snow's still blowing, and the bus is still locked in place, but me, well, I'm getting there, and you're helping me—thank you. This gut sense of what I have to do is growing clearer and more complete. I will admit that in my head it's still ill-formed, but that's what this whole journey is about, that age-old battle of Apollo and Dionysius, sense verses intellect, passion versus reason. But this is not technically a battle so much as a peace negotiation, and for the first time in my life I'm confident that one will be reconciled with the other before too long at all.

You know how they say the journey is the destination? In my case, *this* case, well, that's somewhat true, but it's more true that if I fail to achieve my destination on this journey, all these miles and all these minutes, everything I've thrown away and everything I've taken, all will be for naught. But, I promise you, I intend to do all in my considerable power to get there—for you, for her, for him and me, and for everyone else. And then, *then*, well, we'll see, you and me.

Tokyo, Japan: My Past
The light of December's low-slung daytime sun seems artificial

and contrived here—the blinking neon brightness of night
better illuminates the essences of Shinjuku. But regardless of
the stage lighting, there are the usual hordes of people upon
the boards. The separate and distinct bodies flow past me,
parting and converging like the waters of a river flowing round
a stone, a connection made then instantly lost, the attraction
too weak to overcome the current of time, but leaving its mark
all the same. As they brush by, they fill me with excitement that
builds and builds like a static charge. It suddenly snaps, and I'm
ecstatic. Lost in the masses, I'm seized by my selfhood.

But my euphoria, as ever, is ephemeral. I begin to notice:
owners out walking their expensive shoes and hats. Sharp and
shiny product bags hung proudly from shoulders like medals
of honour. Small packages of tissue free to anyone willing to be
sold on something. It's all prosperity here.

Or that's how it can seem if you don't take the time to look
past it. If you can see through all the designer purses and ties
tied too tightly, you'll notice the youth, defiantly strutting
their stuff in their pursuit of the moment and the deciduous
pleasures of the callow age. Beyond them you'll find the lives
that have been left behind, caught up in the shuffle, wrapped
up neatly in wood-framed cubicles of blue tarpaulin and
cardboard, Pandora's boxes of misplaced dreams and a society's
broken promises. There are too many.

But my friend Yosuke, currently having trouble controlling
his desire to fall on the ground laughing at the jokes God
is telling only him, is oblivious. You see, due to the time
constraints of his job, a real vacation is an impossibility, so I've
accompanied him on this, his virgin excursion to purchase
mushrooms, which he'll use in lieu of the unattainable tropical
beach. But originally scheduled to leave tomorrow, he's decided
to seize the moment and hop aboard today, here and now—
even though he knows I'm going to have to abandon him and
go teach my evening lessons in two hours.

As we walk past the vendors of cheap steel jewellery and even cheaper steelier watches, I'm overcome by a chill and the need to relieve myself of the few beers I had earlier. We're approaching the Mitsukoshi department store, and I decide it's my best hope for relief. "Yosuke, I need to find a washroom, okay?" I try my best to empty my communication of any and all humour.

"Yeah, yeah, whatever. I like to find somewhere to...*eto... dame!*" he blurts out.

As I step through the doors, the commingling fumes of expensive scents ram themselves up my nose, and I quickly deduce the laws of the dimension I've slipped into. Clearly, there are harsh penalties to be paid by souls daring to cavort in cloth coloured other than brown, black, or grey and stitched together by any designer whose embroidered initials alone do not raise the value of the fabric at least a hundredfold. I'm in trouble. In law and order, ignorance is no defence, and other than myself, there's no one (not even Yosuke, thankfully) who dares disobey. Other than me.

Even if I'm not on them myself, I stand out like a sore thumb on mushrooms. Here I am, a tall white foreigner in an upscale department store, in perhaps the most fashion-conscious country in the world, in the cosmetics section no less, everyone in death-tones, and me wearing a red fleece pullover, jeans, long hair and old Docs. I couldn't blend in if I had a crack team of graffiti artists armed with an arsenal of grey spray paint. I try anyway.

Of course, Yosuke, being Japanese and a part of all this—and stoned—is having fun travelling around inside his own head, mindless of this madness. I'm happy for that. Prompted by him bumping into me, I continue toward the unseen goal. The few signs I see are all in Kanji and lack any sort of recognizable washroom symbol. Yosuke, stumbling around behind me like a dumb dog, is no help. The more I think about having to go, the more I have to go. There's one thing that will definitely render my blending attempts totally useless, and that could happen if I don't remain focussed.

"Yosuke. Yosuke, listen, I really have to find the washroom, okay? Where the hell is it?"

"Hell? Ho-oo, what is that?" he exclaims, and laughs.

"Toire...Toire ga doko desu ka," I say with mocking condescension. In response to my attempt to speak his language, he laughs even harder, so I grab his shoulders, turn him around, and force him to walk in front of me, as though I've a gun to his back.

I'm scanning the far walls for toilet signs when he suddenly turns and latches onto me, saying something I can't understand and giggling like a drunk schoolgirl. Looking around to divine the reason for his actions, I see that we've inadvertently walked into the clearing of a mini fashion show. I try my best to meld into the crowd encircling the show and finally push through to the other side, generously giving the spotlight back to the models.

I pause for a moment and catch a vision of one of the girls— her makeup caked on in the manner suitable for television cameras but so monstrous when seen before your eyes. What a perfect modern statement: reality must now bend to reflect television. A tacky impasto portrait of herself; all traces of her messy human biology are coloured over and hidden. She hasn't the slightest hint of a smile on her face, or her soul. Her eyes seem to reach out to be rescued. I turn away quickly.

Yosuke is up ahead, standing under the glorious pastel pink and blue colours of the toilet signs. At last! Grinning from ear to ear with tears streaming down his face, he gives me a huge hug, as though we're the only members of the platoon to make it to the Hewie. You have to love the squishy id-like innocence of people on mushrooms

After finishing my business, I bang on Yosuke's door and tell him I'll be waiting outside. I find a bench full of waiting husbands just outside the washroom entrance, and as I rest my legs, my attention is pulled to the plastic-like saleswoman showing a customer various products, handling them like a priest holding the Eucharist. I'm enthralled, as is the young woman, who appears literally in awe of each miracle product she is shown. I try my best not to stare, but the full force of what I'm witnessing is coming to bear: No alternative. The ubiquitous religion. The commandments plastered on every building, bus, banana label, and any other square inch of sellable space.

I look down at my Doc Martens and see that there is no hope. But I close my eyes and make a vow anyway: I will not fall prey to this dismal, mind-numbing religion.

A moment later Yosuke comes out, and after this brief moment of clarity, we merge once again with the masses.

~~~~~

As I sit here going nowhere, I'm forlorn. Modern human society seems to have advanced to a state where our individual brains can no longer decipher it. We've outwitted our own adaptation. In terms of the collective human intellect, the whole is *less* than the sum of the parts.

ANCHORS

I awaken from my daze awash in the stale smell of fresh
smoker's breath and notice the contented air of the upper-
middle-aged man settling back into his seat diagonally behind
me, his face etched with the expression of someone impressed
with his own genius and cunning. He notices me and hands
me a self-satisfied grin, his glowing eyes beaming behind their
glasses. He flicks his head a couple of times in the direction
of the washroom. I twist to look down the aisle to the rear of
the bus then back at him. He gives me a conspiratorial look of
encouragement.

So I fish around in my bag for my package of cigarettes and
get up from my seat, swing out into the aisle, and give him
a thumbs-up on my way past. As I approach the door to the
washroom, the young girl sitting in the last row gives me a
knowing look and wink. I slip inside, closing the door quickly
behind me. I've never felt more a part of a team.

It's cold in here. The window has been left open, so only a
whisper of cigarette scent lingers, easily overpowered by the
stench of the chemical toilet trying unsuccessfully to cope
with the human waste being forced down its throat. Particles
of snow whip in, linger and disappear. I sit on the tiny toilet
and light up, partaking in the frigid air of contentment. As I
sit smoking and smiling and freezing, I worry a bit about the
other passengers. It's admirable that this older man is willing to

break the rules, but visions of Piggy and Ralph and commanding conches fill my head. Will these people hold out? The group solidarity seems strong so far, but if this lasts much longer, I can picture some of the more desperate smokers staging a mutiny and turning this into a smoking bus. I hope things remain civil and calm, but something much closer to my core longs for revolt. Regardless of what transpires, though, I promise you one thing: It's going to take a lot more than a gunless putsch on a stranded bus to prevent me from completing this masterpiece for you.

Some people sleep, some play cards, and many read, while a few simply stare at the two dimensional whiteness of the window. Which makes me think of the roll of toilet paper you're supposed to picture if you want to clear your mind. I never could do that. What works for me to some extent is semantic satiation: Pick a common word and say it fifty, or a hundred times in a row quickly:

HELLO HELLO HELLO HELLO HELLO HELLO HELLO
HE LO HE LO HE LO HE LO HE LO HE LO HE LO HE LO
HELL O HELL O HELL O HELL O HELL O HELL O HELL O
HELL O HELL O HELL O HELL O HELL O HELL O HELL.

The sounds are familiar but disjointed; their connection to a meaning is severed. You are without language. You are free. It's the exact opposite of those Magic Eye Stereograms, where you stare at the pattern long enough, and eventually a 3D image jumps out at you—the chaos becomes ordered. With the hello exercise, the order becomes chaos.

This principle is often used in meditation to clear and focus the mind. Maybe this is what we all need, some means of putting our beliefs through semantic satiation. Maybe we could get past the old structures, the blinders, and see some truth, some universals. I'll have to work on the logistics of this one.

And just like that, there's cause for celebration on the bus. On this, the fourteenth hour of our ordeal, the compassionate bus driver has just informed us that the storm is far from over. This is not the cause of most people's joy. It's what he said after that that got us excited:

"Now folks, I want to thank you for being so patient and hospitable with each other, and I hope we can keep it up for however long this storm lasts—"

"We'll give you two more hours!" calls out Iain, and everyone laughs.

"*So, ne!*" I add in Japanese for his benefit, then feel instantly stupid. He replies with something I can't make out.

The driver waits for everyone to stop, then carries on without comment. "And toward that end, you know how they say it's cruel to keep a prisoner in jail without telling them how long they'll be in there? Well, you're in here, and I think the same applies to keeping a smoker from smoking. So, in order to ensure the ongoing safety of the passengers, I've decided that, insurance be damned, it's safer to let the smokers out for a cigarette than to risk having them turn into raving lunatics from lack of nicotine. Just ask the Missus. Since this is the situation we're in, all people who want to be let out for a smoke go ahead and line up at the door. Let's all step out quickly and let in as little cold air as we can."

The longwinded announcement has made many people's day—not that that's a tall order. I'm not going to miss this chance to go outside. I might as well have a smoke too. Along with me, about half the other passengers are willing to take the driver up on his magnanimous offer.

The young girl sitting across from me asks if she can bum a smoke. I wouldn't have taken her for a smoker, but anything

to break the monotony I guess. I hand one to her and in return
receive the faintest hint of thanks from her face, but no words.
It's a captivating face, familiar somehow. I make up my mind
to try and talk to her, but not now. I've been handed a mission.
Well, a sub-mission.

Having donned every ounce of material we have for battle
against the madness outside, our excited horde marches quickly
toward the door. I'm toward the end of the procession and can
hear the men on the front lines groaning as they step out into
the frenzy. As I lurch into the blackness, fine particles of snow
blow past me, and I imagine I'm zooming through the starscape
of space. It hits me just how long I've been deprived a sense of
movement, advancement through anything other than time. It's
disconcerting.

Usually the temperature will rise when snow falls, but not
this time. The wind stings my face, and I'm forced to stare at the
ground through eyelashes embracing one another. It blows right
through my layers of clothing as though they're not there, and
I question the brightness of this decision. Why do I smoke? For
something to do, I suppose. It's not an everyday thing for me, but it
is a thing. I pull out my lighter and, like an amateur contortionist,
try to get inside the front of my jacket to block the wind from the
flame long enough to light up. At last I see it take, and I feel the
smooth warm smoke enter my lungs and fill me with unhealthy
pleasure. It's too cold and loud for anyone to talk, so we're a silent,
huddled mass, standing strong against the weather.

I'm one of the first back inside, and walking down the aisle,
I feel the other passengers' thoughts: "What an idiot! All that
just to kill yourself." I remove my coat and resume my post.
Through the window I can just make out the fuzzy forms of
those stronger than me still outside. Seconds later the last of
them come in with the blowing snow stuck to their clothing, like
white noise, and I think of our group: the few, the fit, the proud.
The smokers.

The pleasure of smoking is about more than the nicotine, much more. Lighting up a cigarette is a *start,* and is there anything more invigorating and inspiring than the *beginning* of something, the opening bell, that moment at which everything lies in the future and nothing in the past, nothing to lament or long for? It's the same as sitting down at the bar and having the first pint of the night placed onto the crisp and dry cardboard coaster in front of you, the head dripping down the side, the glass as full as it gets. I think for chain smokers *this* is the addiction, the power to generate one fresh start after another.

I'm suddenly acutely aware of how I'm now past the start of this undefined work of art I'm feeling my way into. The flame has caught, smoke is rising, and I'm happy for it. I am potent and affecting change (even if only with butterfly wings at this point). I allow no thought of sadness and take refuge in the hope that I do the morally "high" thing. History will never be the same. It has begun and it feels right; it almost thinks right— Apollo and Dionysius have agreed to put their weapons down and talk.

I do, though, admit to a sense of homesickness knowing that my last days in Canada are dwindling. *Last days.* What heavy, desolate words. I'll miss it, of course I will, but that won't last long—it's not my home any more; I no longer have one. I have transcended such humble concepts: I am universal.

It's been two weeks since I died.

An eternity.

There's an intriguing atmosphere on a bus in the middle of the night when the other thirty or forty people around you are sleeping. Even though we're all strangers, I feel comforted by their presence—friendship in proximity and strength in numbers perhaps. As I watch the girl across from me sleeping, I'm mesmerized by the rise and fall of her chest and the way her breath creates a foggy bloom on the cold window that gains and concedes ground with each exhalation. I wonder about her family, her loved ones. Is she well taken care of? Are there plenty of people who love her? Or is she alone? Is she one of the many wandering souls on this planet of ours, unable to find anything sticky enough to hold them in place? Can she make it alone?

What would it feel like to let her rest her head on my lap as she slept, run my fingers through her hair?

Who's waiting for her at the end of the bus ride? Who's waiting for her at the end of the line? At the end?

Who's waiting for me?

RUDDERLESS

Three a.m. brings with it the nineteenth hour of our entrapment. In a way, I hope we never leave, that the storm never ends. How much easier that would be.

It'll be interesting to study the personality shifts in my fellow passengers as the time that we're trapped becomes a larger and larger percentage of our life spans. How much longer will it be before the skirmishes start to take shape? I dare say it's been disappointing so far—not even so much as a sideways glance.

For the time being I'll have to settle for entertaining myself by massaging my lower left leg, which has fallen asleep. Isn't it amazing how the combination of a little pressure and time can render a limb completely immune to torture?

~~~~~

Fine, you've seen *The Matrix*, but I think this warrants deeper consideration, since they missed the whole point in that damn movie. Okay, it was a good movie, but also a wasted opportunity, though the "humans are a cancer'" concept was brilliant and unapologetically undefeatable. Descartes, considering what he could know for certain, famously decided to throw away all knowledge derived from his untrustworthy senses, because maybe "God", instead of going through all the trouble of making the universe to see how humans would behave, simply made a computer and a brain, hooked them up to one another, then left them alone together for a while to provide him with answers; deception is infinitely easier to create than reality, and it sits well in regard to old Occam's razor. So maybe you are indeed the only human that exists, and this story is nothing more than a computer program—He or She wants to see what you'll do when faced with the truth about your ontology. Maybe He or She is trying to plant the seed, so it won't be such a shock when you're finally let in on the truth.

Whatever you may get out of this whole concept, the lesson for me is that you and I and her and him can never know anything with absolute certainty, because for all we know, not only is the sun not coming up tomorrow, it never *has* come up. I take knowledge with a grain of salt: probably true, but maybe not. Physics, that most profound of the sciences, has shown that we can never know for certain what is; we can only know what *probably* is.

So where the hell does this leave me? You? How do we know how to act? Or why to act?

~~~~~

I remember, when school was only half a day long and more learning was done outside of it than in, my friend Joel and I would cruise around the neighbourhood on our little bikes, surveying our land. The highlight would always be when the mailman came around, and we'd ask him for elastics. He'd give us a hard time at first, but in the end he always gave in. To this day I can't remember what we did with our elastics, though I imagine they served as projectiles of some sort. Every day that summer, for what seems like a lifetime now, we would engage that man thus. He was always very businesslike and formal with us, but he had kindness in his eyes, and I knew he enjoyed the game. We were thankful to him for dealing with us as though we were adults, and I can just imagine how he must have felt to play a part in the vagaries of youth. Unfortunately, this happy routine was disrupted when my father was transferred to Ecuador and dragged my mother and me there with him. Kicking and screaming.

We lived in Quito for two years, a long time for a young boy, particularly a discontented one. My dad had always spoken to me in Spanish, so there was no language barrier to speak of, but regardless, I made no friends. "They don't just grow on trees," he would tell me. "You've got to be proactive." Whatever that meant. I remember two interminable years of feeling either invisible or on stage, and wanting desperately to be back in my mountains. My mother felt the same. She used to tell me everyday how the brutal heat was killing her. I was never sure how much time she had left.

At last, when I was eight my dream of returning to Canada came true, though not on the terms I'd wished for—the family returned one person lighter, one father figure lighter to be exact. My dad. *My dad.* He was gone. At that age I couldn't understand it and of course blamed my mother—who else could possibly be at fault? But I didn't hold a grudge long, because after all, *she* was there for me. Where was he? We never saw him again. He might as well have died, and after a while that's how I treated it. I realized nothing lasts, certainly nothing good, but probably nothing at all.

From that time on I had great difficulty trusting anyone or anything. I became hypercritical and analytical. I wanted to understand. Everything. It was a consuming hunger, the need to erase all doubt and uncertainty. I drove my mom and teachers crazy. I became reckless and willing to try anything once if I thought it might shed some light on the mysteries of the universe. Besides, if with no advance warning I could be taken from the surface of the earth in trade for a spot beneath, what did I have to lose?

British Columbia, Canada: My Past

It's perfect fall weather, and today Matt and I are riding our bikes to the lookout point on Bruce Mountain. It's a deadly view but one hell of a hard climb. The path zigzags up and up and up, and you feel like you'll never make it without getting off your bike and pushing it, or dying. But we always make it, and as we arrive on top this time (me first), we collapse into a pile of exhaustion.

Once we can breath again, we push our bikes into the bushes and climb the last steep metres to the very top. Settling down at our favourite spot with our feet hanging over the edge, we look down on the world. It's late in the afternoon, but the sun still hovers over the mountains, shining straight onto our bodies. Our sweat glistens.

With my breathing finally back to normal, I feel as good as I ever do. From this spot five hundred metres up from the ground and looking to the northwest, you can see the jagged mountains with their layers like a slanted cake angling up to sharp peaks freshly covered in the first snow of the year, like icing as white as anything you've ever imagined. In the distance to the north the fire watchtower sits like a toy, the only man-made thing in sight up here. A plane scrapes its way across the sky, and I watch it, trying to picture the insides, wondering what the people are doing.

I'm thinking this is as good as life gets when Matt pulls out his pack of smokes.

"Give me one of those."

"Sure, if you want," he says. "But today I've got a special smoke I might let you share." He was the one that got me into smoking two years before, and I wonder what I'm in for now. He pulls out what looks like nothing more than a hand-rolled cigarette. I've never tried one without a filter, but it can't be that different from the store-bought kind.

"Wow, a rolly. That really is something. Where ever did you get it?"

"Just try it and see what you think," he says. He's being very…

nice today, so I'm happy to quit our usual sarcasm and match his mood. I wish hanging out with people didn't always have to be a battle.

Carefully, he twists the cigarette tighter and puts it all the way into his mouth, pulling it out with his lips lightly closed around it.

"You expect me to smoke that?"

"Just chill out, man, it helps it burn slower." Finally he lights the smoke. The end flares bright from the extra paper, then settles into a nice slowburn. He takes a long haul then passes it to me. For some reason he's holding the smoke in his lungs much longer than usual. He looks like he's going to explode.

I take a haul. I have to suck really hard and almost give myself a head rush trying to get the red burn to glow any brighter, but then I find the sweet spot. Without the filter the smoke burns on its way down like liquid fire. I want to choke but manage to swallow the convulsions before they escape. The taste is different from a normal cigarette. It's more natural, grassy, less chemical. I wonder if it could actually be grass he picked or something. I like it. It sure would be cool if we could just smoke grass from the lawn for free.

"This tastes different than smokes," I say after a few more puffs. "It's like smoking grass."

He smiles. "Well, it *is* grass. Not normal grass though…it's marijuana. I stole it from my brother."

I'm stunned. He says it as though he doesn't know full well that I have never, ever, smoked drugs. As I stare at him in shock, I begin to notice a heaviness in my body, a relaxed feeling. I want to say something, but I don't know what. I'm furious that he didn't tell me what it was, but I'm happy to be trying it. I'm feeling excited and playful. I jump up and pretend to be mad.

Leaping on top of him I grab his shoulders and yell, "Why didn't you tell me you lousy fucking bastard? I'm gonna—"

That's all I get out before he shifts his weight underneath me and sends me flying over his head. Within a second he's on me. I wish *I* had an older brother to play fight with like he does. He's bigger than me, and as is usual for boys, our relationship is defined by this size difference. I wonder how it works for girls.

"Chill, you bastard, or I'll fucking kill you!" he yells into my face, pinning my arms painfully under his knees.

"I'm just kidding, man! Get the fuck off me!"

"I've done it before! Just calm down and feel your stone! It's fine! All right?"

"Well maybe if you'd quit trying to *hump* me, I'd be able to relax," I tell him. At this he begins to laugh, hard, then falls off of me. I laugh too, and for the next few minutes we're rolling around on the ground bawling. Something is very funny. Uncontrollable waves of laughter roll over me, leaving me doubled up in tears. I never knew I could laugh like this. I feel like I might suffocate.

We eventually settle down, and Matt says to me, "It's pretty cool, eh?" I agree and want to say more but can't decide which one of my thoughts to turn into words. I stare out at the view and feel added meaning in everything. I see the flowers, plants, trees and mountains as one huge interconnected system, each dependent on each other in some way. I read once that a butterfly flapping its wings changes the world forever. I understand what it means now.

Matt is playing his harmonica: some song I don't know. I never know the songs he plays, but it sounds perfect. I imagine we're in the old west, camped out for the night on our way across the desert, bounty hunters after some fugitive from the law. My brain seems to be on overdrive, filled with so many amazing thoughts I can't keep up with them, one thought spirals out of control as it's pushed out of the way by the next, and the next. I try to keep track of them, like the way I use my fingers to hold all the different paths in those "Choose Your Own

Adventure" books, but it's useless. My brain is like a rolodex gone berserk, it keeps turning and turning, each file card coming into view for just a second then falling away, replaced by the following one, rolling away, off into the sunset.

"We better get going before it gets too dark to ride down the path," Matt says.

The thought of the wasted climb almost scares me. "Jesus! Let's go!"

The trail is already full of ever-darkening shadows that grow and expand into one another, trying to fill in the spaces between themselves. This means that we really better hurry.

I start rolling and feel like I'm floating. I'm full of the urge to go faster and faster, and I pedal as hard as I can. It's like I'm in a video game, my physical body and mental control have been melted to the bike. I am the bike. I float over the rocks and rail around blurred corners. I'm going faster and faster, it's all automatic now, no thinking involved—no time. I have tunnel vision as my full concentration is directed to my eyes, scanning the trail for bumps and lines as what before was an out of control, rapid-fire mind, is now completely focused on the task, a supercomputer concentrating all its energy and power into this one job. I'm the best mountain biker in the world right now; no one can touch me, or even see me. Nothing can go wrong because I'm completely in control of everything, and I won't allow it.

Suddenly, of course, the spell is broken. I'd be smart to remember that I can only control so much of what happens in this world. A bed of sharp rocks has punctured my rear tire, and now also my front. That doesn't throw me though, or slow me. As I fight for control, the stem twists and my handlebars are now turned sideways. I know I'm going to crash. Pain is coming soon. I feel the rear of the bike kick up over the taco-ed front wheel, and now I'm truly floating, weightless. As I glide through the air, my body rotates, I'm facing the sky, laid flat out.

Time comes to a standstill. I notice the early stars in the sky as they peek from behind the clouds, looking on in fascination as I prepare to meet my maker. What will it be? Grass? Dirt? Rocks? Small broken tree stumps that I'll impale my head on? I even have time to pray as I wait for the impact. "Dear God…"

As soon as I hit the ground, time switches back to its regular pace, and all my questions are answered. Rocks. I slide forward about four metres before they decide I've had enough. My body finds a nice place to settle, fitting the shapes of the stones by torn skin and broken bones. I lie still, drowning in a pool of the most intense pain I've ever felt in my life. I can't guess at the damage. I try, but my brain decides to let me pass out.

I awake to the sound and sensation of Matt slapping my face and yelling at me. Beyond the ringing in my ears, I can hear, "Holy shit! Fuck man! Wake up! Are you alive? Oh shit." Once he's certain that I'm definitely not dead, his worry changes to awe. "Holy shit man, you're fucking crazy! That was so cool! You're nuts, man! You should start racing!"

I would rather have remained unconscious, as the pain has only gotten worse. Why on earth can't pain receptors just shut the hell up after a while? I mean, what do they think I'm going to do, try and run away? Maybe I'll be a biologist or chemist some day and figure out how to remove the part of the brain that causes pain.

After my first ever ride in an ambulance we arrived at the hospital, where I was given some drugs that did a good job of blocking the pain, and making me feel as stoned as the marijuana did. So, the final injury tally?

-Five days in hospital

-Internal bleeding and bruises

-Twenty-seven stitches

-Five centimetre hook-shaped scar on my upper back

-Broken collarbone
-Broken left femur
-Sprained left wrist
-One broken and one sprained finger on my left hand
A good day's work.

The five days in hospital were better than school, but I had to be in a wheelchair, which was fun before it became quite literally a pain in the ass. The day we got home from the hospital, my mom sat down with me for a talk. She informed me that the doctor had told her they had found drugs in my blood. To this day I don't understand how. Were they looking for it for some reason? I wonder now if she wasn't just tricking me into it. I wouldn't put it past her.

But she was awesome. All she did was give me the speech about how I should think about my actions beforehand and basically not be an idiot. I guess she thought I'd suffered enough. She also didn't make a rat out of me by calling Matt's mother. I couldn't believe she was being so understanding. I guess in the end she knew I had a head on my shoulders— either that or she figured the accident would have conditioned me never to want marijuana again. Pretty cool mom, eh?

I wonder what she'll have to say about what I'm doing now. I hope she'll understand.

And I hope you will too.

~~~~~

Seven fifteen a.m. Hour twenty-three. That makes an entire day of going nowhere, other than one day closer to whatever end this universe has planned for each of us—if that's how you look at things, anyway. Including the original thirty-four hours before we stopped, we've been on this bus for almost two and a half days now. I wonder how much food we have remaining. I haven't really been eating much since we got stuck. All my time

and concentration has gone into this writing, which I've been
doing almost non-stop. I sure hope I don't run out of paper. I'd
better start writing smaller.

A quick survey reveals I'm in pretty good shape for food:
two ham and cheese sandwiches that I better eat soon; one large
bag of chocolate raisins (unopened); one large bag of salt and
vinegar chips (unopened); one package of generic chocolate
chip cookies (half left); three bananas; no gum (I *hate* gum).
And that's it. My remaining victuals aren't exactly what you'd call
health food, but they'll certainly sustain me for more than long
enough. Water and paper, on the other hand, are more pressing
issues: there's about half left of my litre bottle of water, and only
about thirty pages left in this book. I can probably stretch out
the paper, but the water is a problem. Of course there's plenty of
snow outside, so there's no real concern. I certainly am thirsty
all of a sudden.

I take a sip from my bottle and am confronted by the horrid
taste in my mouth as the water serves to liquefy it. I have to
brush my teeth. Stepping into the aisle, I give my stiff muscles
a satisfying stretch. A few sleeping people have their legs
protruding out into the aisle and all the way over to the armrest
of the chair across. I walk carefully through the obstacle course
and slowly cover the short distance to the back of the bus and
the washroom.

The window is closed now, and it's warm, but this is not a
task for those among us suffering from severe claustrophobia.
There's hardly enough room to sit on the toilet and have your
legs in front of you at the same time. And don't forget that lovely
scent, angered now by its confinement. After relieving myself,
I stand up—well, half stand—and am conveniently already at
the sink. The wall slopes up to the roof above the sink, so I can't
quite get vertical. I turn on the water to wash my hands and
assume it's safe to brush my teeth with it—no chemical is up to
the task of fighting my burning mint toothpaste. After finishing,

I use my own precious water to rinse my mouth.

I move aside for the door, open it, and step out into the marginally fresher main part of the bus. Nothing has changed. Rather than a bus, it appears as though we're in a plane travelling through clouds. I wonder which part of the bus is statistically safer. I bet it's the back; the most common accident must be a head-on collision. On the way back to my seat, I look at the people sleeping, all basically strangers to me. But to see a person sleep is to see them at their most vulnerable. It always makes me feel uncomfortable, as though I'm sneaking a peak into the bottom drawer of their dresser, far too intimate a moment to share with strangers.

Or, maybe it's that I feel responsible for them, I want to protect them, and I know I can't.

~~~~~

In the beginning, living in small groups, we were dependent on each other for survival. Everyone was part of a family, caring for one another. Like the people on this bus: If there were a woman here who'd run out of food for her baby, we would all donate freely of our supply out of simple concern and compassion. If anyone here ran out of food, or became sick, we all would do our best to take care of that person. It all *seems* so simple.

Imagine: A ship sinks, and two survivors find one another on a deserted island. They run toward one another sharing hugs and kisses. Then they realize one is a Palestinian and the other is an Israeli. Maybe they will scuffle then hurry to put as much space between themselves as possible. But if they're dependent on each other for survival, one of two things will happen, both equally profound: Either they will die alone, loyal to their hatred, or they will overcome it and survive. Surely they would come to see their common humanity, their familial bonds, and overcome their differences. Even if they have diametrically opposed personalities and nothing in common, over time they will establish such a bond that even after they've been rescued, they will care about each other for the rest of their lives.

Because they will see themselves in each other's eyes, and they will have polished the diamond of truth.

Put Hitler as my seat partner, and I promise you, either he'll end up a humanitarian, or I'll be hankering to make a lampshade out of the next Israeli I see.

This is exactly what the world needs: to be stuck on a bus together (and *aren't* we?); to realize we're all dependent upon one another—even if only for happiness, because what sensitive, loving person can truly smile while so many cry?

So? What kind of people are we? Do we live solely for ourselves, or for others as well? Will we give up some illusory freedom to distribute real freedom more equitably? It's all about knowledge and imagination. We human beings, through evolution or creation, possess a brain capable of thinking beyond the limits of its biology. We can live another person's life; starve as they starve and cry as they cry.

But it hurts.

COURSE

It's about time. It's eleven fifty a.m. now, hour twenty-seven, and the driver has just proclaimed another smoke break. This time I feel an actual need for a smoke. I offer one to the girl across from me before she has to ask, and she accepts. She's been reading a thick hardcover with its dust jacket removed, and I can't make out what it is. A voice inside says, "Don't let it be Stephen King." We all want people to be what we want them to be.

We step out of the bus, one by one, likely happier than anyone has ever been to go outdoors in such conditions. Like a stubborn grandfather refusing to use a cane, the storm would seemingly rather die than slow down in its old age. It is getting warmer, which is a good sign, though it could mean yet more snow.

I light my cigarette and walk a few steps to the outskirts of the group, looking out into the blowing snow. In the distance I fancy I can see the dark outline of a house or barn, but I'm probably just seeing things. Standing here reminds me of the time I was out sea kayaking with a friend on the north shore of Lake Superior. A thick fog blew in, and soon we couldn't see each other at all. We kept near one another through constant calls into the blinding grey, human foghorns. The water was as still as ice, opaque, like the fog. I was floating in a cloud, and the world had disappeared, gone up in a puff of smoke. I wondered if someone was trying to hide it from me. I feel the same way now.

Perhaps it's that old evil genius again. Maybe there's a glitch in the system, the computer has a virus. He has me on a standby loop as he works on the problem. It must be quite a problem that takes so long to fix. Maybe I'm getting close to something I shouldn't? I feel alone as I stare out at the desolate nothingness with this thought in my mind. What would it feel like to learn that you are the only human being that has ever existed.

Limitless loneliness and longing.

I imagine this is what it must have been like for the first astronauts on the moon: no one else to be seen in every direction, a whole planet of solitude, completely isolated.

All back inside once again, I look at the girl. She looks cold, and I wonder if she'd counted on such conditions when she packed for this trip. I try to imagine what she's thinking. What are her youthful opinions about the world? Would she prove me wrong about anything? Everything? Who knows, she's harder to read than a closed book, and I have a hard enough time with open ones.

A planet of solitude—that's me now.

I'm wakened once again by an increase in the muttering and movement around me. It's twelve fifteen p.m. That certainly wasn't the length of rest I was hoping for, but we're slaves to our environment. The window greets me with the sight of a storm that refuses to go away. Everyone is looking to the front of the bus, where there is a man in a shiny dark blue jacket leaning over talking to the driver. A patch on his shoulder says "RCMP" in yellow block letters. A moment later our driver switches on the intercom and tells us that the cop will give us an update on the situation.

The cop forgoes the microphone, choosing instead to bellow: "Well, good afternoon everyone. My name is John, and I'm an officer with the Royal Canadian Mounted Police. *Est-ce qu'il y a quelqu'un ici qui parle seulement le français?*" he asks with a typically bad Canadian accent. We all stare blankly at him, as if he's speaking French or something. He carries on in English. "This is quite some storm we've got, eh? Actually, what we have here is a low-pressure system about one thousand kilometres wide, and just as long. It's moving very fast south by southeast. This speed is the reason why the winds are so strong, and it also means it will blow over faster. Right now we're more than two thirds of the way through it. As long as it doesn't shift directions or slow down drastically, it should pass in about four hours."

With that the murmurs start again, relief or otherwise I can't tell.

"The good news is that there's not much snow on the ground. The wind is blowing it all away. The bad news is that a tractor-trailer is overturned about ten kilometres up the way, and it's blocking the road. No one was hurt, but we will have to move it before the flow of traffic can resume. That could take a couple of hours. Bottom line, our best estimate is about six or seven hours until you're on your way." Everyone is sharing the same thought: It's a long time still, but at least there's an end in sight. "If you need water or emergency supplies, your driver can radio us, and we'll come on our snow machines. Our headquarters is about twenty kilometres up the road at the next town. Now, are there any questions?" Surprisingly, no one has any; we all accept our fate stoically. "Okay then, just stay calm and try to enjoy the downtime." With that he thanks us, throws more words to the driver, and is out the door.

The driver comes on again. "Well, that's pretty good news, eh, folks? And just think, when all this is done you'll have a story worthy of the *Reader's Digest*." We accommodate him by groaning. "We'll stop at a diner in the next town, and your meal will be on us," he says with a flourish, as though he's expecting applause or something. "We won't be staying overnight, though. Don't want to waste any more time in getting you to your destinations. We'll be there about an hour, and then we're on our way." With a final clunk the intercom goes silent, and we're left once again to the voices in our heads.

Despite—or maybe, because of—the crash landing with Ian and the woman and the flask, I'm in the mood now for some real conversation. I'd do well to get my mind off this writing for a while, no matter how well it's flowing. I must take advantage of this opportunity to interact with people.

Vancouver, Canada: My Past

I can't help feeling sorry for cab drivers. I'm sure many are very happy and would be embarrassed by my sentiments—some even angry and insulted—but I can't help it. Absurdly long hours, little money and even less respect, all manner of idiots and miscreants, thievery, tight traffic and the crap driving of you and me, this is their lot. And this driver, having great trouble talking to me, stammering and tripping over his words, summons my perhaps misplaced pity to an even greater degree than usual.

Then I see that he has a picture of a young girl tucked under an elastic stretched around the sun visor. Looking at her smiling, joy overcomes me. I imagine the happy family life that he perhaps has waiting for him at the close of every too-long day, the oiled smoothness of his speech as he interacts with his beloved wife and child. As quickly as the feeling comes, it goes, replaced by a sickening sadness that stings my eyes. Thankfully, we've just pulled up in front of the bar, and my attention is diverted.

Before getting out, I hand him his money, doubling the small fare with a tip, and he mutters a gracious thank-you. I know giving money away isn't going to solve any real problems, but it can certainly make someone's day, and a day's a fraction of a life.

As I step into the dark familiarity, I'm greeted by blurred whites set aglow by black lights and the funk rhythms of a drum and bass band. After a few minutes of walking around recognizing nobody, I spot Andy at one of the rear tables, surrounded by a cadre of companions. Andy is my roommate, and thanks in no small part to his loud and boisterous Aussie nature and accent, he is very good at making acquaintances. Despite this ability, however, he seems incapable of forming any meaningful relationships, whether with friends or girlfriends. In our short time together, though, we've become quite close and have pretty much become each other's right-hand-man here in Vancouver. Like my other three roommates, he's an arts major at UBC, and I must say, I'm quite impressed by the amount of studying he doesn't do.

"Hey, man! What are you doing here?" Andy yells at me, as though I've never come before.

"I was out with Fred—"

"Gay bar?" he inserts, and I smile. Andy is an unabashed gay-basher and refuses to go out with Fred. He says he *knows* it's not contagious, "but it just makes my skin crawl. And I worry that thinking about it will turn me off sex as a concept. Could you imagine? Nothing but softness for the rest of your life!" Come to think of it, Andy's unabashed about everything.

He pulls me away from his people and toward the perimeter of the dance floor. The band is impressive. There's no guitar but two bassists, three drummers, an electric violinist, and one extremely skinny guy on vocals—his lack of physical stature more than made up for by his sonic capacities. I watch in awe of the musicianship through three songs, but the highlight comes when the bouncers clear the dance floor, and a shapely girl in a shiny chainmail bikini stakes her claim to it.

The band works its way into a complex tribal rhythm with all three drummers joining in, the singer hammering a drumstick against a cowbell, and all eyes on the fluid motions of the girl so full of grace in steel. With time, she begins to move with more urgency, flowing from one end of the empty space to the other, as though searching for something.

"A lot better than watching poofters kiss kiss each other, I presume?" says Andy, and I can only nod in agreement.

She runs off to the side of the stage and re-emerges with two flaming balls connected by a length of chain. She swings them around her like a baton, dancing joyfully with the throbbing sphere of light, as though she's found what she'd been looking for. The ceilings are quite low in this place, and it's unsafe to say that this is the first time I've ever seen anything like this. The pounding beat pulsating in my ears combines with the hypnotic poetry of the firelight in my eyes, and I find myself in a beautiful trance; I am sold. I feel like a kid at the circus, in the area of my brain that I like a lot, fully concentrated, stimulated and assimilated.

Unfortunately it all ends, and I hear Andy behind me. "That's it, mate. Let's get out of here." I follow him through the pliant mass of bodies out the front door and onto the street. We walk a block and turn a corner to get away from the crowd. "So where do we go from here then?" I ask.

Andy sits down on the sidewalk to think and lights a smoke. I join him. "I know an after hours club in Gastown," he suggests, knowing I'll take the bait. Andy and I make a reckless pair, both of us up for anything and feeding off each other. Of course, that's part of the reason we get along so well and why I wanted to meet up with him tonight.

He pulls a joint out of his pocket and lights it. Alcohol is my drug, and I can't get over how strong the B.C. skunk is, but to keep Andy company, I take small, shallow drags when he passes it over to me. Finally I flick it out onto the road, and we watch the people coming and going from the strip club across the road for a while.

Before long, Andy's explaining emphatically how stoned he is. He's no green leaf, so I take him seriously and am thankful that I didn't have much of what was obviously a powerful joint.

"Where did you get it from?"

"Some guy..."

"Are you going to be okay?"

"Yeh, let's just get walking."

In order to get him started toward our destination, I have to help him to his feet. Propping him up on my shoulder, I steer us toward Gastown. He's muttering unintelligibly. Images of war movies flash through my head, where the hero is carrying his injured buddy through the jungle as bullets whiz past and shells explode all around. Of course, the worst thing we have to worry about is an anal cop, but I haven't had to carry anyone around on my shoulder like this for quite some time. Actually, I never have. Here's to novelty.

By the time we reach Gastown, he's feeling a bit better. Thank goodness, because I haven't the slightest fucking clue where this place is. He leads us through some back alleys and eventually stops at a heavy steel door set two feet into a brick wall. The setting is as you can imagine: cracked concrete, rusty garbage containers and skeletal fire escapes doubled up in black puddles. Andy knocks on the door. I'm sceptical, imagining an extremely large and angry man, wakened from his sleep, throwing open the door and bludgeoning us with the two-by-four he keeps by the door for just such occasions.

"What do you want?" questions a disembodied voice, far away on the other side.

"We're not done partying yet!" is Andy's answer, asinine but to the point. The door eventually creaks open, and the distant sounds of Sonic Youth meet my appreciative ears.

A pair of eyes sizes us up, as though we're applying for a position. "That's ten bucks each, guys," says the doorman, pushing the door fully open and scanning the alley in both directions. He's of medium build, of forgettable appearance, ready for action but seemingly not unfriendly. I fumble for money, but Andy is quicker on the draw and hands him a twenty.

We enter a tiny vestibule, which quickly ends at the top of a steep, wrought iron staircase leading downward. I notice a painting on the wall, a beautifully conceived, sparsely executed portrait of a man, weathered and weary. He wears a dark overcoat, and his head is angled down, denying a cold wind perhaps. It's all black and shades of grey, his dark form standing against a background of nothing more than a few oddly angled lines, perhaps representing an anonymous cityscape. The desolate isolation is palpable, and I stand and stare, stuck between floors. There's something about the style that's eerily familiar to me, for some reason, almost as though I myself might have painted it in a past life.

Andy walks past, intent on meeting the music, but I comment, "That's a fantastic piece."

"You like it?" replies the doorman. "I know the artist." There's a touch of pride in his voice. "Ray Mason," he adds, almost as an afterthought, and I'm bowled over.

"Did you just say Ray Mason?"

"You know him?"

"I went to high school with the guy," I tell him. "He sure is good," I add, more to myself that anyone else, still absorbed by the man in the painting. I now also notice the tiny "Ray" scrawled haphazardly in the lower left corner.

"I see him all the time. If you like I could give him your number?"

"No…no, that's all right," I say, thanking the guy and heading down the stairs. I don't want to tell him that Ray suffered from manic-depression and who-knew-what other ailments and eventually became incapable of maintaining the façade of sanity. I always liked him, but you never knew when he was going to go off, like an unwinding jack-in-the-box. Maybe that's why I liked him. He definitely has talent. What a wild coincidence. I hope he's well. Then I feel guilty for my shallow sentiment, and I try to summon some truly positive vibes to send to him.

I find Andy at the bar. "I've got beer, five dollars each, or mickeys of C.C., twenty-five dollars," says the bartender in a manner that leaves little doubt that he's gay and available. Thankfully Andy is past noticing such crimes.

"Give us a mickey then," says Andy—probably not the best idea.

"Hang on, Andy," I interject, giving him the eye. "Maybe we'll just have a couple beers, eh?"

"But that's a bloody rip-off."

"Well, so is the mickey. Besides, do you want to get a bottle of hard stuff, pain it down, and then go home sick? Or would you rather sit pleasantly sipping beers and make it through the night?"

He mulls this over for a second then asks for two beers from the patient bartender. I feel a tinge of guilt over my responsible behaviour tonight but manage to get over it quickly enough.

With our beers we head into the depths of the club. There really isn't much to the place. The lighting is dim, non-intrusive, and very effective in setting the mood of in-for-the-long-haul-ness. The walls are concrete painted black and covered over with chain link, set off here and there by pieces of mixed media art. Some of the work is all right, but all pale in comparison to the portrait by Ray. Comfy couches line the walls, separated by small coffee tables holding enormous glass ashtrays and an eclectic assortment of old lamps. The whole place feels like a chill-out room at a rave, and it suits me just fine.

We find space on a couch near the back, and settling into its softness, I lose myself in the music. After a while, the girl sitting diagonally across from us distracts me. She looks about nineteen or twenty and is pretty far from beautiful, but even further from sober. She's staring at me. Noticing that I've noticed her, she leans over the coffee table between us, and the lamp shines above her such that her long eyelashes create fine shadows down her cheeks like scratches bleeding black blood. After a moment spent looking deep into my eyes, she asks, "What are you passionate about?"

Now there's a question. I feel silly, juvenile, hackneyed. "Do you want me to be serious, or do you just want me to tell you the most off-the-wall thing I can possibly think of?"

"The truth is all that matters, isn't it?"

I've often wondered about the validity of that sentiment. I wonder where her father thinks she is? I guess it could be worse. But it can always be worse.

"I'm afraid the only truth I know is that I don't know any."

Her eyes narrow as she continues to look at me, harder now. I see she's trying to decide whether I'm being serious or just playing her. Deciding on the latter, without a word, she slides herself back across the table and into her private perusal of her own mind. I feel bad, but I'm not really up for any abstract conversations, deep or otherwise. I wonder, though, how I'd have reacted if she'd been more attractive. Pitiful.

Turning to look at Andy, I see that he's busy window-shopping in his own head. I feel maybe the slightest bit stoned, but not really, mostly just drunk.

After almost an hour spent reading faces and postures while revelling in the masterfully selected music, I'm nudged by Andy, recently arrived from the dead. Then he's standing over me, appearing perfectly lucid. "Maybe we should split? We still have a good buzz on to make things interesting." I concur, and we head to the bar to get one last beer for the road. The club is quite crowded now, and we stumble out to the sounds of some very early Cure. After conducting my business with the doorman-cum-art dealer, I step out into the warm early morning, eyes squinting, holding Ray's painting under my arm.

We walk through the maze of streets, purposefully keeping to the back lanes and discussing various these-and-those until we find ourselves at the top of a long gradual uphill that we've climbed without even noticing. The bottom of the hill is about seven blocks below us. Deciding to sit and rest for a while, we sit ourselves down on a curb. As far as the sun is concerned, the night is over, but we refuse to give in. We share a cigarette, and the pre-dawn light reminds me of glum, overcast winter days. There's something depressing about light that signals an end rather than a start.

"Let's get more booze and just drink all day," I suggest.

"I don't think so," Andy simply says, and I recognize the cosmic reciprocity.

Looking around me, I notice an old tire, abandoned. It looks as though it's from a pickup truck. "What'll you give me if I can launch this thing to the bottom of the hill without it falling over?" I ask Andy.

"I'll give you some applause, if you're lucky," is Andy's best offer. It's not exactly the most enticing motivation, but it's enough for me—I don't really ask much out of life. I pull the tire into the centre of the road, line it up, then give it a good fling. It looks good and rolls straight and true through the first two intersections. A car appears on the fourth street but proceeds out of sight just as quickly.

"Man, if a car goes by and hits that tire, I hope you're in the mood for a jog," Andy says, more as a challenge than a concern. Oblivious, the determined tire continues on through the third, then the fourth, fifth and sixth intersections. By the time it rolls through the seventh, it has some good speed and is still travelling right down the centre of the road as though it were on rails. I swear it's revelling, ecstatic to have been given a second shot at life. Having reached the bottom of the valley, it begins to climb the hill on the other side. Another car drives by on one of the streets, but the tire is still rolling fine as it crosses the eighth, ninth and tenth streets.

Just beyond the eleventh street, the fourth of the uphill section, it slows right down and comes to a complete stop. For what feels like an eternity, it seems to be deciding whether it should stop there, or roll back down the hill. Then, without giving so much as an inch, and with an apparent air of satisfaction, it falls over, flat and dead in the middle of the lane. And it's as though it was never anywhere but there. At that precise moment, a car turns onto the road and drives slowly past it. The whole time, Andy and I watch, transfixed, mesmerized, as though watching our own futures play out, and longing for longevity.

"Holy fucking shit," Andy whispers. "Nice goddamn shot, man." Somehow I feel guilty taking the credit for this, it all feels so beyond me. I don't even know what to say, so I just start laughing. Andy joins me, and soon we're out of control.

An old tire rolls along with no more or less free will than any of us, precarious but unwavering, impossible but unstoppable, and after a long trip it comes to rest, for no reason other than it decided to. Perhaps it was just tired. Whatever this experience wasn't, it was Zen.

HARD OVER

Well, they didn't know euchre, but were up for some hearts. I was very happy when my partner, Christian, started passing around a bottle of rum. How fitting. It's not my favourite drink, but in the absence of anything else, it is. If it were mine, it would've been gone a long time ago. I wonder what on earth he was saving it for. I thought about offering him good money to keep the whole thing to myself then realized how badly that would come across. At any rate, I had enough to achieve that warm, contented glow that puts frames around your problems and calls them art; that glow that always leaves you wanting more.

Christian was working in the mine in Sudbury and is on his way to Victoria now. He says he has no idea what he'll do there, but it's home, and his mother is sick, so he wants to be with her. I wonder how serious it is and how it must be affecting him. His face has an overwhelmed look about it that's obvious the moment you lay eyes on him. It's as though his subconscious is warning everyone in the vicinity to be careful, because given any more pressure, it just might decide to pack it all in for good.

The other two of our foursome, Sam and Sam—short for Samuel and Samantha, how cute—are a happily married couple of seven years. They say that they're on their way to Vancouver as well, where they plan to stay indefinitely. She has a teaching job, and Sam is going to try to find work as a bartender. I told them that I'd lived there for a while and that it's a great city. I also warned them of the wet winter weather. They're moving from Winnipeg, however, and say that anything would be better than that. I had to agree. They hope to have kids within a few years if they're settled into jobs by then. I'm happy for them, but they remind me that loss is the only end. We're going to the same city, but very different places.

~~~~~

I'm paranoid. I've killed someone in my past. I never remember when or who or how, but I know I've indeed done it. This awareness consumes me, as I know I'll be caught and made to pay. All my friends and family, everyone that ever knew me will hang their heads in disgust. I'm no longer human; I'm in the sewer, and everyone gives a shit. And there's the acidic burn of guilt. I've taken a life, a breath, a dream. I can't run away from my own mind, which is paralyzed by fear and self-loathing. In no sense am I aware of the fact that I'm only dreaming, but I am, and upon waking, the relief and solace is indescribable.

There's no hidden meaning or symbolism here. The meaning of this me-as-a-killer dream is obvious: I should never kill anyone, because I will be wracked by a guilt that will consume my life—easy, obvious, and redundant. I already know this about myself; it's one of the few things I'm certain of. I've never been able to understand how a person can take a life. Let alone enjoy it. Or not enjoy it, but do it all the same. But if I never could, what makes other people able to do it? Different experiences, different chemical balances in the brain perhaps. But can these chemical balances be changed, or are some people capable while others simply are not?

Lately, though, my brain seems to be tuning into a wider range of human emotion and perception. Am I becoming wiser with age? Does wisdom mean being able to empathize with the motivation behind any act?

~~~~~

After drifting in and out of broken sleep, I feel alive and aware again, as much as possible without the aid of a shower anyway. It's six thirty in the evening and our thirty-fourth hour. As I look out the window, I'm amazed to find I can actually see something. Yes, something, as opposed to nothing. The creaks and murmurs on the bus are livelier now than at any other point during the course of our entrapment. The blizzard has passed, like a massive paintbrush dragging a blanket of white behind it, covering the land. The glare on the window of the bus's internal lights leaves visible only a faint trace of the heavenly spectacle that is the prairie sky at night, but it *is* there.

I can at last *see* that we are on a stretch of highway somewhere in the middle of nowhere. Amongst the white here and there are a few scatterings of pine trees, strong and defiant, like the last hairs to go on a bald man's head. Ahead of us in the approaching lane of traffic is a Taurus with what looks to be a man and woman huddled together in the front seat. They're wearing heavy parkas, fake-fur lined hoods pulled tight by drawstrings around their faces. They look cold. I wonder why they didn't try to come onto the bus? The most pertinent thing to be noticed is the snowdrift on the north side of the car, angling from the ground up to the roof, conscientiously following its profile as though worked by the dedicated hands of a master sculptor.

I feel a chill.

The road is clear, a cold grey in the darkness.

The warm isolation of the storm is gone and the vast expanse of the prairie presses in on our domain.

Faint traces of agoraphobia feel their way around my mind.

The insulation of the snow is gone, leaving the bus bigger, emptier, subsumed by the desolation.

Everyone is craning their heads toward the windows to observe the white wonderland, laughing and joking like little kids.

The girl across from me is not laughing. I wonder what she's thinking.

I hear the intercom crackle into life once again.

"Okay, I hope you're all still with me. We should be on our way in no time. I just got word from the RCMP that the rig up ahead has been cleared, and there's only a little bit of snow removal to be done. I estimate we'll be on our way in about half an hour if things go as they should, and it'll be about a half hour's drive to the next town. We'll be heading to a restaurant there—it's my favourite, mainly because it's the only one. But if you're anything like me, you'll be happy to know that it's a buffet dinner, so you can have enough to make up for lost time. And it'll be no charge, as Greyhound Canada will be happy to eat the bill, pardon the pun." Chuckles and sarcastic comments reverberate around the bus. "We'll be there about an hour, so that the bus can be refuelled, and I can be replaced. So now it's smoke time, come one, come all." Most on board seem to appreciate his attempts at humour this time.

As people start to get up, I wait for them all to get ahead of me then join the back of the line. Now that the snow has stopped, everyone wants to go outside and see the situation firsthand. I look back at the empty seats behind me. They look like slept in beds, newly abandoned. I quickly turn away from the sight.

I can feel the cold burst of air blowing through the bus from the open door up front. The fresh air will do wonders to improve the atmosphere on the bus. Sweep out the cobwebs.

I step down the stairs and onto the layer of hard, wind-blown snow surrounding the bus.

It's colder now. I see the girl putting a pack of cigarettes into her pocket and feeling around for a lighter. Curious. I walk over to her.

"You had cigarettes?" I ask, handing her my lighter.

Looking at me with perhaps the faintest trace of guilt in her eyes, she replies, "Well, I only had a few left, and since you kept offering, I figured I'd save mine. Who knew how long we'd be stuck." Reasonable enough, I guess. "I would have given you some if you had run out, don't worry," she adds, maybe feeling a little embarrassed, though I get the feeling this girl doesn't care much about such things.

"Fair enough, I guess," I say and turn to look out at the prairie.

The snow is hard, and the wind has swept it into tiny steppes like the contour line patterns on a map. The sky stretches around me fully 180 degrees, towering between both horizons, smothering me in its vastness. On a clear night like this, you almost get the feeling that you're floating in space. I can discern clearly the bright patch of the Milky Way, our own flat spiral galaxy, a frozen breath of glittering stars. Standing here on the dry snow, I'm receiving gifts of light from 200,000,000,000 of our closest neighbours, spread across 100,000 light years of space. It can make you feel very alone thinking about the amount of empty space there is between bodies. How can a person look at all this and not feel their ignorance pressing down on them with the weight of a billion solar masses? Shaking my head, I attempt to dislodge this load on my shoulders, but the weight of the universe cannot be shirked.

Finishing the last of my cigarette, I flick it into the ocean of white I stand on the brink of.

British Columbia, Canada: My Past

The usual brown dirt of the trail is covered in leaves that crackle and crunch under my feet. The red, yellow, and orange colours that surround me are broken only by the scattered evergreens and the bright blue sky. I come out here almost every day in autumn—I have to make the most of my forest before the darkness starts coming too early and the snow seals up my favourite trails for another long winter.

Today I'm walking along a different path from my usual one. A while back I saw a porcupine waddling through the leaves and having as much fun as I am. It's always nice to have a friendly run-in with an animal while out here. Thankfully though, I've only seen a bear once, and that was from far away. I was so scared, I couldn't even move for ten minutes. Of course, I was a lot younger then.

My mom wants me back by four thirty today, because we have to go to her friend's house for supper. I hope it's going to be good. It's only one thirty now, so I have lots of time. Stopping for a moment, I gather the leaves into a pile with my foot, showing the damp dirt below to the warming rays of the sun.

Getting on my hands and knees, I collect more leaves and eventually end up with a pile about three feet tall. I sit in it, and my weight squishes it all the way down to the ground. I feel the cold through my jeans. Despite what the cartoons would have you believe, you'd need a lot more leaves than this before you could hope to dive into the pile without breaking your neck. I haven't got time for that, so I give up and continue along the trail. Looking back, I feel a little guilty at having made such a mess, but not very.

After another ten minutes of walking over streams and boulders, I come across a small clearing with a couple of logs arranged around a blackened pit that was once home to a fire. I sit down on one of the logs. The wood is cold and damp. A strong gust of wind blows through the trees and proves too much for the weakest of the leaves, which flutter through the air, dead. I catch one in my hand, a blazing red colour. The pattern of the veins is so perfect, so human-like. I squeeze it in my fist, but it stays together, not dry enough yet to crack and disintegrate.

Behind the log across from me, I notice a pile of soggy paper that looks like a stack of magazines. Walking over to it, I see that the top page of the first magazine is not the cover, which is gone, but an inside page, on which sits a picture of a body. I've seen pictures of ladies before, but never like this. This lady has no clothes on! I've heard of this kind of magazine, but I've never actually seen one before. Why would I?

Now, I know all I need to know about sex from my friends— Matt even knows one guy who's already done it—but I've never seen anything like this before. Standing perfectly still, I listen closely to the sounds of the forest but hear nothing out of place. Stretching my head around, I look up and down the path and see no one. So, sitting down on the log, I peel the top magazine off the pile. It's a little bit damp underneath and wrinkled all over, but the images are more than clear. The first picture is of a woman with brown hair, curly, and hanging loose. She is sitting on a pink rug, with a pink bed behind her and a blue dresser beside her. She holds a red phone to her ear and is staring at me like something hurts. The phone is connected to a cord that hangs down from her ear and across her boobs, which are big, like water balloons. She is sitting cross-legged and wearing red underwear. As I stare at the page, I feel it happening in my own underwear.

Turning the page, I see the same girl, this time sitting in a different position. After five more pages, she has taken off her underwear, and I'm grossed out, but I can't stop looking. So that's what's down there. I feel butterflies in my stomach, and my heart is racing like I'm going to make a speech or something. My own privates are growing bigger, as they've started doing lately, and I wonder if it's possible that they might burst. That would sure hurt, and I would have no one around to help me. The danger of even this can't stop me from turning the pages.

Soon the first girl is gone, and in her place is a blonde lady with dark red lipstick. Her boobs are not as big, and there is space between them. After the first page a man joins her, and I'm even more grossed out. Something forces me to keep digging deeper into the magazine. After a while the man and woman are gone, then all of a sudden, there are two girls doing things to each other that I never would've believed if I weren't seeing it for myself. This is gross too, but at least the man is gone. Do girls really do this to each other? I think of the girls in my class and feel very weird thinking about them doing these things. One thing is for sure—I'll never be able to look at them the same way again.

Suddenly I hear a noise and look around, but nothing is there. Feeling too nervous to stay here any longer, I peel off the next four magazines and stuff a pair into each arm of my sweater, holding them in with my fingers. I run back down the trail as fast as I can toward home. My heart is racing, but I run even faster. It feels good, and my mind is filled with amazing images. Finally, twenty minutes later, I reach the end of the trail.

I've got to show these to Matt; he'll be blown away. I sure hope he's home. Reaching his house, I find him there and tell him he has to come out. He can tell from my red face and heavy breathing that it must be important, so putting on a jacket and shoes, he follows me outside.

"Come with me. Man, have I got something crazy to show you," I whisper.

"What, what is it? Show me now."

"No man, just wait! Come on!" I say again, growing more excited as I lead us into the bushes behind his house.

"What the hell is it!" he yells from behind me, and I'm happy to be in control of such an exciting situation. I don't answer him, leading us further into the trees. Stopping a safe distance from his house and figuring a picture is worth a thousand words—these ones are probably worth ten times that much—I pull the magazines from my sleeves and hold them out to him.

"Deadly! Where'd you get these?"

"I found 'em in the bush, a whole pile of them, just sitting there!"

"Where exactly?" he questions further, flipping through the pages and turning the magazine sideways sometimes.

"Well, you know my regular trail?"

"From the end of your road?"

"Yeah. About ten minutes in, it forks off to the left. The path is grown in, but it's there. They're about half an hour down that path in a camping clearing." I announce all this feeling very proud of my find. "Have you ever seen a magazine like this before?"

"Sure man, my brother has tons of them." He pauses, and his eyebrows rise as he says, "Why? Haven't you?"

"No way, man!" I exclaim, still feeling the odd pressure in my underwear. "It's pretty gross, eh?"

"What? Fuck no man, these chicks...oh man, someday you'll dream you were with someone like this," he says, pointing at the page. I still don't really know how I feel yet, but I think that the someday he's talking about might be tonight.

"So, that's where we go, eh?" I say, pointing to the otherworldly area between the girl's legs.

"That's it, man," he says, growing more excited. "And where the baby comes out nine months later."

It takes me a minute to realize what he has just said. "What?"

"That's where the baby comes out."

"No way!"

"Yes way, you retard."

"How the hell is an entire baby gonna come out of there? It's no assembly required, you know."

"Well then, smart-ass, where the hell does the baby come out? Does the stork deliver it?"

"It comes out of the stomach, geez!" I say, matching and raising his frustration level.

"How does it get out of the stomach, you idiot—do you see a zipper!"

"The doctor cuts it open and takes the baby out!" I yell, aware of how stupid I sound, but not as much as he does.

"You think they had doctors like that in the caveman days?"

"Well, they..." I don't know what to say to that, but I know I'm right. I *must* be, because *he* can't be.

He looks at me for a moment with pursed lips, then his expression changes, calms. A moment later he says, "Look, man, remember last year when I told you those lights floating across the sky at night are satellites, and you said it would be impossible to see the light from so far away, then you asked your teacher and he said I was right?" I do remember and don't answer. "Same thing, man, trust me. Do you really want to go ask your teacher where the baby comes out?"

I hesitate, considering. "You know this for sure? Like, for sure for sure?"

"Yes, I know this for sure. Your big head squeezed out of there," he says and points to it again, pushing the page into my face. I shove him and the girl away.

"That's fuckin' gross," is all I can say.

TAUT

Throughout my life there have been numerous occasions when I have felt the hand of mortality with disturbing lucidity. I'm not referring to dreams here, but wide-eyed, conscious reality. The moment is always accompanied by profound loneliness, inescapable, convincing me there is nothing else. This feeling most often comes when I've had a late afternoon nap and have wakened to the darkness and solitude of the early evening. With nothing to look forward to but a late night of introspection and isolation, it's as though I have wakened to a world where the sun shuns me and no one else lives. From here on it's just me and the darkness and the suffocating ennui. The sensation itself passes within fifteen or twenty minutes, but an odd cloud lingers in my thoughts, like an aftertaste, or a ringing in the ears. It's almost as though I can feel death lurking. It used to be that in daylight, around others, I didn't notice it; it was blocked out by all the noise and colour. Now it's creeping into the daylight hours as well. I'm better able to handle it now, though; the frequency has diluted the intensity.

Toronto, Canada: My Past

Is it possible for a person's very existence to slide out of phase with reality? For the last month or so I've been feeling like my life is out of synch with itself, like a poorly produced DVD when the voice track is out of time with the movements of the actors' mouths. Sometimes I'm watching the checkout lady's mouth move, and I don't know what she's said till her eyebrows draw together in confusion; other times I know what she's going to say before she even says it. Could it be that somehow the alignment has slipped between my mind and body, or myself and my surroundings, beginnings and endings out of phase like two piano strings out of tune with one another?

It started six weeks ago. I woke that morning ahead of my alarm clock with a stomach that felt as though it was going to implode. I spent the first hour of the day hugging the toilet bowl and wishing I had cleaned it the week before as I had planned. I've never felt so sick in my life. I had to call out from work and the noxious feeling stayed with me all day. By the evening I was beginning to worry that this state of pain would become my new normality.

I considered going to the doctor, but they've never proven worth the wait in the past, so I decided in the end to deal with things on my own. With Scotch and pills as escort, I finally managed to fall into sleep for the night. When I woke up the next morning, my stomach was back to normal, but the pain had migrated to my brain, giving me a headache more intense than I had ever imagined possible. After half an hour I realized that the pain was intent on staying awhile, and I called out sick again. All I could do for the entire day was lie motionless on my couch, trying my hardest not to use my brain at all. The only mental energy I expended was in attempting to separate my mind from my body, which I wished to leave alone with its misery.

I became enveloped in a certainty that the cause of my suffering was not biological in nature, that there was no reason to concern myself with my own physical health, that the problems were rooted in some kind of mental or spiritual crisis. This didn't exactly make me feel any better. It did, however, lead me to the conclusion that going to the hospital would be useless and that I had better find my own way of treating my condition. The only thing I could think of was to try and meditate, turn my brain off, and become nothingness.

I must have fallen into a deep sleep sooner or later, because I woke up the next day free of pain and with no physical side effects other than severe hunger. Replacing the pain, however, was a shatteringly morbid sadness that permeated my brain and body like a disease of the blood. I felt as though in combating the pain of the last two days, I had spent all my dopamine and serotonin, every last molecule of positive neurotransmitter in my brain, and all that remained were those responsible for depression and pessimism. Along with the contents of my stomach, my entire happiness had gone down the toilet. I was steeped in negativity and melancholy such that I truly believed I had never even known happiness; that it was all an illusion that had been blown away like cigarette smoke in a storm and could never be retrieved. I was paralyzed by desolation and pointlessness.

It being Saturday, I thankfully didn't need to concern myself with work and decided that I needed to get out of my apartment and into the real world. Maybe the sight of some flowers or children or dogs would spark some positive thoughts in my mind. Down the street is a pub that I frequented now and again, and I decided to go there and have some breakfast. I hoped some food might lift my spirits. Not even bothering to shower, I put on clothes that were the most handy and made my way down the four flights of stairs to the street below.

The weather was fine, a perfect May day, about ten degrees enclosed within a crisp and cloudless blue sky. As far as my mental state was concerned, however, there was a damp winter fog wrapped around me, shielding me from warmth and light. I could not be consoled. The four-minute walk to the pub did nothing but push me further into despair, and as soon as I arrived, forgoing the menu, I asked for a neat double Scotch. If ever in my life I'd needed a drink, I needed one then.

~~~~~

A sudden lurching of the bus awakens me, a sensation that most of us here have forgotten even existed. It seems odd, impossible, as if we've actually somehow slowed down even further and the earth has decided to get going without us. The sounds of hoots and hollers and general celebration fill the air, then clapping. Looking out the window seals it—we're on our way! I'm disappointed that I missed the exact moment when the wheels started turning, like jerking your head in reaction to the sound of an accident and seeing the tangled cars and glass raining onto the ground, but missing the actual impact.

My watch reads eight fifteen p.m. That makes close to thirty-seven hours of entrapment—a day and a half. I look over at the girl, searching for a definable expression on her face that might betray her feelings about moving closer once again toward her goal, but find nothing. What is she about? Where is she going? To do what? Her clothes provide no clue as to her social standing or even her style—pure comfort clothes for travelling: big green cargo pants and a blue fleece pullover, under which is a white t-shirt of some variety. This time she strikes me as exceedingly beautiful, as though the scenery passing by the window behind her has stirred up and activated her beauty, like mixing reactive chemicals together. She's the kind of girl I would have gotten quite excited about when I was younger. Such a long time ago. Those feelings are lost now, buried under a mountain of experiences I could never have imagined then.

I try to discover the title of her book but again come up with nothing, as the cover is partially visible but obscured by shadows. As we pass by a highway light, I can make out "Martin E". Unbelievable. It's *Martin Eden* by Jack London, one of my favourites.

Toronto, Canada: My Past

Three double Scotches later, only forty-five minutes had been swept aside by the minute hand of the clock, and I was feeling no better. I began to despair. For the first time in my life I feared that my brain was taking me on a trip that I was truly unprepared to take and had no way of returning from. I tried to think of what I had done differently in the last few days that might provide some possible explanation for the way I was feeling. I could think of nothing. Finally concluding that it would be pointless to continue drinking, I decided to make an academic exercise of the whole business.

Returning to my apartment, I locked the door behind me and headed straight for my bedroom. Opening the door to my closet, I plunged in. Digging through the abandoned clothes welled up in the far corner, I burrowed deeper and deeper until I located the hard edges of the shoebox I was searching for. I removed it and myself from the dark closet and observed it resting in my hands. Closed with duct tape, the contents had been sealed away for perhaps fifteen years, and it took a great force of will to convince myself that this was indeed a good idea. I carried it into the living room with the respect afforded an urn and placed it ceremoniously upon the coffee table.

The distant sound of a police car's siren stole my attention long enough for me to decide to put on an old Billie Holiday CD. As the first song came on—"Strange Fruit"—the atmosphere in the room changed such that I felt as though I had stepped into another body and time. The heaviness of the song and the air helped me realize that it would probably not be such a bad idea to have another drink. Taking the bottle of Scotch from the top of the fridge, I brought it and a sharp knife into the living room and sat down in front of the box waiting on the coffee table.

I couldn't exactly figure out why it was that after so many years I was finally ready to face this part of my past that I had shut away for so long. It was something in the air, something in the very essence of matter that had reconfigured itself and turned me upside down and inside out. Somewhere a button had been pressed, a line severed, a bridge crossed, and the present was no longer my own. It was time to look back.

Picking up my bottle, I took a long drink and realized that I still was not quite ready. I went back into the bedroom and fished through the middle drawer of my dresser until I located my emergency reserve of cigarettes, thankful for the lighter tucked away inside the package. I pulled one out and lit it, the stale smoke filling my lungs and providing me with the briefest distraction from the weight in my brain. Bringing the pack with me, I made my way back into the living room and made the decision at last that it was now or never.

Running the knife neatly around the lid of the box, I removed the top and gazed at the white plastic bag inside. Pulling it out, I unwrapped it from itself and without looking, reached inside and felt around the sharp corners of the photographs within. Deciding on one, I closed my eyes and pulled it out, holding it delicately in my two hands, trying desperately to get a handle on my thoughts. Why on earth was I feeling so profoundly miserable? Had someone been spiking my water supply with some kind of Anti-Prozac? I slowly opened my eyelids and focussed on the image.

The photograph I clutched in my hands seemed to pull and drag me beneath the surface of a sea of painful emotions and forgotten memories like a lead weight. I wanted to let go, but my fingers formed a death grip as I clung to it for life. I grew colder and colder as I sank to the depths of the ocean of my past. I remembered every aspect of the image and time portrayed as though it was the only day I had ever lived, a summary of life.

My father's face, almost completely in shadow as the sun set behind him, was the main subject. Haloes of light filled out the photo as the camera soaked up the glare of the sun, lending him an angelic air and complementing his easy smile which lay in shadow. The stubble on his chin sparkled silver while his unkempt hair shone brilliantly as it caught the light that seemed to pass through him. Here was the man who made me, my creator, my reason for being. It was as though I was looking at myself. I felt a stunningly tragic punch of loss.

A combination of the chemicals in my brain, the Scotch, the cigarette, and the image, made me violently sick to my stomach once again. I sprinted to the kitchen sink to rid myself of poison.

~~~~~

All the blinded vehicles have been healed, and the highway is scarred with the snowy shadows they've shed. This makes for slow going, but at last we've entered the confines of a small town. The name is not obvious, but its unimportance is. No sight exists more spectacular than a couple of streetlights, a "reduce speed" sign on the highway, and a few nondescript buildings peppered around here and there. Imagine, this is a city, and London is a city, but that is where the similarities end. What different atmospheres, experiences, worlds.

We slowly roll past a tiny Canada Post office attached to a small convenience store and turn left into a parking lot. I can see a plain brown-brick building, windows all along one side glowing fiercely against the blackness that taunts them. The Venetian blinds are almost shut, but evidence of a restaurant lurks behind them. I make out the outline of sugar containers— with the lids you can loosen as a gag—beside the unmistakeable generic plastic ketchup bottles. It's nine thirty p.m., and besides us, there are two pickup trucks in the frozen gravel parking lot, one old and one new—probably the whole town—getting together to discuss the storm.

We pull up alongside the building such that from our

position all we can see of the restaurant is the flat roof. Once we're stopped, the driver delays for about two minutes for the usual reasons unknown to anyone outside the brotherhood of bus drivers. I think it's to let the anticipation grow, particularly suitable on this occasion. He stands up and faces us, and all we can see is his upper body over the partition. He looks at us for about five seconds, probably stunned by the fact that the death of the longest shift of his life is at hand, then simply says, "Hungry?"

Amidst a chorus of "yeah"s and "you-better-believe-it"s, we all get out of our seats and prepare ourselves physically and mentally for the fact that we're about to step under a new roof for the first time in what feels like an eternity. We excitedly file toward the door with all the anticipation and wonder of plane crash survivors missing in the mountains for months. As we step off the bus, we're greeted by a cold wind and the driver reminding us that the bus will be back in one hour sharp. We all shake his hand and offer token thanks to him for performing a modified version of his job for so many hours in a row.

It's bearable outside, about fifteen below, but the wind is still strong. A few footsteps in the dry creaking snow that sounds like styrofoam, through the door, and I'm in. It takes a few moments for my eyes to adjust to the bright fluorescent lighting. Able to see again, I look around at the tables and see that all of them are already occupied. The three locals at the counter watch us as though anticipating an attack, whispering to each other their battle plans. The restaurant itself is your usual small town diner: white walls yellowed by years of cigarette smoke and grease fires, adorned with cheap frames housing even cheaper paintings. There are two rows of three vinyl-seated booths side by side down the centre of the room, with tables and chairs around the perimeter, and a counter with stools at the back—or front I guess, depending on how you look at it. On the end of the counter near the door sits the cash register with a display of gum and chocolate bars.

Deciding the place for me is back here with the townsfolk, I sit down on one of the red vinyl stools, two removed from said locals. I hope I'm not invading their territory. The smell of grease and gravy permeates the air, creating pangs of hunger deep within me, and an extra ounce of saliva in my mouth. The buffet is set up in the space between the counter and the row of booths. I eye it like prey. I assume it's mob rule, as some of our crew have already staged a full frontal assault on the bank of food. Never lacking in courage, I scramble over to them and choose as my weapon a clean (enough) white ceramic plate with a thin brown stripe around its circumference.

When all is said and done, my kill total is three of these plates and six glasses of orange juice. I wonder what our group total is. Could the restaurant have possibly turned a profit tonight? I look around and see that there are still a few people eating. They must be pretty slow eaters for me to beat them. The bus should be back soon, and surprisingly, I look forward to regaining my home. As I get up, the vinyl of my stool groans in anticipation of being once again afforded the opportunity to assume its favoured shape, and the creak of rusted bolts calls to mind a tired old man. I make my way to the door and seeing again the point of purchase display, stop and buy some chocolate, surprised to learn that I don't have to pay extra for the aging.

I step outside, light a cigarette and wait for the return of the bus. It's cold. Very cold. I start to hop around to fend off the shivers. This is how so many of them die on Everest, sitting down and slowly being erased by the cold. I read about one climber who got stranded in a storm near the top. He was out of reach of the would-be rescuers down below, who could do nothing to try and save him until the storm ended. The most insane part was that he had a radio with him and was in contact with the other climbers throughout the whole ordeal. Near the end they managed to get his wife on the line. He was speaking with her in his last moments; she was listening as his words finally faded. Their voices were able to interact, across a universe, but that was all. How would it feel speaking to your loved one on the phone, listening as they freeze to death, and being absolutely powerless to do anything to save them?

They found his body the next day, sitting upright and frozen into position, the radio in his hand still, batteries long dead, just like him.

Toronto, Canada: My Past

I poured myself some more Scotch and proceeded to roll myself a joint. Now I was really scared. My joint was lumpy and misshapen, like a body rolled up in a blanket, but it was all I could do to keep my hands from shaking. Something was going on in my head. I had never experienced such feelings before, and I knew getting stoned was the last thing I should be doing, but my mind wasn't functioning properly. I had to do something. Before I lit up, I turned the music off and the television on. Something mundane and pedestrian might bring me back to normality. Finding a baseball game, I left it on and lit my joint.

The first few puffs seemed to actually make me feel better as the black fear lifted somewhat, and I felt a bit of sun enter my thoughts. With elation, I smoked more, almost convincing myself that it was all over, just an episode. Ten minutes later, however, I was back in it, worse than ever. I couldn't control my mind; I was losing it. The darkest, vilest thoughts were flooding my mind, drowning me in mental madness. It was as though all of a sudden I was seeing the reality of the world, that good does not exist, that all there is is evil and that I myself was part of it. I didn't deserve to exist, and all there would be from that moment on was hell, an eternity of mental anguish.

I was filled with an inhuman fear that seemed to tear my mind to shreds while it hacked to pieces my former self. I was positive there was no going back, that once a brain thinks these thoughts, they become set in the foundation and can never be forgotten—they will grow and strengthen and overpower everything else, like weeds growing through cement. My heart rate began to increase, and I started to hyperventilate as I felt the beginnings of my first ever panic attack. I didn't know what it was, but I knew my chest was going to burst like a balloon, that my heart would tear itself apart from the exertion. Before long I was convinced with absolute confidence that I was going to die. I was certain that my brain was forcing my heart to beat faster and faster until it would seize. I could feel it pounding out of control deep within me. I was giving myself a heart attack.

"Hello?"

"Julia...Julia?"

"Yes, hello?"

"Julia...it's me...listen...aw, fuck! I've smoked some really bad shit, and I'm really fucking fucked. I...I can't talk."

"Holy shit man, are you all right!"

"No...you have to come over right away, and...and take me to emergency, okay...Julia?"

"Emergency? What's going on?"

"Julia! I'm fucking serious! Just come now...please."

~~~~~

The one thing all these people share is an overpowering tiredness. It's been a long pull, and now that they're satiated, the strain of doing nothing brings itself to bear. Like waves of the sea travelling for miles and miles then finally meeting land, they are crashing, their simple cycles disrupted, the carpet pulled out from under them. I cannot include myself among their ranks. I feel alert, ready for anything. The anticipation of reaching Vancouver fills me with the dreadful happiness of a man who finally realizes what he must do to be made complete. There is of course the fear of finishing the journey, but it's mixed with the elation of discovering long-sought-after knowledge. I wonder how many others on this bus have come to such a realization? How many anywhere?

The new driver trails behind the last person to the back of the bus. From there he slowly walks up the aisle, checking people's tickets. This is not a transfer point, so he doesn't really need to do this, but I suppose he's the thorough sort. Just as he reaches me, I find my own ticket in my back pocket and hand it to him.

"Hmmm, one way eh? You movin' there?" Inquiring minds want to know.

"Maybe," I say. Who really knows what the future will bring. I'm impressed that the question raised no anxiety in me this time.

"Well, it's a nice place, I'm sure you'll like it," he says, finishing with me and turning away to continue rooting out nonexistent illegals.

Vancouver is a great city, everyone knows that, but I won't be staying long. I hope it's not raining the whole time, as is usual for winter. It's late in the year for that, though. If you've only been to Vancouver in the summer, you can't possibly imagine how different the atmosphere is in the winter. You begin to wonder if the sun actually even exists any more, as it's been gone for so long. "Out of sight, out of mind" does not apply when you're talking about blue skies and the warming yellow sun. At first you think you can handle it—you like rain anyway, you tell yourself. It'll vary for different people and what climate you happen to have grown up in, but it will happen; even the bubbliest personality is popped. But it all seems worthwhile as soon as the first hint of spring and summer arrives to wipe your memory clean once again.

PORT

Well, I think it's time to start getting to the real heart of this matter, this matter of the mind, this mind of the heart.

New York, U.S.A.: My Past

It's still very cold. For March, anyway. The air is crisp and clear outside, but here in this bus it's stagnant and warm. Through the front windshield I can at last discern the vague outline of a collection of tall concrete pillars that can be none other than New York. It feels odd to gaze upon this sight. New York is perhaps the one city that everyone in North America—and much of the rest of the world—feels they know intimately without ever having been there. Now, approaching the real thing, I feel nervous and anxious. Will it be all that it has promoted itself to be, all that I've imagined?

I arrive at the Port Authority bus terminal at six thirty in the morning, Sunday. Despite not having slept all night, I don't feel tired, just excited. I get off the bus and follow the signs leading me out onto the streets, where I start to walk with neither map nor direction. I like to do this when I first arrive in a new city; it's like opening the cover on a brand new book. I love the feeling of being completely immersed in something new and foreign. Every corner promises novelty. It's the natural state of our lives really, though the longer we hang around, the more certain we become of the street names. Eventually, though, something happens to bring our assumptions crashing down on us, along with the realization once again that we are after all, lost. Only then do we know where we are.

Where is everyone? Other than the buildings boxing me in, this could be a regular small town for all the people not milling about. Has this tourist somehow mistakenly been allowed to stumble onto the truth? Is Manhattan really just an elaborate set for a movie? Here and there is the occasional jogger or woman walking her dog, but that's it. It's as though a neutron bomb has gone off, vaporizing all biological life and leaving intact only glass and concrete longing openly for their return.

After a short while I arrive at a convergence of streets that looks a lot like my mental image of Times Square. Up until now, my only experience with that famous corner of the world has been watching a million revellers willing the ball to drop three hours early on New Year's Eve. I imagined Times Square to be a place where people constantly gathered and lingered, but right here, right now, other than the larger than life faces staring me down from the billboards, there is no one.

On either end are the media towers, huge pedestals offering their massive TV screens to the heavens, going over everyone's heads. Over there is the rolling news banner board that has proclaimed the headlines since well before man landed on the moon. All the biggest brands are represented here one way or another, chain restaurants and stores fill every building and garish logos cling to every surface like leeches. It's not hard to imagine every corner of every city in the world looking like this someday. It all seems so ridiculous and pointless with no yellow cabs threading the streets, no life, no one to be convinced. It seems stripped, deracinated; it has just wakened and hasn't had time yet to put on its makeup.

I walk out into the centre of the intersection and lie down on the pavement. I close my eyes. The only sounds I hear are pigeons, the wind. I can almost imagine that I'm in a park or a forest. Here I am lying in the middle of Times Square, alleged crossroads of the world, and I'm not getting run over, or yelled at, or anything. I wish I had a beach towel and a beer to make the surrealism complete. If only there was someone to take a picture. Getting up, I promise myself I will come here for New Year's someday so I can stand in this exact spot and compare.

Other than lying down in the middle of the road, there isn't really a lot to do, since everything is closed. My lack of sleep is stalking me now. It's time to start looking for somewhere to stay. I probably can't get a room until one at the earliest, but I should start looking, it could take a while. Out of curiosity, I decide to check out some of the fancy hotels.

"Excuse me. How much is a single room for a night?"

The well-manicured front desk clerk looks at me with a knowing expression on his face; he's been here before. He presses some buttons on his computer, affecting great purpose and import, then looks up at me. "For tonight sir, that would be $469. Plus taxes, of course." He enjoys his job. I can tell.

"I see…and when would check-in be?"

"That would be eleven thirty a.m. sir," he answers, still on to me.

I look at my watch briefly. "Oh, too bad. Thanks anyway." I turn away and walk out before he has a chance to say anything else. Well, that was silly, but kind of fun.

Four hundred and sixty-nine, American, for one night! The way some people live. Can you imagine? Obviously what I'm looking for is a hostel. I begin my search for a phone booth, and after finding two barren of books, and one with a book missing the "H" section, I find one containing hostel listings and a dial tone. A thousand are listed, so I phone the one that seems best located. After phoning this one and three more, the only fruit of my labour is the knowledge that all are full. The man at the last hostel, by way of explanation informed me, "That's March break for you, friend. You don't come to New York without a reservation at the best of times, never mind this time of year. Unless you're happy being homeless, that is."

I hadn't even realized that it was March break. Thankfully though, he was helpful enough to provide me with a number for a hotel in Newark—yes, New Jersey. He told me that it isn't really that far, and that unless I'm loaded, it's my best bet. According to him, all I need to do is catch a bus from the Port Authority to the Newark airport, and then get the hotel shuttle from there. Calling the hotel itself seals the deal as it's a reasonable seventy-five dollars a night. As long at it's generally stench-and-cockroach-free, I'll be fine.

After yet another hour on a bus, the driver makes the announcement that this is the stop to get off at if you're going to Newark Airport. He further informs us that a shuttle bus will be along any minute to take us to the terminal. So about eight of us stand up and shuffle toward the door, trying our best to look like we know what we're doing, but only managing to resemble lost sheep.

As we reluctantly step off the bus, I notice that one amongst our ranks is a rather attractive young girl with a backpack… hmmm. About twenty minutes of watching and waiting pass before the shuttle comes, and we all board. Finding a seat near the middle, I take it and commence staring out the window, but not before noticing that the girl is sitting two seats behind me. After ten minutes of craning my neck and eyes to follow the paths of the airplanes slicing up the sky, we arrive at the terminal. The girl stays on the shuttle. Oh well.

As I wander looking for hotel shuttles, I come across a help desk and concede defeat. I'm informed that the hotel shuttles only go to terminal three, and I'm currently at terminal one—this journey just keeps getting longer and longer. The monorail, a glass-enclosed driverless affair—like a roller coaster minus the speed and sharp turns—at last drops me off where I need to be. I

work my way out to the shuttle pick-up and drop-off area. Here
I stand amongst a clockwork rotation of other weary travellers,
watching shuttle after shuttle come, but for some reason they're
never mine.

Looking vacantly at the people around me I'm amazed to see
the girl again. She's sitting on her pack, leaning against the wall,
busy turning something over in her mind. Hearing yet another
van pull up, I glance at it and am happy to see the name of my
hotel written in block letters along the side. I'm a hundred times
happier when, walking toward it, I see the girl is doing the
same. This is some coincidence. Just like that, a real element of
adventure has been added to my trip.

~~~~~

So, we'll arrive in Vancouver at six thirty tomorrow night.
It's eleven thirty p.m. now. With the time change that makes
another eighteen hours, a long time to be sure, but considering
how long we've already been stranded, it sounds almost rushed.
I boarded this bus at eight p.m., three days ago! When I finally
arrive in Vancouver, this trip will have taken ninety-two hours.
Almost four entire days sitting on a bus. Not many people
can claim that among their travelling stories. If we had been
told at the beginning of the storm that we would be stuck for
a full thirty-six hours, we likely would have lost it—I would
have anyway. But little by little, not knowing what's coming, it's
bearable, like life.

The bus jerks and jars out of its well-deserved slumber,
swaying side to side over the bumps in the snow as we turn
onto the highway, on our way again at last. I look over at the girl
once more. Wavy brown hair, just past her jawbone, swings in
tune with the motion of the bus as though polishing her milky
white skin. It directs my attention to her strong, muscular neck.
There is just something about a well-sculpted neck—you can't

place a beautiful sculpture on a cheap pedestal. Once again her beauty strikes me—green eyes, perfectly manicured eyebrows and delicate nose and lips. No guess as to her nationality.

I turn to the window and watch her reflection. She's reading her *Martin Eden* again, almost finished now. I wonder what she's making of his self-created alienation. Only her eyes move as she sits with her legs tucked to her side and her book resting on her thigh. What is it about this girl that's drawing me to her? It's not her beauty; I'm past that now, and besides, I could practically be her father. There's some kind of deeper connection here, I'm sure of it.

I remember in Japan, it was uncanny how many students there were who looked like Japanese versions of people I knew in Canada. I began to wonder if maybe every continent had the same collection of people, each group differentiated only by slight regional physical differences that manifest themselves in a sharper jaw or folded eyelid. I mean, could there really be six billion different faces and personality types in the world? I wondered if I would run into the Japanese version of myself. How strange that would be.

But it's not her appearance; her mannerisms perhaps. The reference point for such a thing is not easy to define, and as hard as I try, I'm coming up with nothing. Changing focal points for a moment, I turn my thoughts and my stare out the window. Nothing out there yet, just flat darkness. I focus on her again, and a minute later she turns away from her book and looks around, surveying the same old scene.

Then she turns to look out the window, and suddenly it's as though she's looking right into my eyes. Whatever she's looking at, her reflected sightline is precisely in line with mine. She is gazing directly into me. It's one of the most intimate moments of my life. It's as though we're staring into each other's eyes just before we kiss. I realize now that she hasn't been reminding me of a person, but a feeling. It's a strange, foreign sensation that has been long hidden within me. It fills me with the melancholy of a life lived in a minor chord. My heart pounds within my chest and weakens my foundations, like a hammer and chisel chipping away at the stone wall of my resolve.

I know now that I cannot talk to her, she could get inside me too easily, steer me onto the wrong course. I've never been as certain of anything as what I'm doing now, and I can't afford to allow even a drop of doubt to bleed in. I feel the tinge of confusion, the trademark of human existence that was once so common in me. I have not missed it, and I do not welcome it now. For once in my life, I actually *know* something, and that sentiment I must follow, I can't let it become clouded.

Innocently, she turns back to her book, unaware of how close we came to colliding.

Toronto, Canada: My Past

So that was six weeks ago now. I did not die, not really. But, I am a different person, of that I am certain. I can't explain it. I can't explain anything. None of us can. But we try anyway, don't we?

The dope was a bad idea. Very bad. Booze has always been my drug, and while I've had some great experiences on other drugs, I've always found them essentially counter to what I'm trying to achieve in life. After this near-death experience, I promise you one thing: Unless someone holds a gun to my head and forces me, I'll never set off on a drug trip again.

But this whole thing did bring existing matters to a head. That Thursday when I woke up, I felt that some cosmic balance had tilted, some tragic change had been affected and I would never be the same. It seems I was right about that.

And now here I sit at my desk, trying my best to carry on as usual, but I still feel it. It's as though I've gained another sense, or lost part of the others. The visible spectrum of light has been reduced, and there are no more reds or blues or greens, only darkness and brightness. But even the brightness has been muted. Like a home stereo with blown speakers, there is no more sharpness or clarity of sound, no more crispness or definition of shape. Sights, sounds, voices and feelings are all a flat blur.

I try to get excited about things, but I can no longer convince myself of anything. I feel as though I'm on autopilot, steering my body through the day, concerned with nothing more than getting to the end. I haven't touched my guitar since that day; I haven't even been listening to music. I used to hate silence, but now the music fails to change the atmosphere sufficiently enough for me to even bother with it. I can't carry on like this.

I knew I was living a delusion, trying to convince myself that I could control my mind and my perception of life. It was getting to the point where most days I was able to do it. I wasn't what you'd call happy or satisfied, but I had already accepted that, and I was getting by. Under the circumstances that was all I could ask for, and I felt very lucky to be finding success. But somehow the strength gave out, the mist lifted, and the camera was put in focus. The sleeping pills are the only thing allowing me to hold on now.

New York, U.S.A.: My Past

I've never been good at approaching complete strangers and initiating small talk, especially when that stranger is an attractive girl, but this should not be so hard. She was, after all, on the same bus as me all the way from Manhattan. As luck would have it, my task has been made even easier, as we're the only two passengers in the van. It would be strange if we didn't talk. There is the driver of course, a short man who sounds and looks Latin American, but he's none too talkative.

While I'm busy tossing around ideas of what to say to this girl, she angles herself around to face me and says, "I sure am glad you're here, or I'd be a bit worried about this hotel." The sound of her voice is like a symphony.

"Don't count on my hotel savviness," I reply. "I was just happy to find somewhere so close."

She smiles, and I am soothed by its ease and warmth. "I saw you on the bus from the Port Authority. Couldn't find a hotel over there either?" Her voice is soft, yet strong and confident, seasoned, with a touch of an accent I can't place.

I'm pondering her age as I reply, "None for less than the down payment on a small house."

"I had the same problem. It's terrible."

"Maybe one of these days I'll learn to make reservations." I'm trying my best to sound natural and calm, but my brain isn't buying it. "Oh well, at least now we get to see two states instead of just one, right?"

"Yes, I suppose you're right," she says, smiling still, eyes locked on me. "Any idea when the last bus leaves the station?"

"I think around midnight."

"I guess that's not too bad. Nothing like having to be home early though. My mother would be happy at least." Her English is perfect. My mind is racing off into the future to see how this new relationship is going to turn out, leaving me behind to fend for myself in the here and now.

"Well, maybe there's a happening lounge in our hotel," I try to joke.

"Hey, you could be right. Maybe it's the coolest Seventies lounge in town." I feel a tingle of excitement as she responds to my attempts at humour.

After a few seconds of silence, I take up the torch again with, "So is that a French accent?"

She shakes her head. "It's Norwegian. But everyone over here always guesses French."

I laugh. "Everyone just assumes French when they hear an accent. Your English is flawless though."

"My father studied computers in America and spoke it fluently. He used it with me a lot when I was young. He doesn't really like using it any more, though, so he's forgotten some of it. I also lived in England for a couple of years as a teenager. Plus, I've been living here in America for the last five years. In fact, I've just finished my Masters thesis two months early, so I'm travelling for a while until I head home."

"Well, congratulations! Cheers," I say and make like I'm holding a mug of beer up in the air.

She does the same, and we touch knuckles. "*Skal*," she says.

"What?"

"In Norway we say *skal*," she explains. Then, lowering her voice, "If you don't say *skal* first, it won't matter how much you drink that night, you might as well be drinking water. And, as if that weren't bad enough, you'll wake up the next morning with an epic hangover that will last for seven days and seven nights."

"Really?"

"No. But you won't be allowed into Norway ever again, especially if my dad has anything to say about it."

I'm very happy to hear her let out a gentle, yet honest and incredibly endearing laugh. I try to make mine sound as natural. "You're from Norway, wow. I hear it's the most beautiful country in the world."

"Well, I haven't seen every country in the world, but it has its fair share of beauty. I'm definitely looking forward to getting back for a few months to relax and figure out what I want to do with the rest of my life, I really just…"

Her voice trails off with her gaze, and she's not here any more. She's staring through me. Her pale blue eyes sparkle with effulgence. Shallow waters reflecting the northern sun. I feel an overwhelming need to pull her back to me, as though I'm already addicted. "Well, that certainly sounds good. I'm afraid Amsterdam is the closest I've ever been to Norway."

She comes right back to me. "Well, you ain't seen nothin'

yet then," she says, imitating an American accent. "Imagine a country made up of nothing but mountains and trees and mile after mile of coastline cut by fjords."

"Sounds kind of like Canada, if you add mile after mile of glass flat prairies and a lot more room," I offer.

"I guess you're right. Cheers to beautiful places," she says, offering her delicate white fist again.

"*Skal*," I reply.

"That's very good. I see you're a quick study. You can come visit Norway any time," she says, flashing me a toothy smile that could launch a thousand Viking ships, all willing to fight to the death.

"So what and where were you studying?"

"Buffalo, political science and economics. But I don't know if that's what I want to go into," she says, almost defiantly. "And what about you? What's your story?"

As we roll along the highway, I tell her the salient points. The words tumble out, but I don't know what they mean. I know only the effect they have on her beautiful face—the tensing and easing of muscles enthralls me, as exhilarating as music, as compelling as poetry. I realize I've stopped speaking, yet she still watches me. Waiting. Reading. I need to say something.

"Oh, you're Canadian, *eh*?" she says finally. "What part did you grow up in?"

"A smallish town in B.C. Have you ever been to Canada? I mean, other than Niagara Falls and Southern Ontario—they don't count."

"Well, I've been to Victoria and Vancouver, but not really deep into the mountains. That sure is a beautiful area. I've also been to Montreal and Toronto a couple of times. Montreal is a fun city." She's obviously happy to tell me she has seen some of my country.

"I'm living there now, as a matter of fact."

"Really?"

"It's got a great vibe. Very artsy."

She nods in agreement, then slyly adds, "So shouldn't you have been able to tell that my accent isn't French."

I grimace in defeat. "Well, I didn't say I'd been living there long. And Canadian and French French accents are two very different things."

The driver interrupts, informing us in his thick Hispanic accent that we're only a minute away. Our conversation is left hanging as we both turn to look out the windows and watch as our new neighbourhood reveals itself to us, one window frame at a time. We're nowhere near the main part of Newark, whose few tall buildings can be seen congregating off in the distance as though they're the outcasts, not allowed or wanting to join the overachievers across the river. We're driving down your basic cookie-cutter suburban main strip, resplendent with the plastic primary colours of fast food joints and gas stations. And there's nowhere else I'd rather be right now.

"Talk about 'Excitementville'," my new friend says to me.

"No, no, I think this place is called 'Kicksburg'," I hear myself say.

We turn into the driveway of a single-storey, grey brick building, coming to a stop under the overhanging roof in front of the main door to the lobby. The hotel isn't much to look at from the outside, but it could certainly be worse. The driver pulls our bags out of the van, and carrying them both, gestures for us to follow him inside. The lobby is a small room with three chrome-framed vinyl chairs and a television playing a loud program in Spanish. The smell is pure hotel: a mix of cigarette smoke, laundry detergent, and mouldy carpet. It all appears clean though, and that's the most important thing as far as I'm concerned.

We individually register and receive a key, not speaking to one another the whole time, yet already feeling together, a unit that requires formalities to break apart. "So, what floor are you on then?" I ask her.

"Oh, they offered me whatever I wanted, but I always like to be on the first floor. It's a fire thing, you know."

"Hey, me too! Wow, what a coincidence," I reply, struck again by just how beautiful her smile is. "So, do you mind if I ask you your name?" I say.

"Of course not. It's Kira Andersson," she says, offering her hand to me as I tell her my own name. Her shake is on the soft side, but not feeble. It occurs to me that this is the perfect female handshake.

Summoning up all my courage, I venture on. "Well, Kira, are you heading back into town once you get settled?"

"I think so. I think I'll have a shower and change first. How about you?"

"Well, I was planning the same thing. If you like, we could go in together, probably be on the same shuttle anyway. Maybe we could get some food?" I'm growing bolder by the minute, spurred on by her easy demeanour.

"I was hoping you were going to suggest that," she says in a tone more serious than any she's yet given me. She seems somehow distracted, as though fending something off.

"Well, awesome then. How's three thirty? I'm pretty damn hungry."

"Three thirty it is," she says, picking up her bag as she makes a move toward the hallway.

"Let's meet right here, okay?" I agree and we both head off to our respective rooms. Well, my body does anyway. My mind is somewhere else.

OVERBOARD

At the moment I'm reading *The Birth of Tragedy* by Nietzsche, a book that's not sitting well with me. Existentialism rings true to me for the most part. From what I can tell, it states that the best guess for life after death is that there isn't any, and as such we should revel in our daily existence, because that's all there is. In "believing" this, I'm just going with the odds, as they seem best to me. But I don't know about ol' Nietzsche.

Maybe I'm reading this all wrong, but he seems to be saying that all life is a pointless swirling vortex of pain and suffering, and that the way to make the most of it is to live a life of selfishness and impulse. He says that to experience artful tragedy is to be face to face with the reality of our existence. Seeing as how our lives are so tragic, the experience of art in all its forms is the greatest and most profound act of life. In as much as he ascribes any meaning whatsoever to life, he proclaims that meaning to be art. I'm not trying to say that I know something that was not obvious to one of the greatest human minds of all time, but to put art above the concept of morality, above compassion, well, think about that.

More than any other art form, music does it to me. When I listen to certain pieces of music—especially loudly—I'm overcome by a sensation of... I don't know what. It's almost like I'm in touch with a side of the universe that I don't normally see, and am unable to rationalize or define. Other than dancing, I don't know what to do. It's so immediate and overpowering. It's as though the sounds are getting inside of my being, filling me with pure uncut inspiration. I'm never sure how to read the message but am always somehow convinced that it's there. I suppose it's like the feeling I get when I experience an act of kindness, or a beautiful scene in nature, but in those moments it's diluted, the sense of urgency is removed somewhat. This is the power of art.

But what precisely is the value of art? To help answer this question, think of the piece of art that speaks most fluently to you, inspires you the most. Now imagine that the person or persons who created it derived their inspiration from a war, or murder, or something more extreme. You can even pretend that the piece of art was inspired by the artist's own feelings about a murder that he or she personally committed. Now, would that killing have been worthwhile? In your mind, would the ends justify the means?

Was the act justifiable, and even desirable since it provided you and perhaps many others with this invaluable work of art? Make a decision: either one person is executed, or all the famous art that has ever been created is destroyed. What is your answer? Maybe killing one person would be a small price to pay for Vivaldi's "Four Seasons". Or maybe getting rid of all that tired old art would be a good thing, freshen things up, lift the weight off the shoulders of all the aspiring artists out there trying so hard to find a new mould. The answer to this question doesn't come easily to anyone, if at all. I think Nietzsche, however, knew how he felt about all this.

New York, U.S.A.: My Past

The dangling light fixtures spill only dim light onto the floor and walls, and I have to strain to make out the highly-stylized brass numbers screwed onto the doors. Reaching 117, I insert the key in the doorknob. After receiving a static shock I not only feel, but see and hear as well, I push open the door. I'm greeted by the same smell as the lobby, and turning on the light am afforded the first view of my new quarters. The single bed lies against the far wall in the wake of the only window in the room, its view kept in confidence by dark green curtains. Directly on my left is an open door with a small washroom behind it. Stepping in, I'm happy to see that the chrome faucets are cleaned to a shine, and the water pressure in the shower is ample. Back in the room, I turn on the television and find the news. The screen does not flicker, and the colour is even tolerable. Against the right wall is a dresser, upon which sits a plastic vase paired perfectly with a dusty plastic flower. I appreciate the thought. The room is nothing to write home about, but the bed is comfortable and other than the dust on the flower, all is neat and clean.

I look at the bed and know that if my body gets anywhere near a vertical position, I'll immediately fall asleep, so I force myself into the shower. Afterwards I feel worlds better, particularly as it gives me some time to come to terms with the Kira situation. I will take this for what it is, and if it isn't what it needs to be, I will make it that. I will steer in close enough to the falls to feel the cooling mist, but I will not let the currents suck me in.

She's already waiting for me, and within ten minutes we're both on the shuttle again and heading toward the Newark airport. We talk the whole way, and after a long, interrupted journey, find ourselves at the New York Port Authority. As we wander around looking for a timetable for our bus, I once again note her simple beauty. Of typical Scandinavian stock, she is a tall five foot ten and slim but athletically built. Wavy blonde hair caresses fair skin, and blue eyes headline upon an assured face that refuses to give even an inch to age.

Other than her smile, the thing that strikes me most about her is the ease and grace with which she carries herself. If she has felt even the slightest anxiety or nervousness around me, I most certainly haven't registered it. This doesn't seem to come from any sort of overconfidence. I sense that it results more from the calm core of her nature, an acceptance of things as they are, that she knows what will happen will happen, and there's no sense getting on about it. This is quite the opposite of my short temper and tendency to get frustrated, a character trait my mom always said was due to the Spanish blood in me.

"So what shall we do then, mister?" she asks in what I'm quickly discovering is her usual playful tone.

"Well, I'm pretty hungry, and seeing as how it's already six, maybe we ought to go in search of food," is my more serious response.

"All right then, you lead the way," she says, and I comply. We end up all the way down in the Italian quarter before we finally find something that suits our fancy and budget. The restaurant is on the corner of two narrow streets thick with foot traffic and ambiance. It's tight and crowded, but we hold out for a window seat, which we get after waiting only twenty minutes. The lampshades hanging from the distant ceiling cast a dim red glow around the room and are nicely accented by the single votive candles on each table. Such a romantic setting in such a romantic city has us both feeling loose and talkative, and the warm red wine we share does no harm either. Throughout a fantastic dinner, our conversation flows easily, though we do not drift too deeply into any particular subject, perhaps not wanting to be smothered by the weight of it. We open up to each other the various boxes of our lives, and I learn that she feels somehow unfulfilled by her university experience. She tells me that what she really wants to do with her life is some sort of humanitarian work, and she explains how the politics and economics courses she took went nowhere near any of the issues she cares most about.

"That's university for you," I say. "Of course, I must be honest and warn you that my opinion is biased, since I never went."

"What?" she says. "But didn't you say you taught English in Japan? I thought you had to have a degree to do that?"

"Well, I couldn't very well let that stop me now, could I?"

"What, so you lied or something?"

"That's right."

"You're joking! I don't believe you."

Clearly she really doesn't, and I laugh. Of *course* an educated person such as herself has a hard time accepting this reality. "I'm serious. Almost every time you apply for a job out of the country, they never bother to do any research; it's just too complicated from so far away. I mean, I'm sure it's different if you're applying for a real job, but teaching English in Japan? Most places, as long as you show up speaking fluently, that's all they care about. Of course I did have to borrow my friend's diploma so I could photocopy it."

"So you forged a friend's diploma and lied about having a degree to get a teaching job in Japan?" I nod casually, and she considers for a few moments before saying, "Way to go!"

We order another bottle of wine, and she tells me that besides her mother, she is the only girl in a family of six, and the youngest. "So you don't want to mess with this girl," she says as she flexes her biceps. I learn that her father is a computer programmer and that her mother is a small-time organic farmer, doing it mostly as a hobby. She tells me that she plays piano poorly and violin even worse, and I tell her about my own limited capacity for artful things.

"So you're a writer?" she asks.

"Well, kind of, but only in the way someone who paints houses for a living can call themselves a 'painter.'"

"Have you written any books?"

"Oh sure. I wrote a novel once. But by the time I was through editing out all the sentences I didn't like, all I had was a blank screen staring back at me."

"Well, I'm sure it'll come sooner or later," she says, and I can only smile.

Soon our second bottle of wine has evaporated, and we

decide to head out into the open air.

Walking along the still-crowded sidewalk, Kira asks, "So what are the main things you want to do while you're here?"

"Well, I guess I definitely want to go up the Empire State Building. And I'd like to go to the MOMA, and the United Nations. All the typical tourist stuff, I suppose."

"Oh no, no. The Empire State Building really isn't that popular with tourists," she says.

I throw her a sideways glance and add, "But it's too late for any of that now, so I'm up for anything. We could always just walk around and enjoy our first night in New York."

"Actually, I was here once when I was eight. My dad brought me on a business trip, but that was ages ago. I can't remember anything except the traffic and the noise, it all seemed so crazy."

Having made no decisions, we continue to walk, turning wherever we please and ending up in Chinatown, then Soho, then Greenwich Village. I try to imagine what it must have been like to live in Manhattan at the time when so many visionary artists like Warhol and Kerouac were deriving their inspiration from its streets and cafés. Now these neighbourhoods are too expensive to contain such a vital artistic tone, not that I can imagine how different it was or wasn't. It's all in my head.

Restaurants and bars and stores neatly line streets that seethe with an endless stream of people artfully trading places with one another every second. The night is suffused with a fresh chill that we hardly notice, warmed as we are by the wine and the energy of Manhattan, and one another. We do, however, make note of the fact that it's already ten and decide to head back up to the bus station. This is a disappointing reality, as I would love to find a lounge or pub and just sit and talk all night. Our attention wanders with our steps, and we get lost a couple times. By the time we get to the station, it's already past eleven thirty.

Looking around for our bus, we can find no sign of it, and asking at the counter reveals that we've missed the last one of the night. It's now eleven forty-five, and the last one left at eleven forty, which is great news.

"Should we look for another place to stay?" Kira suggests.

"That could take all night. And even if by some miracle we did find a place, it would probably be cheaper to just get a cab back to Newark," I say.

"Well, do you want to do that?"

"How about this. Why don't we go have a few more drinks somewhere and just come back for the first bus at six?" I suggest, rather daringly. "We'll do it the Tokyo way. If you miss your last train there, you just find a bar to sit in until the first train comes in the morning." I worry for a moment that I'm being too obvious, pressing our new relationship a little too hard. I can't help it though, I just feel so comfortable with this girl. And even if I do get a little too close to the falls, come Sunday this all ends, no matter what. In fact, it's perfect conditions for me to eat my cake without having to worry about having it too.

"Sounds like fun to me. Are you sure you can handle it though? You're looking a little tired, you know."

"Don't you worry about me. There's plenty of time for sleeping when you're dead." And with that we head off in search of a bar, and each other.

Soon enough we come across a small cocktail lounge playing some early big-band jazz, and we decide to donate some time to it. Settling in, we resume our dialogue, and I'm hard pressed to remember the last time I talked this much in a single day, let alone with the same person. With each glass of wine poured into it, the conversation distends, gets deeper and heavier, but I feel lighter and looser, as though every word is a physical load I expel.

Finally, unable to hold it in any longer, I ask, "So what about relationships?"

She can see that I'm serious and dispenses with any silly answers she might have had at the ready. "You mean boyfriend-type relationships, I gather."

"Well, that's the most interesting, is it not?"

"In some ways yes, in some ways no."

"That's true."

She hesitates. "Well, I've had a few long relationships, but nothing to bring me anywhere close to thinking about marriage. As far as my current situation is concerned, I've just left behind a relationship of five months that was good, but I'll be able to live without it quite easily. And as far as my future plans go, well…I'm a loving person, but to be quite frank, I don't see any men, or women, in my long term future, not in a serious way." This is an intriguing answer.

"Explain."

She hesitates longer this time before going on. "I just feel I have something more important to do with my life. I guess I believe we should all try and do some good with our time here. You know, leave the world a better place than you found it and all that. And for me that means living my life for others, helping others, the ones that need it most. In the West, we like to imagine that we have what we have because for one reason or another, that's the way it should be. We accept things as they are and say we don't owe anyone anything. That's just wrong; we *do* owe something. I acknowledge my debt. It's more than that though… it's really hard for me to explain. The bottom line is that to be attached to anyone, I would have to become too self-involved. From what I've seen, the two paths are incompatible…you know, it's like…fuck, I'm drunk."

What a perfect girl. A silent moment or two passes, giving me time to choose my words carefully. "I can't tell you how much I respect that. That's the ultimate way to live. If only it weren't just you. I think you should do whatever your heart tells you, because no matter what, you have to be happy yourself before you can ever really help anyone else."

"Damn straight," she says, raising her glass into the air in a toast. Silently I lift mine and offer agreement. Afterwards, we share our first awkward silence, bred by the dissonance between what we have just said and what our hearts are feeling. It's heavy; our words seem to be making love in the air between us, and we can ignore it as easily as we could a couple actually making love on the floor in front of us.

The time comes, and we make the bar a memory. We decide that since we're close, we'll take the risk and finish the night properly by going for a nap in Central Park. We walk up Broadway, and by the time we reach Columbus Circle we're practically sleepwalking. Looking up Central Park West, lined with trees standing guard against the imposing cement buildings, I'm amazed by how big this urban wilderness really is. We pass numerous benches, some occupied, some not, and try to decide between bench and grass. Grass wins hands-down, and we soon find a suitable space under a welcoming tree.

I sit down and lean my back against it. Kira, as naturally as if we were an old married couple, lies down beside me and rests her head on my chest. My skin tingles and my heart flutters at this close contact, but not in a sexual kind of way. It results more from the mental bond I feel with her already. We're too tired now for talking, and neither of us even mentions the cold. Five minutes pass, and I can feel that Kira is asleep already. I try to stay awake—an attempt to prolong the moment—but within minutes I too am starting to nod off. And I remind myself: Eat, not have.

ADRIFT

We're an hour closer to our goal now, and writing about being tired is causing me to dream of sleep, but I'm far too edgy for the real thing. The snowstorm was a catalyst, freezing solid my resolve, and now, reliving those first days with Kira, I'm more focused than ever. The rotation of the tires below creates a soft hum that soothes my body and mind. The forward movement of the bus brushes aside the wind, as well as my doubts. With every mile and minute in the history books I feel stronger, as though I'm continually picking up momentum. Terminal velocity will come later.

All this physical and mental progress occurring within and without me seems to exaggerate the inertia of time, which is crawling now, inching along at a snail's pace. I write an entire segment of my life, and only half an hour of real time has gone by. Whole years of my life seem to fly by without break of daylight, which I long to see again. It's as though my life is flashing before my eyes.

It's almost midnight, and we're maybe a half an hour from Calgary. I watch the beams of shadow tracing their routes through the inside of the bus, insatiable, devouring again and again everything in their paths, stopping for no one and nothing. None of the other occupants notices this play of light as most are sleeping while the rest try to, perhaps disturbed by my reading light which shines on relentlessly. I hate it when I myself am trying to sleep and someone has a light on, but I have no choice; I can't stop writing.

I feel as though I'm becoming a permanent part of this vehicle, and I worry that when the time comes, I won't be able to leave. I'll become a legend, the old man of number 225— "They say it all started when he got stuck in a snow storm for thirty-six hours." In some ways I will be staying behind, a part of me anyway. The only things that come on the next leg of the journey are the absolute necessities; there is no room for excess baggage of any kind. I'll leave all excess on this bus, there shall be nothing to weigh me down; I can take no chances.

Now I can make out the small group of high-rise buildings in the centre of town, and the Calgary tower, seemingly a gawky, snub-nosed imitation of the C.N. in Toronto. I've never been in the Calgary tower, but I've been in C.N. many times. I'm scared of heights, and the glass floor kills me, but I love that rush. Whenever I visit a new city I always make a point of going to the top of the tallest building for the view and fright. It's good to remind yourself that fear exists.

But that's lifetimes away from me now. We've just crossed the Bow River. As we turn onto Sixteenth, I recognize it as the street the station is on. If it were daytime, I'd be able to see the Rockies off in the distance; I'm close to home. Like many others right now, I'm anxiously anticipating the fresh air and cigarette I'll soon be enjoying. Once again the voice of the driver fills the air.

"For those of you who haven't noticed, we've entered Calgary and will soon be at the terminal. To anyone terminating here, I would like to offer my thanks and apologies once more for the extended delay. For those of you carrying on, I've just been informed that the bus will be changed here in Calgary. You'll need to gather up all your belongings and bring them with you. Again, we'll be transferring buses in Calgary, so please don't leave anything on the bus. Your bags down below will be automatically transferred to the next bus. It will come to platform eighteen, the same one we'll stop at. We won't stay more than fifteen minutes, so please stay near the platform. Your next bus will be number 1017—that's 1017. Thank you kindly."

A minute later we turn into the parking lot of the station. It's no different than any other bus station really—smells, sights and sounds so familiar. Everyone gets off carrying their things and I wonder how many of us are saying goodbye to this bus in our heads—"You served us well, we'll miss you" and the like. We were forced to spend time together, and we're more caring for it. Even the people we didn't speak to have become familiar and comfortable, we've bonded through time and adversity. If any of us got hit by a bus and killed, the rest of us would feel more sadness for them than we would a stranger. It's funny how it works, but it's predictable and can be used. Familiarity breeds empathy. Let's get that Israeli and Palestinian trapped on a bus.

Standing outside smoking, I can sense summer in the air. It could be a Chinook, but I don't think so. Along with the others, I watch as old 225 is whisked away the moment it's empty, as though the poor bus is ashamed for getting in so late and just wants to get out of our sight. The company wants to erase all memory of the ordeal from our minds. Like a Mafia traitor, it's going to be taken care of. As it rolls away, I fancy that I can sense its fear. We're all a story richer, though, and that's no little thing.

Everyone is lined up and expectantly awaiting the arrival of the new bus. The group is very quiet—perhaps all talked out, perhaps nervous about the meeting. We're a "special service" now, and there are only about fifteen of us left. Deciding I probably have enough time, I leave the line and head into the station to find a washroom. Just as I'm about to reach for the door, I feel someone grab my right wrist and give it a good yank. It's the *Martin Eden* girl from the bus. I hadn't even noticed she wasn't in line.

"Come with me," she commands under her breath, and for some reason—manners, I suppose—I follow. She leads me away from the platform area to a dim corner and stops in front of a garage door that hangs half-open like a slack jaw. Looking around, I see that no one's eyes have followed us here.

"What is it?" I whisper, and she says nothing, just stares at me with wide eyes and furrowed brows. I'm struck again by that feeling of familiarity, very strong now as I stand face to face with her in this tired half-light.

"Do you know what you're doing? Do you really know what you're doing?" she says at last in an insulted tone. I have no idea what's going on.

"Do I know you?" is my meagre response.

"You don't want to do it. You do *not* want to do it," she says sternly, and a strangely surreal feeling sweeps over me. Like a shiver.

"I...I don't know what you're *talking* about. What are you talking about?"

She just stares into my soul, seeing god knows what. "Do you even know where you're going? Do you know what you're doing?" I say nothing. "I'm begging you, please don't do it... just...just don't get back on that bus." She is holding onto my wrist with both hands as though it is a life preserver.

I feel light-headed and extremely uncomfortable. What is going on here? Can lack of sleep cause hallucinations this convincing? "Look, I really have no idea what you're talking about. You...you must think I'm someone else. The bus is coming," I say as I pull on my arm, which she holds even tighter now.

"No, please, don't," she moans, "don't. Come with me, we can go to my apartment. Come hang out with me tonight, we...we can do anything you want...anything!" Out of the corner of my eye, I see the bus pull onto the platform.

"Look, I have no idea who…I've got to go!" I exclaim and pull my arm sharply, tearing it out of her hold.

"Please. Please!" she screams as I turn away. The few people around do not seem to hear it. Looking back, I see her slump down to the ground, tears flowing down her young, familiar cheeks. She's still looking at me, following me with her frightened gaze, imploring me with desperate eyes. Turning my back on her for good, I flee to the security of the bus and feel as though I have just escaped through the bedroom window in the middle of the night.

New York, U.S.A.: My Past

I only woke up a few times over the four hours we lay there, but each time I did I was rewarded with the beautiful realization that Kira's weight was still pressed against me. Usually when I sleep I toss and turn all night, particularly when I'm sleeping in a park under a tree. But each time I woke, I held my ground, not wanting to disturb her. Unbelievably, I don't think she woke up or moved even once. This time, though, the sun is rising, helping the leaves into their green coats for the day, like a mother, and I must move, or I may never do so again.

Carefully removing myself from under her and placing her pretty head on her arm, I stand up, stiff as wire. I notice for the first time that it's actually quite cold out. It seems we did a masterful job of keeping each other warm. The slightest hint of mist levitates above the ground and lends the park a mystical air. Fitting. Through the branches of the trees I can see the buildings forming a sheer wall of glass and steel and stone along the edge of the park, stopped short in its advance. A staring contest rages, but the grass and trees will not be intimidated.

I don't sense Kira coming up behind me until I feel her warm breath in my ears whispering, "Good morning."

Turning to look at her I'm amazed by how fresh and

desirable she looks. I want to hold her in my arms and kiss her, but instead I simply ask, "How did you sleep?"

"Great! I always sleep well outside, especially when I have a good pillow."

"Weren't you cold?"

"Well, it might sound funny, but when I sleep my senses tend to go to sleep as well, so I don't really notice the temperature."

"So I see your wit is a twenty-four hour thing then?" I say.

"Well no, that also goes to sleep when I do," she throws back, a twinkle in her eye.

"Well, I'm afraid it's too early in the morning for my brain."

"Oh, not a morning person, eh?" she says, again usurping my Canadian vernacular. "That's too bad. So how did you sleep then?"

"I can't complain," I say. "Though I kept having this terrible dream that I was lost deep in an evil forest, trapped under a huge fallen log. At one point I was so desperate to escape that I even tried to eat my leg off."

"See, it's not too early for you!" she says, punching me in the arm. "I'm glad you didn't try to eat the log."

"Damn, I didn't even *think* of *that!*"

For a moment our conversation pauses as we yawn in unison and look out at the park, also in the throes of awakening.

"So what shall we do now? Do you want to sleep here longer, or would you rather head back to your hotel bed?" she questions me.

The choice is perhaps not as obvious as it might seem. "I think I'll go for option two, but let's find some food on the way to the station, all right?"

"Okay, but it's probably easier to just buy some," she says with a sheepish look, and I'm in awe of her. I love it.

"Geez, you're making me even more tired!"

We find a convenience store and stock up, and on the way to the terminal I tell her my waking up in the morning history. "I basically couldn't do it under my own power," I explain. "My mom would yell at me, through maybe four separate sessions, eternally optimistic, until finally she would come and rip my covers off and force me to stand. Sometimes I would just get right back into bed when she had left. For the first hour of every day I basically hated the world. I figured there was no way I was going to be able to enjoy a life where so much waking up was required."

"You must have driven her crazy!" Kira says, laughing.

"And when I finally did get up, I'd be in the most evil mood. I used to build a wall of cereal boxes around me at the table so that she couldn't look at me. Learned more French that way than in school."

"You realize that when you have kids, they're going to act the same way. That should certainly be interesting for you to experience."

"Ah, I'll just let my wife take care of it," I reply, hoping for, and getting another punch in the arm.

"As you can see I'm a different story, nothing but my usual charming self in the morning." I grudgingly agree, and soon we're at the terminal then finally back at our hotel. We would surely have fallen asleep on the bus if we didn't have to transfer so many times. We both make our way to our rooms after agreeing to meet in the lobby again at noon.

Of course I can't sleep. Lying on my bed, tired but invigorated, staring at the mildew blooms on the tiled ceiling, I feel inspired. This is feeling so natural, so easy. I'm reasonably certain it's the same for her too. With other girls, even those I'd been with and known a long time, I distinctly remember feeling a bizarre isolation—distance, space between us, moments of realization. Sometimes while watching TV or driving, I would look at the girl's face and think to myself, who are you? They seemed so far away and foreign, so separate and unknowable that I couldn't fathom what had brought us together and why. But with Kira this hasn't happened at all and I feel certain that it won't. We fit together like left and right hands.

Maybe my resistance is, as it were, futile. Or worse, just plain stupid. I look at her and I feel comforted, consoled, as I do when I'm with my mother. She is familiar to me, even though we've shared only one day together. I don't know the reason. I look at her form, her face, and nothing seems odd or out of place. If some God were to float down through the roof and into this room, proclaiming that this girl is the soul I've been matched to for all eternity, it would seem to be a reasonable explanation.

And shoot me if she doesn't feel the same.

The sound of the phone ringing awakens me. It's an old-style phone, with real bells, so pleasant compared to the scientifically-formulated-to-grate modern annoyances. The finer details of my current situation flood over me like a warm breeze as I recall the face of my new acquaintance. It's the exact opposite of that feeling you get when you dream you've won a million dollars then wake up to the stack of bills marked "overdue" sitting on your bedside table.

I think of the anxiety, the old fear of the pain. But it's all below the surface now, under the water. I have to set my gaze on precisely the correct angle to see it. My happiness obscures these thoughts under a film of bright light, and all I can see are the warming rays reflected back at me. Negative thoughts are as contrived as sandcastles, and the high tide of my joy razes them, leaving behind not a trace.

Having gotten dressed after a quick shower, I'm heading to the lobby enveloped in the hotel smell, which has become the scent of happiness, anticipation and adventure. I'm ten minutes early, so I sit and watch the Spanish soap opera bellowing away. It's hard for me to understand all that is said, as they speak so incredibly fast, but I get most of it. From where do televisions summon their power to attract eyes as though they are the sewer-grate at the bottom of a hill after a lively rain? We cannot escape it. I've always hated television, but even still I watch it

infrequently. Television and its prescription of laugh tracks
and mediocrity is counter culture in a literal sense. Counter to
culture—against culture, the destruction of culture and mind.
It's the conditioning of my youth that draws my attention to this
box, even as I sit in excitement waiting for my Kira.

And then she appears, looking as fresh and clean and
beautiful and appealing as anyone ever has. She's wearing a
heavy wool sweater, and I want to join her inside it, feel her skin
against mine. I'm falling faster now.

The driver is waiting for us, and we pile into the van to
complete our third circuit of this merry-go-round of pleasure.

To save time, we take a taxi, and I experience my first ride in a
New York yellow cab, which is really no different than any other
taxi experience, except that you can watch New York passing you
by through the window. We drive along the east side of Central
Park, and I can almost see the place where we slept last night.
Arriving at the Guggenheim, we pay the driver and step out.

Frank Lloyd Wright's masterpiece is a New York landmark
and a must-see—quite a feat for a building that is only five stories
high in a city famous for its skyscrapers. Its layered rounds have
a weightless feel, as though made of paper or plastic, a cloud or
dollop of whipping cream. The inside is even more impressive.
We pay our admission and walk into the open area that the
spiral encloses. Looking up through the lofty curving lines, I'm
reminded of the grandeur and symmetry of the Pantheon in
Rome. Architecture is such a monumental art form, and I've
always been awestruck by it; I love the way you're able to walk
through it, interact with it, and merge with it. It's almost as
though it's incomplete without you inside of it, the life force and
the soul of the work. Or maybe it's just Kira by my side.

Starting at the spiral, which is basically a long ramp
circling up three or four floors, we ascend and observe the
works arranged along the winding wall. There's a Chinese art
collection on exhibit at the moment, and though we both agree

it's not among our favourite styles, we have an amusing time
pretending to be snobby art critics. After a while, as so often
happens in a large museum, it all starts to look the same, and
my attention wanes. Agreeing we've gotten our money's worth,
we leave, and it's already dark outside. We have vowed not to
miss the last bus tonight, so we can't stray too far from the bus
terminal. We find a place to eat just off Times Square, and by the
time we're finished, it's already eight. Getting some beer first, we
head back to the hotel having decided to have a drink together
before getting a proper night's rest. By nine thirty we're sitting
on the bed in my room, checking the channels on the TV, and
we come across that old classic, *Rocky III*—the one with Mr. T.

"Oh! Oh! Leave it here!" Kira directs me. "I love the Rockys!"
We share a six-pack of beer while watching and inevitably become
excited by the action in the movie. By the time the final fight scene
comes, we're quite wound up and sitting on the edge of the bed
cheering out loud for Sly. Kira starts hitting me playfully while
imitating Mr. T. We spar a little before I finally push her onto her
back and sit on her, smothering her arms so she can't move.

"Now whatcha gonna do, Mistuh?" I tease.

She struggles valiantly beneath me, but I hold her firm. "I
hope you know you're playing with fire here. Remember, I had
three older brothers, and they're all bigger than you. Don't say I
didn't warn you," she says and begins squirming again.

I'm feeling greatly aroused, of course, being so close to her.
Every part of our bodies that touches seems to melt and fuse
together like water seeping into soil. Loosening my grip, I allow
her to squeeze her arms out, and to my great surprise and
satisfaction, she wraps them around me and pulls me into her.
And just like that we're holding each other. It feels like home.
Then we're kissing. Softly at first, then progressively harder,
more passionately, the kind of kiss lovers share when they're
reunited after spending an ocean of time apart. I'm shocked
by how familiar it feels, as though I'm kissing my wife. At this

precise moment, I'm convinced that we have lived past lives together. We roll over, and I feel wisps of her hair tickling my ears. My hands venture under her sweater, and my heart races as I feel her smooth skin stretched taught over the tense muscles of her lower back. But before I know it she is pushing me away, gently at first, then more forcibly.

"No, no, no," she says until we disentangle ourselves. The ordeal feels like trying to separate two massive magnets, and though no longer touching, I can still feel the immense attraction pulling between us.

"What…what's wrong?" I manage to sputter.

"No, I just…" she pleads. "I have to go, I really…" And as she moves toward the door, I fall back down on the bed, unable to move or breathe, a marionette whose strings have been cut. She is taking all my energy and life with her.

"I'm so sorry," she whispers. "I can't do this…I…" As her voice dies away, so does my heart. And then all I hear is the door as it closes behind her, followed by the grave silence of shock. A heavy, crushing aloneness threatens to smother me, as though now that I've experienced perfection, I'll never be able to live without it. I want to cry, but I feel too sad. I must get out of this room, but I cannot find the energy necessary for such action. The only movement I might be able to make is to go to her, but I know it would not be right. I have no say in any of this. It as all beyond me. I am a wandering fallen leaf being whisked along by a cold pre-winter wind.

I awaken to the sight of the clock reading 10:21 a.m. and am instantly awake. The emotions of the previous night saturate my soul, the sleep having provided no respite whatsoever. I'm at a loss for a plan of action but am saved by the presence of a folded piece of paper on the floor in front of the door. I fully expected to wake today and find that Kira had checked out of the hotel and my life forever. I bound out of bed and over to the note, hurriedly unfolding it and devouring the words.

Dear you that has gotten me so confused,

For the past ten years of my life I have had an unflinching goal, a plan to do something important and worthy with my life. I was going to live selflessly, always for other people. There is so much hurt and injustice out there that I can do nothing other than dedicate myself completely to the idea of being a force for good and love. I was content and fulfilled with this plan, this life. The only way for me to dedicate myself fully to such a goal is to be my own complete person, independent and removed from the banality of the emotions and stresses of a romantic relationship. I must be free to live life on a whim, able to change directions at any corner that might lead to the place where I should find my purpose.

Now, here I am on my way home for some down time before I finally set off for Africa, chasing my dream when...

Enter You. Do you realize that in a matter of two days you have me reconsidering and imagining, being selfish? This is unacceptable. If my feelings for you were not so great, then I could be with you, for now. But I can't get you out of my head. I feel a connection with you, as though I'm a positive charge to your negative. Together we make harmony. And I know you feel this too. But if I were to be with you, I would never be able to live the life I have planned. Perhaps you would say this isn't true, but I just know it. Even if we tried, over time I would slowly drift away from my calling.

I'm deeply sorry, but there are too many other people in the world that need me in my positively charged state.

Maybe it could have been so beautiful, but that wouldn't be right.

Love,
Kira

With an impossibly heavy heart, I read the ruinous letter two more times and grow increasingly upset as the words refuse to rearrange themselves into a more positive light. There is no hidden meaning or riddle to provide relief. The paper falls from my limp hand, and I feel insulted that physics has not recognized the gravity of the situation and altered itself accordingly. I collapse into myself, the weight of my sorrow so massive that it pulls my self in whole. How did I not recognize the full extent of these feelings growing within me? I have never felt so out of synch with the universe, so untethered, so disconnected. The trajectory of my life has been an arrow flying through space, and tonight I hit the bullseye, but just as I thought I had finally arrived, I bounced off the wire. Now here I lay upon the floor, motionless, the goal never so far from my reach. I'd arrived at my home after years of searching and doubt, only to have it disappear like a mirage as I crawled to the front door. And I never even knew it was what I was searching for.

SEA

SEAWORTHY

Well, here I am in Vancouver. My hotel. After checking in, I had a much anticipated shower, my first one in four days. After some hot food, I went for a swim in the hotel pool. The pool is in the basement and has no windows, the lack of which is not quite made up for by the cheery palm tree mural painted on all four walls. The affected scene wasn't quite sufficient to transport me to a warm island beach, but you have to appreciate the effort. Regardless, floating weightless in the tepid waters was like heaven after sitting so long on the bus.

Having done all this, I'm now sitting contented in a room that should make a pleasant home for the next week or so while I prepare. It has expansive floor to ceiling windows looking out on Robson Street, with Stanley Park on one end and the city stretching out on all other sides. I have a number of friends here, but I won't see them. It's just too risky to tempt myself like that. It's eight thirty now, and I've been contemplating going out for a walk, but I think I'm just too tired. A long sleep on a real bed will do me a world of good.

"Hello."

"Good morning! Sorry to wake you, Mr.—"

"Yeah, no problem. How you doing?" I reply as I clear my

throat and cut him off unintentionally, still half asleep. I feel as though my brain has been out of business for the last twelve hours. What a difference horizontality makes.

"Great, just great. The wife's driving me round the bend, but we're fine, you know how it is." I don't. "I'm a little sad though at the thought of letting my baby go to you," he adds, sounding very sincere. His voice is disarming and decidedly good-natured.

"Don't you worry, Bill, I'll take good care of her. So, can we meet today then?"

"Yeah, of course, whenever is good for you."

"All right. I'm at the Bermuda Hotel on Robson. Do you know it? Across from the Safeway?"

"Yes, sir. It's beside a really good Indian restaurant too. You should check it out. How about I pick you up in an hour?"

"That'd be perfect," I say, trying my best to match his cheerfulness, a difficult task I am ill equipped for so early in the morning. "I'm in room 2008 if you need to reach me, but I'll be waiting outside for you. What are you driving?"

"It's a blue sixty-nine Chevelle," he says, his voice oozing like liquid pride through the receiver.

"Wow, nice, I can't wait to see it," I feed him. "I'll see you in an hour then."

"Sounds good, buddy, catch you later," he says before hanging up. I try to picture what he's going to look like. Probably has a bit of a gut, short hair no doubt, most likely none too concerned about fashion either. He certainly sounds like a nice enough guy.

Stepping out onto the balcony, I take in a large helping of the cool, dry air. The morning traffic on Robson stretches off in both directions like a long metal snake, or perhaps a slinky would be a more accurate description. The sidewalk is already full of people happy to be seen on the most happening street in Vancouver. In the distance to the east, Mount Burnaby hovers above the slight morning haze. It's an absolutely perfect morning, and I'm filled with a sense of wellbeing that has been absent for some time. It will only be a brief visit here.

Finding a suitable ledge to sit on, I begin my wait for the Chevelle. As most people do in such situations, I occupy my time with that old standby of a pastime known as people-watching. Perhaps more than any other city in the world, Vancouver has all kinds, making it perfect for such an endeavour. But it's not just the variety of ethnicities—it's also the wide diversity of lifestyles and belief systems that make this city so stimulating. A supremely tolerant city, Vancouver is where you'll find business people asking hippies for a light, students, druggies and punks sitting on a shared set of stairs, and freaks, jocks, mods, rich, poor, trendy, hopeless and helpless sharing the sidewalks and parks with a minimum of friction.

But, alas, a mean-looking Chevelle is creeping up from the northwest end of the street. Now here is a nice car, showroom condition and willing like a Harley. The silver grill has been removed, and the four round headlights peer out angrily from the blackness. The driver pulls up to the curb in front of me, and I approach the open window.

"Bill, I presume?"

"That's me!" he shouts, leaning over to open the door. Getting in, I shake his hand and smile as I see that the picture I had painted of him in my mind was not far off target. He's a stocky man of average height, with two or three day's worth of facial hair to supplement a curly mop on top. Clothed in an untucked plaid shirt and old jeans, it's plain to see that all his effort regarding external appearance goes into this polished steel suit on wheels. Pulling noisily away from the curb, he informs me, "It's only about ten minutes from here."

"Killer wheels! It's mint!" I say, not only because it's the appropriate thing to do with car people, but also because this Chevelle really is impressive. He nods in modest appreciation and proceeds to tell me about all the modifications he has made: headers, performance piping, titanium hardware and various other things I know little about. I'm not really a "car guy", but I do appreciate quality, and I have a real soft spot for old cars. Is there any material possession that can elicit more emotion, excitement and fancy in people than an automobile?

"There's nothing like an old car. I love to imagine all the different people that have owned and loved it in the past. I can just picture the teenager who saved up for three years to pay for the half that his dad said he would match. And then the day they went down to the shop and finally drove it away."

"Yeah, man, Norman Rockwell should have painted that," Bill says rather insightfully.

"He probably did," I say. "And of course all the nights spent cruising streets filled to the curbs with other beautiful cars. Going to the race strip, then later on, if you're lucky, maybe getting laid in the back."

"It's so cliché, but that's the perfect life for a teenager, eh? Maybe even men in general," he says, obviously very happy to have his car appreciated and understood.

"Has it always been in Vancouver?"

"No. It was originally bought and owned in L.A. I have all the papers," says Bill.

"How long have you had it?"

"Three years and four months," is his ready reply.

"And how long have you been married to your wife?"

"Oh man! Don't test me like that!" he says, and we both laugh.

I ask him what he does to keep the bank account full, and he tells me he's a cameraman for the hockey and basketball games at the GM Centre. When I express my approval, he informs me that the hours are not that great, but that he makes good money and gets to watch all the games for free. I can think of worse jobs.

A few minutes later we arrive at the marina, and I cringe as he actually parks his car sideways, taking up two spaces. I want to tell him that he's just begging to get his car keyed, but I hold my tongue. We walk up to the gate, and he quickly locates the proper key from the most crowded ring I've ever seen.

"Jesus, do you have the key to every door knob in the GM Centre on that thing?" I joke.

"Well, my house keys are on here too."

From here I can see Grouse and Seymour mountains standing tall over the strait. These north shore mountains are the birthplace and namesake for a completely distinct style of mind-blowing, super-technical mountain biking. I've ridden them myself many times, but I'm a far cry less insane than a lot of the riders you'll find risking life, limb and love amongst the rainforest's tangle of trees, roots and mud.

Turning my thoughts back to this side of the water, I take in the familiar sight of the cruise ship terminal, so reminiscent of the Opera House in Sydney. I remember it was there that I went to a computer-generated 3D Imax show of a space flight. We were stoned, and to this day, I can say that basically, I have been to space. My attention quickly reverts back to the marina itself. I focus on the sounds, all so familiar and universal. Even the most casual of sailors feels a sublime calm when bathed in the sounds of the bells and creaking wood, wires clinking off aluminum and ropes groaning under strain, and the eerie sound of the wind whistling through shrouds.

The sight of all the beautiful sleek sailboats makes me feel almost nervous, anxious to get out on the water and make the most of whatever wind there is before it blows away, wasted and unused. I sailed a bit as a kid, but it was as a teenager that I really got the chance to learn the ropes, so to speak. Every summer my friend's dad would let us be part of his crew in the weekly races. Those were some fun times. Since then the only sailing I've done has been with friends and acquaintances here and there.

"You know, I've always felt that I must have been a sailor in a past life. I just love everything about it," I say to Bill.

"Yeah? So who do you figure you were? Columbus, I guess, eh?"

"No, no one famous, I'd remember something like that. Just a regular everyday sailor working for pay and love of the sea, I suppose."

"And the drink no doubt, huh?" he says, then dives into a drunken sailor impersonation, which is quite amusing, and I laugh. "I don't think I would have liked all the rats and scurvy back then," he says.

"Yeah, GPS is pretty handy too I guess, eh?"

Bill points to a boat up ahead and says, "Well, thar she blows."

I feel a surge of tremors run through me as I anticipate this first meeting, like a performer taking his largest-ever stage. As I approach, it's readily apparent that my new friend Bill here has put every bit as much love and care into this boat as he has his car. It is, well, beautiful, gorgeous, sexy. A dark navy blue body and teak deck are brought to life by gleaming, freshly polished hardware mounted artfully like jewellery. The name, printed on the stern in white script, reads *The Count of Monte Cristo*. Perfect.

Following Bill onto the deck, I feel alive, empowered, free of the weight of the earth. It's as though the boat is its own universe, above and beyond the rules of normal existence, even gravity. Bill can see my pleasure and says, "Almost as nice as the car, isn't it?"

"If you turn that sentence around, I might agree with you," I reply.

The cockpit is large and shaped like a T, making space for a generous wheel at the back. Bill, feeling the need to play salesman, informs me, "So, you know, she's a thirty-five with a nice wide three and a half metre beam. All the lines lead to the cockpit, of course, and she's perfect for solo sailing. You're gonna be happy to know that she has hundred-gallon water and fuel tanks. You can motor all the way to friggin' Japan if you need to, and there's enough water for two people for more than a month.

You're basically your own little island here. And I've taken really good care of her. She's better than new, if I do say so myself. I even replaced all the lines for this sale."

I know all the stats on this model, and I'm almost willing to take him at his word for everything else. "Well, it sure is a pleasure to look at," I offer, not wanting to give too much away, though I get the feeling that Bill, like myself, is the straightforward business type.

"Well, shall we go for a sail?" I say.

"I was hoping you'd say that. No better time than the present, someone always says."

As Bill prepares for launch, I have a look around and notice other details. The self-tailing winches will likely come in handy. I like to exert myself when I sail, but on a solo trip such as I have planned, they'll be welcome when I'm really tired. In awe and wonder I look at all the ropes of varying gauges and colour artfully winding their way to their designated insertion points, tying together an ancient system that has changed little since the very first sailboats plied water. Even the most fastidious landlubber must appreciate the allure of travel by boat, maybe the oldest mode of transportation known to man other than pack animals and his own two feet. There's magic present as a boat slices its way efficiently over the very same water that is the source and sustainer of all life on the planet. Whenever I'm on a sailboat I think of the great tall ships exploring the brackish backwaters of the unknown world so few years ago. Oblivious to where they were heading, they bravely sailed on, unyielding to the omnipresent worry that they would sail over the edge of the world that lay in wait, perhaps just over the horizon.

READY ABOUT

New York, U.S.A.: My Past

The black has finally succeeded in beating the blue from the sky, and the streetlights and neon signs buzz by in a pulsating blur of the garishly mundane. In the shuttle once again, returning to the hotel, I've decided I will check out tomorrow morning and return directly to Montreal. My day today was spent walking around in a daze, a hazy fog of Kira's scent and soul. Every woman I see brings her to mind, whether it's a confident gait or a wandering wisp of hair; she is everywhere yet nowhere. I can't even say where I went today. It's quite simply astounding how a taste of love can turn you from one person to another in a mere matter of moments. Yesterday was full of anticipation and novelty; today is empty, devoid of all meaning other than its lack thereof, like a garbage bag full of crumpled and torn Christmas wrapping paper. Perdition can walk unannounced into your life at any moment, despite how securely you thought you had locked the door.

I wish I could leave tonight, but being at home will probably make no difference in the way I feel; it might even make things worse. At the very least, though, I would have left the scene of the crime.

To protect itself from depression, my brain is donning that age-old coat of armour called anger: anger at myself, of course, only myself. How could I breach my sedulous avoidance of such situations in the past? I could never understand how love could be worth the ridiculous extremes of highs and lows it subjects its sycophantic slaves to. I'm nobody's fool; I see right through it. That was of course before it figured out the proper formula to tantalisingly tease even my vigilant mind.

Arriving at the hotel at last, the driver pulls under the shelter and turns off the engine. I look into the lobby and am shattered for the millionth time today as her absence is confirmed. I feel cold. I slip out the side door and stand and stretch. I should probably go find a liquor store. It's sure to be a long night either way, but at least with the soporific effects of the bottle, I'll fall asleep, eventually. Looking up and down the street, I spot a convenience store a couple of blocks up the road. Huddling inside my jacket to block out the wind, I set my feet to falling in that direction.

Then I hear the sound of someone whistling. Refusing to allow myself any hope, I continue on in forced ignorance. The whistle is soon followed by the sound of someone calling my name. Even over the wind and the passing cars, I know. It's her. I turn to look and see her sitting on a bench beside a bus stop across the road. All my mental energy goes into deciphering the image entering my eyes, trying to read her countenance for any sign, any visual clue that will tell me how this is all going to work out.

~~~~~

Bill pulls me up out of my reverie. Having removed the main sail cover and performed the multitude of other preparatory steps, he asks me to help slip the ropes from the dock. "But before you do that, can I ask you something?" he says furtively.

"Sure, you can ask, but I can't guarantee I'll answer. We did just meet, after all," I joke.

"I just was wondering, do you uh…uh, smoke the herb?" He

asks it with the same nervous shyness that people exhibit the world over when asking this question of people they don't know.

"As a matter of fact, I do," I say to avoid any awkwardness. I'll just take shallow puffs.

"Well, all right," he says, adding, "You never can be sure with you Ontario types."

I laugh. West Coasters think of people from Ontario as uptight and stiff. I would argue that Ontarians are more dedicated to their habit, because they have to put up with so much more official resistance than their fellow Canadians living on the west coast, who can basically walk down the street blowing smoke in the face of the police.

Bill is rolling the joint while sitting on the port bench, and I sit across from him. "You know I was born and grew up in B.C., eh?" I say.

"No shit? Where?" I tell him, and we talk for a while about places that we both know, places that seem as far away as a forgotten dream.

"So have you ever lived anywhere else?" I ask.

"No man, never really felt too much of an urge to go anywhere else, I mean, why would I?"

I can't really argue with that, I suppose. Vancouver is certainly a great place to live. I can see it being more than sufficient to sustain a happy life if you're not naturally inclined to go out and see what's over the next hill.

"Yeah, man, I can see that."

With that I decide to imitate pure Ontario form and broach the subject of the business at hand. "So, forty grand, eh? Seems fair to me from what I've seen so far, and I haven't even seen the cabin yet."

"Oh, yeah, sorry. I totally forgot. Why don't I show you now?" he says.

"No, no, whenever...I did tell you I'm planning a long sail, right?"

"Yeah, you mentioned it. So where you going exactly?"

"Oh, I don't really know yet, just a long way away…you know," I lie.

"That sure sounds good. If I didn't have to work, I might ask if I could join you."

"Yeah… But you know, I'm going to need to get it dry docked and inspected, just so I know what I'm dealing with. I'd hate to be out in the middle of nowhere and have the mast split down the middle like a piece of dry firewood, if you know what I mean," I say, trying my best not to insult.

He's finished rolling the joint and says, "Hey, no worries, man. I'd do the same thing."

"I'll pay for the job regardless, but I can't really commit until after that's taken care of." I can't help but feel a little embarrassed talking such straight business while a joint is being rolled.

"Well, buddy, sounds like you got your head screwed on straight, and that's all more than fair enough with me," he says, obviously confident in his boat in a way that puts me at ease.

His candour provides me with the courage to ask another easily misinterpreted question. "One other thing. Do you smoke on here often? Nothing personal and no big deal. It's just that if you do, I better get a police dog to come and sniff around after it's cleaned. I'll probably be crossing some crazy borders."

"How you gonna get a cop dog?"

"I don't know. I just thought of it now. There must be some way."

"Well, I've given it a good once over, but I guess if I were you I wouldn't take any chances either." I'm very happy and comforted by how this is all going, and it puts me in the perfect mindset to smoke. If the rest of the trip goes as smoothly, I'll have nothing to worry about.

"Well, to speak of the devil and all that," Bill says, eagerly lighting the joint and delineating a timely end to the conversation. He holds it for a few puffs before handing it off to me. I always feel uncomfortable holding onto the joint for longer than one drag and rush through a couple of shallow ones just to get it back to Bill. I've always admired the efficiency of taking one toke and passing it on. This concept of taking a few while the other person waits just seems forced. Maybe I'm missing the point, but it's my nature to feel uncomfortable as all that smoke goes to waste, like leaving the water running while brushing your teeth. Or maybe, as Bill would likely accuse, I've just been living in Ontario for too long.

We smoke in silence, and I'm careful not to let Bill notice that I'm not really inhaling. Other than the odd seagull and the faint hum of cars, all I can hear is the water gently lapping up against the hull. "Fuck man, I just love being on sailboats! Are you getting another one?"

"Oh yeah, of course. Smaller though, a fixer-upper—I like doing that sort of thing. I did my car, and now I want to do a boat."

"I can respect that. I have to be honest though. I understand the gratification derived from getting your hands dirty and making something work again, but I'd rather be out on the water teasing the sails than below decks sanding the floorboards."

"I know what you mean," he says, offering no argument. His explanations have likely fallen on enough deaf ears to last a lifetime. "So I thought you said you'd be here two days ago? I was starting to worry that you might not be interested any more." I re-tell the story of the bus, and he's suitably impressed. "Well, as long as you stay south, the closest you'll come to that on this boat is dead calm, and even still, you got that huge gas tank to take you—"

"To Japan, right?" I interject, and we both smile.

"Well, let's try out our sea legs then," says Bill, standing up. "How about you get on the dock there and push us off?" I step off the boat, feeling a little wobbly from the joint, but Clinton probably inhaled more than I did. Bill fires up the engine, and I'm pleased to hear it start with neither protest nor procrastination. He nods to me, and I remove the ropes one by one from the stern forward, until grasping the forestay and guiding the boat out of the slip. I manage to jump on cleanly just as the bow clears the dock.

He steers us out of the marina past all the other boats that seem to look on in envy, knowing class and refinement when they see it. None of these other vessels seem as perfectly accommodated as *The Count*, though I'm already quite biased, knowing that this cunning craft will soon be my own. I think again about how happy I am with the name. It's bad luck to change the name of a boat, and this couldn't be better if I had chosen it myself. A badly named boat would certainly have been bad enough luck in itself, never mind the added risk incurred by changing it.

Once we clear the other docks, Bill signals for me to hoist the main sail, and without even thinking about it, my hands automatically locate the main halyard as though I had sailed this boat a million times. The lines are in basically the same place on all boats of the same class, and I feel as though I could sail *The Count* myself right now, figuring out the finer points as I go. The main raises effortlessly, the luff feeding perfectly without the slightest pinch or catch. Once it's fully hoisted, I close the jammer on the line and Bill trims the sail. He cuts the engine, and the main uses its bounty to power us silently out of the marina.

As soon as we clear the lee of Stanley Park, Bill calls for me to take the jib sheet as he releases the roller furler. Pulling the sail taut, I cleat it off, and soon we're sailing close-hauled through Burrard Inlet and toward the steel ribbon of the Lion's Gate Bridge. The dry wind is blowing in steady from the Georgia Strait at about five knots and creating perfect conditions. We're heeled over quite a bit, as Bill tells me he's found the optimum heel to be twenty to twenty-five degrees, so

I allow the jib more line and *The Count* responds nicely.

Our speedometer shows us to be cruising at about twelve knots. The waves are minimal, and the bow slices through the one-foot rollers with trenchant determination. When you have steady wind, there isn't a whole lot of work involved in sailing—unless you're racing of course—just keep those sails trim, watch the tell-tails, and keep the heel optimal. There is an indescribable pleasure that comes from moving through the water with no net energy expenditure other than the food energy required to fuel your own body.

I would rather do this than fly a plane, the physics of each being remarkably similar. After all, flying through wind or water, aero and fluid dynamics share many properties. Due to the lack of a jet engine, however, there is a lot more artistry involved in the piloting of a sailboat. The search for maximum efficiency involves an equation that includes hull and keel shape, length and width, sail shape and materials, mast height and number, length of tacks, the reading of sky and water, sail and mast tension and angle of attack, etc etc etc. The variables are endless, like the possible colours on a palette, the meanings of combinations of words, or the arrangements of musical notes. It truly is an art, and people who race sailboats are the master seamen, squeezing every ounce of efficiency from the boat and converting it into forward momentum, progress and speed.

As I sit staring at the water, listening to the splash of the waves on the hull and the willing whisper of the wind, I am almost content, but as we pass under the Lion's Gate Bridge, I look up at the structure and my sense of wellbeing is lost again. From here, down on the water, it seems emasculated, so high and thin and bony; an iron snake slicing through the air, underbelly exposed, as vulnerable as you and I. I think of the people driving their cars across, seduced by the supposed solidity, their rubberized drone audible so far down below. The whirring of each individual tire melds into one soft muted noise, like an amalgam of the linoleum lives laid down and paved over in the combined hum of human advancement. What is the collective consciousness of all this humanity, what is the message? Could it possibly be as mundane as a plea to get the hell out of my way, to get home five seconds faster—please?

"Are you fine at the helm, Bill? I think I'll go check out the rest of the boat, if you don't mind."

"Sure man, go right ahead. Can you find it all right on your own?"

"It's that way, right?" I reply, pointing off the stern out to the water.

Stepping down the companionway, I'm more than satisfied by what I see. The cabin is immaculate, exuding the feel of an upscale hotel room that has just been cleaned by a crack crew of maids. Being in the cabin of a sailboat can often feel like sitting in a glorified closet, but happily, the airy, expansive feel on this boat alleviates any such concerns. Cruisers are a roomy class of boat, and I know this particular model is well regarded for efficient use of its wide beam.

The U-shaped galley is fully equipped with double burner propane stove, mini fridge and even a double sink. Forward of the galley is a couch about five feet long and quite comfortable. Across from it is the navigation and control desk, the rear sleeping quarters extending aft of that. Forward of the desk is the main sitting and dining area. Everything is arranged and organized to prevent a person from feeling as though they're in a submarine.

The décor is pleasant, dominated by the teak panelling and the dark blue upholstery of the couches and chairs. The many portholes and overhead hatches provide a pleasing abundance of natural light. Stepping through a narrow door provides access to the head and the main sleeping quarters. Lying down on the bed, I'm happy to find that I fit without having to hang my feet off the end—very good. Along with an alarm clock and various personal items, on the shelf I notice a picture of a woman I assume must be Bill's wife.

Wearing a soft white sundress with a fine floral pattern, she's leaning against a stone railing with the arid ruins of the Roman Coliseum sweeping off into the background behind her. Her dark hair blows gently in the breeze, and her head is angled slightly to the left as she smiles mischievously at me. She looks very young, beautiful and seductive. The picture itself does not appear to be very old. Gazing into it, I feel light-headed, and suddenly I'm hyper-aware of the slight tilt of the boat under my belly and the smell of seawater. My surroundings become washed out, and fade to black, as though I'm looking into a candle in a dimly lit room. It consumes the existence of everything around me, and it's all I can see. I'm fixated on the picture, sucked into it. Novel and foreign memories are flooding into my head, filling a room in my brain I wasn't aware was there.

Somehow I remember the breakfast we shared this morning as we discussed the heat and studied a tourist map of the city to decide where we would go. I'm happy today, but feel a bit out of sorts as the knowledge lingers just out of reach that this girl is not my own. We've explored the ruins and walked the paths of the ancients, the oppressing Roman sun wearing down our unaccustomed bodies and lending credence to the imagery in our minds. And as she poses, her smile disarms me; I feel helpless, the puppet of the big hand, revelling gloriously in my lack of options. I press the button, and as the shutter closes, a black curtain is drawn over my eyes and I find myself back on the boat, looking at the framed picture of a beautiful girl, frozen in time.

New York, U.S.A.: My Past

She stands up and motions with her arms, more emphatically now that she knows I see her. Finally, I'm able to move, and I turn toward her, my self-respect fighting with my heart to keep me from appearing too excited. Perhaps she just wants the deck of cards she left in my room, or my email address, or some other such unimaginable thing. As I start across the road, she does the same, and I notice her bag, left behind, leaning against the bench. For some reason, I relate to its solidity, the sheer weight of its presence.

Her manner of walking suggests that she is in fact happy to see me, and this observation allows my heart to finally win the tug of war with my brain, and I speed up, desperate to feel her again. We meet in the middle of the road, on the yellow line that normally does a better job of keeping things apart. We have defeated it. She immediately throws her arms around me, and the night, with all its pallid novelty, fades away into a swelling of dimensions. Symmetry at last. I lose myself in the eternity of this thing that I know from this moment on I'll allow myself to inhabit wholly and completely. I feel her weight and her warmth as she buries her face in my chest. Her hair, enlivened by the wind, tickles my neck and chin as I join her embrace.

"I'm so sorry. I'm so sorry," I hear her whisper, almost as though it's not so much directed at me, but rather at existence itself and the physical entity that is us. I squeeze her tighter and feel her heart's fluid beat pulsating through her body, keeping perfect time with my own as though they are two musicians who have played lifetimes together, forever. A moment later a car whizzes by, horn blaring and given texture by the Doppler effect, the driver screaming out the window.

"Let's get off this road before we get killed. That would certainly be a dumb ending, wouldn't it?" I say.

"Maybe, but at least it wouldn't be due to my stupidity," she says, making no movement. We make it to the bench, and taking me in her arms, she pulls me to her, and we share a kiss that sends tremors through my bones and brain, reconfiguring the basic foundation of my life and being, like a shiver of the earth flattening houses and lives. My mind is racing, erasing.

All doubt has been banished, and I am reborn. Kira will be my girl. And I realize that that is how it's always been.

Toronto, Canada: My Past

I wish I could say that I'm back to normal, but what exactly would that mean anyway? It's been five months now since that day, and I still haven't completely overcome that experience. But I have managed to wrap it up and find a place to store it. Time heals all wounds. I guess that's true. It also creates new ones, but in this case I think I'll simply be left with a scar, right across my forehead, that serves as constant reminder. But the pain is easing.

Long before that day, I resigned myself to the fact that my existence would only constitute a half-life, a numbed reality. That day was most definitely an extreme low, but I'm using it to my advantage now. I know what could be, and every day that is better than that one is one to be happy about. I mean sure, maybe there's a constant cloud of depression lingering in my thoughts, but what right do I have to complain? My situation has come about as a result of choices I myself have made— everyone else on this planet should be so lucky!

Regret is such a pitiful waste of time. Once you have made a decision, you must base your entire existence around the new structure and rid yourself of any tendencies to look backward or forward and wonder what might have been. I must have complete confidence in my choices and myself. I am happy. I really am. Maybe not content or ecstatic, but reasonably happy. This is what I wanted. This is what I gave myself.

~~~~~

Sitting here in my Vancouver hotel room, writing when I'm not staring out the window, I find myself torn between staying in and going out. I haven't been here in a while, and there are a lot of old haunts I feel compelled to visit, but I don't feel like going anywhere. Being in this city is quickly becoming disconcerting. There are so many lights and likenesses summoning nostalgia and memories, people and places. All I really want is the solitude of the boat and the sea, not the crowdedness of a bar. Now that I've seen it, I can't get *The Count* out of my head; I love it; it's perfect. There is now that extra layer of reality to my task and situation, and I'm ready.

Certitude is a parsimoniously apportioned gift, and now that I've got some, I know exactly what to do with it. Impulse and analysis are the two oars with which I have paddled through my life, and often they pull one at a time, turning me in circles and affording no headway. Now, though, they pull in sublime unison and propel me smoothly and determinedly toward my goal. The war waged within me has at last, under the direst of circumstances, ended. The practical details of the arrangement have yet to be worked out, but Apollo and Dionysius have agreed in principle to join forces. Still though, I need to exercise extreme caution and steer myself clear of all potential disruptions and distractions, both mental and physical. That includes getting rid of some excess baggage.

There are really only three things of consequence I'm bringing on this trip: My guitar and a pair of Turner prints: *The Fighting Temeraire* and *Rain, Steam and Speed*. I shall put one of these paintings on either side of the cabin, so that I can see at least one from wherever I may be sitting. I also brought fifty of my favourite CDs and had planned on bringing them on the boat, but tonight I cracked a bottle of Scotch and started listening to a disc, then, wallowing in a scary wave of nostalgia, stopped it after the first track, wanting to break the CD in two. Then I did, almost blinding myself with a shard that drew blood beneath my eyebrow. I put another CD in then did the same. By the time the bottle of Scotch was gone, I had covered the carpet with plastic splinters and there was nothing playable left.

I did not allow myself to feel sad; sometimes light has to be extinguished in order for you to see the road clearly.

~~~~~

"Hello."

"Hey, buddy, it's Bill again. How you doing this morning?"

"Fine, fine. What's up?" I ask.

"Well," he starts, "I talked to the inspection guys, and I have some good news and some bad news." Here we go.

"I've always been the bad news first kind of person, so why don't we start with that," I say.

"I'm afraid it's gonna cost fifteen hundred, pretty steep. And then on top of that will be the marina's charge to haul the boat out of the water. I'll pay for that, though." He adds the last hastily, perhaps anticipating an argument.

"That's no problem at all," I reassure him. It could cost five times that, and I'd still be fine. "So what's the other half of the story then?"

"The good news is they say they can do it Friday." That is good news, though it means I have a busy few days ahead of me.

"That's awesome. The sooner *The Count* is off the hard the better. So can I call you Friday morning, and we'll make the final arrangements?"

"Yeah, of course. Hey listen, I'm shooting the Canucks tonight. They're playing Dallas. I can get you tickets if you want. What do you say?" Once again I'm struck by how friendly and utterly agreeable this guy is. I might have been friends with him.

"Ah, thanks, man. I'd love to go, but I'm afraid I've got plans to meet up with some friends tonight. Thanks a lot for the offer though. Maybe if it was the Leafs they were planning on losing to, I'd go."

"Oh, low blow," he groans. "Call me Friday then."

"I'll do that, and thanks again, Bill."

TIME

I've felt a bit like a robot for the last three days, but it's all done; I'm ready to go. Bill called me last night and said that the boat would be back in its slip by three p.m. today. There was nothing at all wrong, not even a frayed rope or a rusted rivet. I've decided that given this proof of Bill's pedantic maintenance, I'll trust his cleaning skills as well and forego the drug-sniffing dog—I haven't got the slightest clue how to find one anyway. If anything were to happen, at worst I'd be delayed. No one would seize the boat on account of a few isolated grains of marijuana, even if they found them. One other problem is my lack of a radio license, but that also is at worst of minor consequence.

I had thought about going to the dock to see *The Count* put back in the water but decided against it. It would certainly be a good idea to get a visualization of the shape of the hull and keel, so I almost did go, but it just doesn't feel right, I suppose like the tradition of the groom not seeing the bride until the ceremony.

I'll meet Bill at four p.m. I hope to invite him for one last cruise on his boat while I sail her solo—it would be good to get in a dry run with him there to answer any questions that come up on my first sail. I'll leave tomorrow morning—the sooner the better. Luckily, leaving from Vancouver, I have about two hundred kilometres worth of the Juan De Fuca Strait before I hit the open ocean. I'll take it slow, and it should be more than enough time for me to get a good feel for the basics of the boat. The finer details will come later. Most sailors would say I'm rushing things, but I'm operating primarily on instinct here. So far everything feels right.

"Where'd you get the dog?" Bill asks, surprised to see my new friend.

"The pound. I figured I'd save one. They keep people sane, you know?"

"That's a damn good idea," Bill says, impressed, though I'm not sure if it might be because he's genuinely concerned about me coming unhinged. "I've got a pure bred Lab myself," he says as Len runs over and starts jumping up on him, licking and writhing in excitement. He has an exuberant tail wag, the kind that involves the whole body and leads me to worry that he might embarrass himself by falling flat on his snout.

"He's still wondering if it's a dream that he's out of the pound," I say. Len is a smaller than average two-year-old mix of border collie and husky, jet-black with white chest and paws, as well as faint rings of white around his eyes like make-up. I know he'll calm down once his excitement wears off. He seems exceptionally good-natured and happy, at the moment anyway. Bottom line of course is that he's a gamble, but it can't be helped. I need a first mate. I don't want any imaginary friends coming along with me.

We cruise out of the harbour under my control. I'm tentative at first, but the water slipping under the hull and the winds fondling the sails seem to do so with affectionate respect, and I gain confidence quickly. We sail into Deep Cove this time, looking for light wind, which we find to some extent, but even here in the sheltered Georgia Strait, the winds are healthy tonight. The only problem with the evening is that it's cloudy, and Bill tells me it might rain tomorrow. The marine forecast on the radio supports his claims. If it is raining when I wake up, we'll delay departure. Like turning your back on a weeping lover, setting out in the rain would be wrong.

My ship sails well, and I'm more than pleased with my purchase. The large rudder provides precise steering and holds course effortlessly. All lines pull smooth and true, and despite her wide hull, the bow slices efficiently through the water. *The Count* is built and designed more for cruising stability and comfort than speed, but it's nice to see that performance was not sacrificed to any great extent. I never even once need to ask Bill for help or advice; the language of this boat comes to me so naturally, it seems as if it has been hiding in my brain all along. He offers useful tips now and then but mostly just tells me how he'd never guess it had been so long since I last sailed a boat. This is going to be quite a voyage, one for the books.

Docked at the marina after a fantastic evening, we settle our business, and I give Bill my sincere thanks for his honest and respectable manner. I decline once again his offer to go out, telling him that I'll be heading off early and would much prefer to be well rested. Besides, I still have a lot of work to do between now and tomorrow morning in terms of rigging and stocking the boat. I've said goodbye to Canada already, and there is no need to go out and therefore necessitate doing it again.

The atmosphere here on board tonight is quite cozy. The dark wood interior combined with the soft glow of the lamps makes me feel as if I could be sitting in a mountain cabin by the warm glow of a fire. I can hear a few other people on the boats around me—nothing more than a smattering of words and muffled laughter betray their presence. What is happening in their lives? Everything is as ready as it needs to be tonight, just perhaps an hour's worth of set up tomorrow morning, and I'm off.

I think Len is going to be just fine. When I throw the ball

overboard, he leaps into the water fearlessly and brings it back for as many times as I care to throw it. I've bought a car seat belt that I put on him, and I can easily haul him up out of the water by grabbing onto it. I've also bought a bunch of leashes that I'll attach to the railings in various places so he'll always be secured when on deck. What's amazing is how he already seems to know who his master is. And the best thing is that he plays hard, but he also rests hard; he'll go hours on end just lying there, not moving, like a dead dog.

Now it's time for me to try that.

Of course it's raining. A grey gloomy sogginess inhabits the air and everything in it like an evil spirit, the all too familiar spectre of the Vancouver winter. I suppose it's only fitting that I should face at least one day of this before I leave. I was definitely living on loaned time for the last five arid days of sunshine. Thankfully though, we're far enough away from winter that there is little worry of the wet weather imposing itself upon us for too long. Turning on the radio to the marine forecast, I learn that it will persist through the day, but will clear tonight.

So, a one-day delay before I've even left the dock, no problem. I can use the time to double-check stock, study the charts, and various other minutiae. In fact it could very well prove to be a blessing in disguise. Perhaps I'll even take Len for one last extended walk on dry land. One thing is for sure—I want to leave under the warmth of my favourite star. It just wouldn't do to leave without bidding my Canadian sun farewell.

After a productive day, everything is set. All supplies are checked once, then again, including dog food and booze, the latter taking the form of fourteen bottles of twelve-year-old single malt Scotch—I can afford it. I've got my course plotted for tomorrow's sail, though it won't be necessary to follow it too closely. Sailing out of the Juan De Fuca will be straightforward enough due to the well-marked shipping lanes and heavy traffic. I'm aiming to be out on the open sea by Tuesday, tomorrow being Sunday. It's a conservative estimate, but that's how I'll be making this trip, nice and easy. The main goal is to get there.

The rain has already stopped, and the barometer is rising. The marine forecast is still calling for partly cloudy skies tomorrow with a high ceiling and moderate southwesterly winds—perfect. Nothing takes the glow out of a sailor's eyes like the absence of wind, and I hope I won't experience that for some time, not until I deserve a good rest anyway. Len is off to bed early, comfortable in the quarters he's already chosen for himself—the aft starboard berth, which extends underneath the cockpit. Presumably he likes the security of a small confined space after his time spent in the slammer.

Staring at the painting across from me, I find myself lost in thought. I'm happy on this boat, but it's frustrating to be going nowhere, especially as this train bears down on me, reminding me of what's possible. The black steam engine, its knife-edged smokestack the only point of sharp definition in the whole scene, wills itself out of the smothering heaviness of the atmosphere as though striving for clarity and focus, just like the rest of us. Its determination is a tangible object, you can reach out and touch it; it invades you. What's it dead set on?

EMBARK

Sunday, March 17th, Day 1: Victoria, Canada

A great workout for the first day—I had hoped to get a good one in, and we managed to cover a fair distance. Irregular winds provided good test conditions for all three of us. The weather was warm with scattered cumulus cloud and intermittent sun, but the westerly wind, gusty and variable, was really wild. We averaged about eight or nine knots per hour sailing into the weather for the most part. This feels very fast, particularly for a boat so weighed down with water and fuel. We're still all getting used to each other, but it's coming along nicely. *The Count* is predictable and responds well, especially at speed.

Tonight we'll bed down for a much deserved and valuable rest, even if not a very long one. We'll be up at five a.m. and ready to go by six, in keeping with the daily schedule I have made. This should provide the maximum number of daylight sailing hours while affording us adequate time for rest. I anticipate that tomorrow may need to be a shorter day, as my muscles feel sore already, but that's to be expected at first. I'm comfortable and confident.

Monday, March 18th, Day 2: Port Renfrew, Canada

Conditions today much the same as yesterday. I'll need to slow down a bit, as my muscles are protesting, not quite used to the amount of exertion I'm demanding of them. They'll come around in a few days. Today we made about eighty-five or ninety knots, quite good. Tomorrow we'll sail out of the Juan De Fuca Strait, and after rounding Cape Flattery, we shall say goodbye to Canada. I'm prepared.

Namsos, Norway: My Past

After the shortest week of my life, the time had come for me to head back home. Kira still had a few more days planned in New York, but I had to be back at work. We had discussed her coming to Montreal instead of staying there, but for the most part we had avoided the subject, unwilling to make the predicament more real by paying it lip service. However, right from the night I had come back to my hotel to find her waiting, I knew what I was going to do. I knew she would be thrilled; it was just a matter of broaching the subject. The moment came as we were relaxing in a coffee shop, soaking up the vibe and critiquing the various people flitting by.

"So you know I'm supposed to be back at work the day after tomorrow, right?"

She looked at me for a moment as though unsure how to respond. "Yes, of course I know. It was the Secret Service right? Or was it Interpol? I can't quite remember." After a week together, I could see through her fronts like polished windows.

Despite her unease—and the fact that I already knew them—I wanted to hear her ideas vocalized, so I pressed on. "So, what are your thoughts?"

She stared into her coffee for a few long moments before looking up at me with her piercing eyes and finally saying, "You know I told you I never wanted to get seriously involved, and I meant what I said." With this she stopped, and I let the silence hang. "But I also meant what I said outside the hotel the other night. I mean…I guess I realize now that it was ridiculous to assume I could ignore my heart…but it's only because my heart has never yelled so loud before. I think maybe to be with someone, with the right person…with you, doesn't have to be a sell-out. Someone like you could maybe even give me strength, the strength to cope. Maybe I wouldn't even be able to do it without you." She paused again, her voice becoming strained. "And I know you're game. I see now that I don't have to be alone to help people, that to make myself happy is not selfish." Finally she reached the heart of the matter and blurted out the words I so needed to hear. "Oh, the hell with it. What I'm trying to say is, I've fallen for you. And I need you. It's so deep, it's—"

"I'm going to phone my boss tomorrow morning and tell him I'm not coming back to work, that I've fallen in love and I'm not coming back." Staring into her eyes, I watched my words set off a spark deep within. The expression on her face cycled through shock, disbelief, then amazement. But then, strangely, a look of resignation stole over her countenance. So unexpected was it that for a moment I feared we had suddenly turned to different pages.

"Kira, what is it?"

"I knew it. I don't necessarily believe in fate, but I just *knew* it about us. I guess it just feels strange to be faced with the idea that this magic we feel might be entirely beyond our control, that we're just somehow along for the ride."

Unsure how to respond, I gave the soft touch a try. "Well, that sounds good to me. I'm certainly not going to complain about a chauffeured trip through heaven."

She looked at me for a moment, her lips quivering as though she might cry, then finally she burst our laughing. "Man, you sure can be cheesy sometimes!"

"Yeah, yeah, I know. The bottom line here, Kira, is that I want to be with you too. I want to be with you whatever you do. I don't know what the hell I'll do, but I don't care." I was feeling giddy just thinking about it. "Maybe I'll write. I do call myself a writer, after all. Maybe it's time to write something more substantial than another freelance article for bloody *Men's Health*."

My excitement was catching as Kira jumped out of her seat, and throwing her arms around me, engaged me in a long, sustained, French kiss. Or should I say, Norwegian kiss. Then she looked me in the eyes and said, "I've never heard of a more exciting plan in my whole life. Let's get out of here and go celebrate."

We went to a club. It was early, so there wasn't much of a line outside, and the inside was just as empty. The dance floor was virtually empty at first, but we could not be deterred, and we found ourselves just as alone as the place steadily filled. Having drinks during the shitty songs, we danced the night away and got a loud and sweaty start to our new shared life. We managed to keep an eye on the time, however, and made the last bus back to our hotel, which was beginning to take on an air of home. We were excited to tell the front desk lady that as of the next day, we'd need only one room.

We spent one more week in New York doing more sightseeing and exploring, except now officially as a couple. Kira didn't really have any firm plans for the rest of her trip, so we just took it day by day. As I'd already told her, I had some money saved up—not a lot, but enough to get by on for a year if I had to. Neither of us had ever been, and Kira really wanted to go, so we decided to go to Australia for a little while, then to Thailand, where we travelled around a bit then spent a week on the beach. It was a good opportunity to relax and allow ourselves to be ridiculously and sickeningly romantic. From there we got a cheap ticket to Los Angeles, and after renting a car and buying a tent, we did a road trip around the Southwest and into Mexico. And now, here we are in Norway.

The weather has been warm considering how far north Kira's hometown of Namsos is. I'm told that it's normal though, resulting from the warming winds of the Gulf Stream. Winter is another story, but I haven't read it yet, and thankfully, it's a long way off.

From what I've seen so far, it wouldn't be too much of a stretch to call this perhaps the most beautiful country I've ever laid foot or eyes upon. Dominated by rugged mountains, icy-cold aquamarine rivers and vibrant little towns, the landscape is relentlessly stunning. The abundance of awe-inspiring, glacier-cut fjords results in more than five thousand kilometres of breathtaking coastline. It's a nature-lover's paradise, and I feel as though I'm undeserving of all the beauty and happiness that have been injected into my life since I met Kira. But beauty begets beauty, and once you see it, you find it in every cloud and under every stone, a state of being, a synonym for life itself.

I can think of no more perfect place than here, basking in the warm sunlight with the faint smell of Kira suffusing the fresh winds that blow in through the open windows of her bedroom. The curtains flutter and bloom on the gentle gusts as careless and joyful as the beating of my heart. Through the large window, I can see farmland gently sloping up and away until the angle becomes such that it's more accurate to consider it part of the mountains.

We've been back here for a month now, and Kira is thriving. It must be something to do with being home, though I sense that, more than that, it's a function of her being out of the big city. More so than myself, she's defined by her surroundings, shaped and moulded by them. She's perfectly relaxed and carefree here amongst the mountains and trees and flowers. It's much easier to be human in places like this where a person feels like they're living with and because of their environment, rather than in spite of it.

Kira's parents make a very happy couple and have taken well to me, obviously trusting Kira's judgement to the end. They have welcomed me into their home as though I'm her husband. Her mother cannot speak English at all, so Kira often translates for us when we try to talk. Hearing her speak her native tongue is quite enticing, I must say. Her father pretends to have forgotten much of his English, though he clearly understands everything I say. He's a colourful and lively speaker in Norwegian, but when he uses English, his speech is laboured and lifeless. His true ability is betrayed when he gets onto his favourite subject, Norwegian history—from the Vikings, right up to the succession from Sweden in 1905. He's obviously fiercely proud of his country and for good reason. Their standard of living is among the highest in the world, thanks in large part to the North Sea—Norway is the world's second largest oil exporter after Saudi Arabia. I do like to tease him though and tell him that Canada rates higher on the UN's list of desirable countries, to which he responds by telling me that it's nothing more than a matter of time before Norway takes over. He does concede that he has great respect for Canada, being, like Norway, so far north and all.

So far we've done little more than explore the surrounding area, which Kira knows like the back of her hand. We've also spent a few evenings hanging out at the local bar, where everyone seems to know and love her. Most of her friends have left, though, and I can tell she misses them a lot. I joke with her that she merely wants to show me off, and she sarcastically assures me that I'm right. We did take a trip down to Trondheim to visit two of her brothers who live there now. They look just like her, and it was amazing to see the strong similarities in personality as well. I thoroughly enjoy watching her interact with other people, like watching a kitten playing with a ball of string; every laugh and every gesture amuses and touches me.

I feel at peace, and I'm beginning to think I could happily stay here for the rest of my life. It's been a desperately long time since I have felt anything even approaching the satisfaction I feel every minute of every day here. I worry that I won't want to leave, but I know that wherever Kira is shall be my home, and my peace. We've spent time here and there discussing our plans for after Norway, but nothing concrete has been decided yet. Most likely we'll stay a couple more months then head off. It's just a matter of clearing our heads first, particularly for Kira; she has a lot of expectations. As far as I'm concerned, I will follow her wherever she wants to go. I know as much about Africa as most people, which is very little when you get right down to it, so I'll leave it up to her to choose the place that most fits her needs. I want to see the world, all of it; the order doesn't really matter.

My only fear is of getting in the way. Despite all that we've discussed and shared, I still worry about this. How could I not? I'm a romantic at heart, but faced with the reality of this intense relationship, I find I'm sometimes at a loss on how to handle things. A romantic only because he knows he will always be alone; up to now that was how I defined myself. I always dreamed of finding Miss Perfect, I just never really thought I would. I mean, who the hell am I, anyway?

Wednesday, March 20th, Day 4: Seaside, U.S.A.
The boat is running magnificently, and Len seems to be enjoying himself—beats the pound, I guess. We really pushed it hard the last four days, especially today and yesterday. Northerly winds have been brisk, between fifteen and twenty knots. Running with them and following seas, the boat is flying, and I'm finding it hard to tame my excitement. I'm hardly even taking the time to eat lunch, and my body is complaining now. I'd better make tomorrow a rest day, or I may be in danger of running myself down to a point that will require more than a day to recover from. It's just so tempting to crank the miles out at the beginning of a trip and get a good start under your belt. It amazes me when I think about how much of the earth's surface

you can cover simply being blown about by the wind, like a fallen leaf or a discarded paper bag.

Being out here on the sea, almost totally isolated from all other life forms, a person really has the time to think about his own existence relative to that of others. I've only been on the water for five days now, and all the massive collections of human beings in the cities with all their concerns and dramas and rents feel a lifetime away. They have ceased to exist for me. I wonder what effect this trip will have on my connection with my fellow man.

Could it not be said that as I sail this boat along the surface of the ocean, adjusting the trim of the sails and the angle of the rudder, that it has become an extension of my body, that I have in fact become one with it? What is this concept of separation, distinction, the space between us? What are borders and limits? If you look at an ocean, does it not seem to be one entity? And landmasses appear to be distinct, but what if you drain the oceans? What about the separation in time between myself now and in the past, as well as the separation between myself and the others on the boat that passed by me yesterday? They're going their way, and I'm going mine. I'm me, you're you, she's she, but what mechanisms keep our existences wholly independent of each other? Am I really a separate and distinct entity, or are we all just a part of one larger form?

Do you know that there's a certain fungus that appears above ground as separate growths like any other plant, but when you dig in the earth to locate its roots, you find that it's actually just one head of a massive organism that spreads for kilometres under the ground? Maybe we're like this, except with non-physical ties; one and the same in another dimension we cannot see, like the underground dimension of this fungus. Plato said the common bond between like objects is a "form" existing somewhere in the heavens that we all aspire to. Maybe this "form" is similar to the underlying fungus growth, and each of us is connected to it. Maybe our apparent isolation from each other is nothing more than that, an apparition of distinction. Are we all islands in a vacuum, or is it just that we can't see the connections?

Two balls colliding with each other will change directions. We know that all matter—including our bodies—is constructed of atoms and molecules continually interacting with each other. Isn't it possible that like the chain reaction of falling dominoes, we affect each other on a molecular level just by being near each other? If I tell you I hate you, those sound waves will travel through the space between us, enter your ears, and have an effect upon your brain. We are linked.

What of individuals themselves, how do we maintain our own singular identities from one moment to the next? In terms of material composition, you are an entirely different person now than you were fifteen years ago. So how do we remain constant, how do we age? Our genes comprise the map for our makeup; they are the immortal foremen of the construction project, dictating how each new cell will form and behave, ensuring that the song remains the same. As for aging, whether telomere-controlled cell division is the ultimate mechanism for it or not, presumably someday science will figure out how to keep our cells multiplying afresh forever. How would you like to be twenty for the next sixty-five hundred years, or at least until you get killed in a car crash?

But DNA is always mutating and changing, this is the key to variation and survival. DNA determines how my physical makeup manifests itself, but what does it have to do with my perception of my own existence? What keeps my consciousness contiguous through time? I wonder if maybe I'm in fact a new person every second, every millisecond, a new self each time, but unaware of any change because I retain the same memories. If I had the proper tools and could trade all your memories with mine during an operation, then wake you up, essentially you'd believe you were me and that there had been no break in your temporal existence. So what mechanism keeps me as me, and you as you?

It's more than fun to imagine that there is no such mechanism, that every moment we're blinking in and out of existence in different bodies, like the flashing lights on a Christmas tree, one minute you're you, the next minute you're me. We're nothing more than little sparks of electricity floating in and out of different body systems, unaware.

Fine. It's far-fetched. Sure. But only because it goes against our sense of things. Yet you only have to think about how the earth is in fact not stationary, to see how our sense can be grievously mistaken about reality. Just imagine that all people are part of the same system, different consciousnesses bobbing in and out of different bodies, like a sophisticated whack-a-mole game. We're not aware of this process because when we switch bodies, it's instantaneous and we're immediately hooked into the new system. No one would ever know the difference. I wonder if this is what death is like? Maybe when we die, we just lose this false individuation and become once again part of the cosmic oneness. Perhaps I'm on the wrong side of Occam's razor this time, but who really knows the truth about anything. It's at least possible, and it can never be disproved.

Sydney, Australia: My Past

"So what sort of trouble should we get into tonight?" Kira asks while gently setting down her wine glass, her face lightly flushed from the Australian red.

"How about that flyer we saw for the noise show?"

"What, you want to go?"

"Maybe. It could be interesting."

"All right. Let's pay and get out of here."

Stepping out onto the sidewalk, we join the many people out

to enjoy this fine late summer evening. We've been in Sydney for three days now, having come straight from New York. It's my first time here, and I'm impressed. What a beautiful city. I've often heard people say that Australia has a distinctly Canadian feel to it, or vice versa. I'd have to say I notice it as well. It's hard to explain exactly; perhaps it's the easy multiculturalism, or the cleanliness, or the friendliness, or perhaps just the palpable "non-American"-ness.

"What was the name of that place?" asks Kira as we stand on the street watching for a cab.

"I think it was the Eliminator…Terminator…Masturbator, something along those lines."

Kira looks at me as though trying to decide whether or not to respond. "Oh great, 'Yes, driver, Masturbator, please.' I can see it now."

Finally we succeed in getting a cab to stop for us, and we climb in. The driver turns to face us and in a heavy Aussie accent asks us where we want to go. He's young and hip looking, so hopefully he knows the place. "Well, we're not entirely sure. Do you know of any clubs called the Eliminator, or something like that?" I ask, giving Kira a wink.

"Oh, yeah, mate, no problem. It's about fifteen dollars from here." I give Kira an "I told you so" look, but she ignores it. The driver turns away, and putting the car in gear, steers us out into the traffic. He's not through with us yet though. "So where you from then?" he asks, as most everyone has. Usually it's Kira's accent that prompts the question though.

"I'm Canadian, and Kira here is from Norway."

"Ah, cool, mate, cool. I have a brother living up there in Toronto. He's been there for two years now, works with computers. I'm going to visit him as soon as the money piles up high enough."

"Great… Canadian women really go for the Aussie accent, you know."

"Is that right? Well, I'm going for sure then. Hell, maybe I'll move there too! John says the winters are pretty rough though." For the next ten minutes, we talk about Canada's fabled cold until we finally reach the club. "Well, here you go, folks, you have a good time. That's thirteen-fifty, please."

"Keep it, myte," Kira says, handing him some money.

"Cheers. See you later then," he replies, smiling.

Stepping out of the cab, I walk over to Kira "I hope this accent thing isn't going to be permanent."

"Ah, gud on ya, myte," she says, and I laugh.

An eclectic assortment of people mill about outside the club. There is no accurate way to classify them as belonging to any particular style or cultural subset, just a mix and match. One of the two glass doors is propped open, and behind it can be seen two large bouncers talking to each other, looking like twins with their shaved heads and tight black T-shirts. Eminently more noticeable than any of this however are the sound waves emanating from the brick wall. The sounds do not seem to fit together in a way that could be considered music, given even the most liberal usage of the word.

"Ten dollars each, guys!" one of the bouncers yells over the noise as we step into the entranceway. Kira beats me to the draw again and hands him the money. "Earplugs?"

"What?" I ask, betraying my ignorance of the whole scene. He doesn't reply, just reaches under the counter and pulls out a bucket full of small packages. I notice both of them sport the jaundiced sponge in their own ears. I've never felt the need to wear earplugs for a concert. When my mental state matches the music just right, I've been known to dance right in front of the speakers. Then again, I've never been to an event where earplugs are offered at the door. It could be a sign.

"They're included in the price!" yells the other, even bigger bouncer.

"Take them!" yells Kira. How motherly of her. I accept her

advice and the earplugs. I hold off putting them in though, and we proceed down the dimly lit staircase, the noise getting louder with each step. At the bottom is another door, behind which is an unmanned coat check area then another pair of doors. Through these we enter the club itself. The noise falls on me like a gigantic cartoon anvil.

TEMPEST

Sunday, March 24th, Day 8: Gold Beach, U.S.A.
One week, and all's well. The view is amazing tonight, the sun setting a spectacular scene as it hovers low over the serrated edge of the Coastal Range. Draped in a thick layer of fresh snow, and so proud, each peak stands tall, calling into question the purity of each cloud that sails by. It makes me think of home. The mountains are a visual reminder of my personal beginnings, but the ocean brings to mind things even further around the wheel of time, something beyond memories and boundaries, something primordial.

We've gone over one thousand kilometres already, averaging about ten knots in winds usually between five and fifteen knots. The fact that the oceanic current along the Pacific coast of North America—the cold California Current—flows south helps out in the speed department. The winds have been northerly for the most part, allowing us to run with them and head almost directly toward our destination. Running downwind like this can be dangerous, as the tiller is hard to read, but I'm keeping us well off shore. The boat is performing spectacularly, as well as I'd hoped and even better. *The Count's* fast, and that's even without the spinnaker, which I'm not about to bother with. She feels exceptionally light in the water, yet tracks with determination and solid resolve. I can't understand where all her speed is coming from—with her wide beam and

full tanks of water and fuel, she simply should not be this fast.
Perhaps the Kamikaze is blowing for me.

Originally I hadn't planned on making any port calls, but
I'm now leaning toward spending a couple of days on the hard
in San Francisco or Los Angeles. It would be nice to give the
boat some rest, rent a car, and drive into the desert for a few
nights. Part of me wants to continue sailing all the way through
and make the trip in one run, but I don't know. Something is
drawing me.

Len has found his sea legs and seems to be perfectly happy
with his new home and master. The weather has been favourable
so far, and he loves the sun. I let him have free run of the deck
when at anchor, and he busies himself with his exploration of
the boat. And he just loves being in the water! When the wind
and waves become playful, however, I'm forced to relegate him
to the cabin. I'd like to allow him more freedom, but it's pretty
much impossible, and he doesn't seem to be holding it against
me. I certainly don't relish the idea of performing a rescue
manoeuvre for a panicking dog that has just fallen into the
drink, especially given how long his nails are getting. I'll go at
them with the wire cutters soon.

As far as the sailing goes, I've been keeping it pretty basic;
I haven't even changed a sail yet. The spinnaker is still below
decks in its bag, where it'll stay for the entire trip. I like to move
fast, but the boat seems to be doing it on her own regardless
of what I do. Besides, it's not like this is the "Around Alone"
race or anything like that. There is no rush, and I'm trying to
simply enjoy things. This is the trip of a lifetime, and I'm not too
concerned about having it end before it should. I have all the
time in the world.

I've been following the shoreline for the most part, but not
too religiously. I try not to get more than fifteen kilometres out
though, and land is always in sight. At night we find the nearest
and best shelter on the chart and head for it. We've had no

problems finding suitable places. It's still low season, and there's always plenty of room in the marinas.

The only problem to speak of so far occurred a couple of days ago as we were trying to secure ourselves for the night. We were in a bay with no marina or mooring buoys and were forced to sleep at anchor, but for the life of me, I could not get the anchor to hold. It was well after dark before I finally succeeded. So as to make sure the anchor held, I gave it about eight to one scope, which leaves a lot of swinging room for the boat. Even after it was set, I wasn't able to relax completely. I was worried about depth at low tide, but there was nothing I could do, it was already dark, and I was dead tired and frustrated as hell. *The Count* has a bow roller for the anchor, so the manual labour was minimal, but the mental strain was heavy. In the end, though, no harm was done other than wasting a lot of time.

Getting the proper amount of sleep is of the utmost importance on a venture such as this, and I've established a routine that is working well. Our usual pattern for the day begins with waking up at about five a.m., or just as the sky is beginning to lighten. Once we're up, we have breakfast right away. For me the morning rations are instant oatmeal and coffee or tea, for Len they're dry dog food. After checking the marine forecast and some general housekeeping, we're ready to pull anchor by six a.m.

We sail straight though to eleven a.m. or so, when we break for lunch. This generally involves heaving-to for about half an hour. When the sea and skies are too restless, we must keep sailing through lunch, and I'm forced to eat on the fly, so pop tarts and granola bars from my pocket are the only things on the menu. By three p.m., we're looking for a place to dock for the night; it's important that we're all set for the evening before the sun goes down. Thankfully, the days continue to get longer and longer as we head south and nearer to the summer solstice. We greeted the vernal equinox three days ago.

Secured for the night, we have a nice cooked supper, and Len passes on the Scotch, my nightly ritual. After dinner I'll usually clean up, check my position on the GPS and plot a rough course for the following day. I haven't been too pedantic about tracking our course—it just takes more energy than I can usually manage to muster at the end of the day. Being close to shore, lines of position are easy to establish, and I can easily track myself. Of course, if you're going out of view of land, you'd better make damn sure that you're vigilant with your navigating, or you could find yourself receiving your fifteen minutes of fame posthumously.

Physically, I'm feeling fit: no sickness or extreme tiredness. My muscles have recovered from the initial shock and now perform efficiently. Often, before I go to bed, I have an hour or so worth of spare time in which I write or play guitar, or just stare at the stars with Len by my side. It could all be so idyllic.

Sydney, Australia: My Past

The sound consists of an inhumanly bassy Rotterdam-style beat propping up what sounds like a chainsaw cutting through a dying Harley Davidson. Over top of this is a high-pitched squeal such as I'm sure I've never heard before, most likely because to hear it results in paralysis and amnesia. The volume is, well, insane. I don't think it could physically get any louder without the vibrations transforming the room into a cage full of people doubling for Mexican jumping beans. In the five seconds it takes me to get my earplugs in, I feel like I've advanced a good twenty years closer to the day I'll require a hearing aid. I turn to Kira and see that she already has hers in and is trying in vain to say something to me. She might as well be trying to talk through a jet engine. Taking her hand, I head over to the bar at the back, the farthest point from the speakers.

The place itself is small and unassuming. In front of the bar there are tables and chairs and a few couches—all full of people. On the walls flow a few tubes of purple neon to match the liberal distribution of black lights, and I feel like I'm trapped inside an electric circuit. There are a surprising number of people in front of the stage, all cheering for one solitary soul who is the unlikely maestro of the cavalcade of sound. Behind him a large TV screen displays a grainy, unstable image of his form.

I scan the various empty bottles on display such that, in lieu of human speech—which is of course inaudible—the customer can see what is available for sale. I point to the strangest bottle and hold up two fingers. The bartender nods and returns shortly with the drinks. He holds up all five fingers of his left hand and three on his right. Taking this to mean eight dollars, I hand over a ten and give Kira her bottle, marvelling at the efficiency of the transaction and the limitless ability of human beings to adapt to novel environments.

When I'd read the flyer advertising a "noise" show, I'd imagined a number of potential manifestations of the term, all of which hinged on the idea of music. I realize the word "noise" in no way implies music necessarily, but I figured there would have to be some point of connection. What assaults the airwaves in this room leans much more toward sound in general; there is no defining melody or time structure, no key, form, or pattern of any kind—beyond of course the blurred 220ish BPM beat of this "piece" the only piece to have "drums" at all. All there is is noise, deafening noise. For the first time in my life I have earplugs in my ears, and they feel odd and unnatural, but I really see no point in sacrificing my hearing to this.

The plugs remove the high-pitched sound so completely that I have to loosen them every now and then just to make sure it hasn't stopped. We stand and watch as the first guy is cheered off the stage and replaced immediately with another performance. This act creates the same screeching blob of sound waves, but with a twist. A person in an elaborate cardboard robot costume walks into the overzealous crowd in front of the stage and egged on by another "band" member, the crowd proceeds to tear apart his outfit. Each piece gets tossed around from person to person until the robot suit is nothing more than so much recycled paper. And then it ends, and everyone is cheering, including Kira; not including me. The whole thing is more performance art than anything else, but I refuse to appreciate it as such. That isn't what I signed up for tonight.

The next act is a guy playing some kind of homemade electrified contraption that looks like the aborted offspring of a guitar effects processor and the leaf springs of an old truck. He's dragging a chain in and out of the steel coil, producing violent static sounds each time the metals contact each other. It reminds me of "Operation", that old board game where you had to perform surgery on the patient whose nose would light up like Rudolph and buzz in pain every time the operating tweezers touched metal. After this he moves onto an electrified toaster with two screwdrivers stuffed into each slot. He bashes and beats the toaster with ever-increasing intensity until finally the power connection is severed and the noise cuts out cleanly to silence. And the crowd cheers on.

We've been here for over an hour already, so I find Kira and steer her into the coat check area for a talk.

"You want to go? We could probably hit another place if we leave now," I say.

"Sure, all right. Are you sure you want to leave so soon?"

"Yeah, let's hit it." Ascending the stairs, we remove our earplugs and emerge into the omnipresent beauty of the night.

"So, where shall we go then?" she asks, taking me into her arms and looking up at me, smiling. I love looking at her face from this angle.

"I don't know. Let's walk a bit. All right?"

"I'll go crazy, or anywhere else, as long as it's with you," she says, and I laugh. And she says *I'm* corny.

As we're walking along the sidewalk, she decides to broach the subject at last. "So, what did you think?"

"I'll say it was interesting," I offer. But I can't resist adding, "Insofar as it's truly amazing how creative human beings can be in their attempts to invent new art forms."

"Is that all you got out of it?" she says, sounding very much like she's going to disagree.

"Well, possibly some acute ear damage too," I say, only half-jokingly.

She doesn't hesitate to disagree. "Well, I thought it was great."

"Oh yeah, how so?" I'm dying to hear this.

"What do you mean, how so? I can't believe you didn't get anything out of that," she says.

"Oh, come on, Kira. It's not like I'm an art snob, it's just that that was definitely stretching the boundaries."

"Well, for one thing, you *are* an art snob, and secondly, I don't know how you can say that and not cringe. You do realize how many other people throughout history have said that exact thing to so many fantastic artists?"

"All right then, let's hear it. What did you get out of it?"

"I don't know, lots. Like take the volume for instance, overpowering, inescapable. You can imagine it as a metaphor for human fear, of death maybe, or any number of things. Or the fact that the whole concept is basically a form of anti-art—like the whole Dadaist movement—a form accessible to all, a people's art. It's like they're saying a big 'Fuck You' to all the Yngwie Malmsteens and Slashes of the world. Or the uncertainty of it all, the unpredictability of the lack of form, like how in life you can never really know what's coming, everything is a jolt."

The more she says, the more passionate she becomes; it's time for me to join the battle. "Do you really think that guy on stage actually thought of all that? I mean, I could place a blank piece of lined paper in a frame and someone might say it represents all the hidden meanings in the universe, or all the truth that exists but remains unwritten, unknown or suppressed. Or maybe it's about potential, the potential in everything to become great or mundane. Am I really to be lauded and respected for putting the paper in the frame when it's the viewer that's doing all the analyzing and thinking?"

"Of course, interpretation is a huge element of art," she replies. "But an artist is doing just that. They're opening the faucet, turning on a light, providing and becoming a conduit for such things. The artist doesn't necessarily think of all that stuff, but she provides the means for it to be brought out of hiding. That's art."

"How about the guy with the toaster? All he was doing was smashing a toaster hooked up to an expensive sound system."

"How about that?" she asks, incredulous. "Maybe you just turned off right from the start, so you didn't even try to get inside of it." She turns away, looks to the wall of buildings, then presses back at me like a sprinter off the blocks. "Torture! He was giving a voice to all the pain and suffering in the world that goes unheard. It was as though the toaster was alive and responding to all the violence we commit against ourselves and nature. When a tree gets cut down, it doesn't scream because it can't. Tonight that guy made me hear those screams. He beat that thing and it screamed until finally it died, just cut out, like we all do eventually. And then the silence was like a negative; it spoke louder than the noise it was juxtaposed with. It made some of us, maybe for a moment, think, about the totality of death— 'that's all folks, hope you didn't want anything more because it's all over. Don't even bother clapping for an encore, the power has been cut and the memory erased, and there's no getting it back. Just go on home.' But the fact that you didn't open up to it is significant as well. There is no true art form or one type that will speak to everyone. Some people feel calm when they listen to Beethoven, others need to listen to

Malmsteen or Slash to relax." She's on a roll, and I'll admit I've been put in my place.

I look at the ground and think about it a moment, watching my feet racing one another. "Maybe you're right," I say. "I went in there expecting to see at least some musical instruments, and all I got was shapeless disgusting noise, so I turned off, turned away from what was being offered, like a pouting kid, I guess."

"Aw, it's no biggy."

"No, you really are right. Cynicism is the antithesis of an open mind, of hope itself. It's like with visual art. When it came to abstract art, I couldn't get my head around it. It just seemed purely decorative. If you have a white room with aqua accents, you get a piece with colours that will complement. But then I read a few books and everything changed. I love the way you're forced to think, to go beyond line and colour, to go beyond conscious thought and analysis. I love how intellectual and cerebral it all is. With the Mona Lisa, you see amazing skill rendering profound depth of feeling and expression, but with an installation piece I'm captivated, captured by it, almost like a drug, Every element becomes part of the intrigue. And now modern abstract is by far my favourite."

"Ah, no warries, myte," she replies, again in the Aussie accent.

Laughing and punching her in the arm, I say, "Okay, one-nothing. You better revel in it now, though, because I'll even the score soon enough."

"Oh no, you won't. I'm untouchable. Don't worry, though; it's not your fault. You just haven't known me long enough to know that yet. The sooner you learn it, though, the better off we'll both be," she tells me, feigning seriousness.

"Yeah, yeah, yeah. So shall we go back to the noise show then and wait for a slow song to dance to?" I say.

"Hilarious. Where the hell are we going?"

~~~~~

I sit, caressing the contours of my stainless steel rigging knife. Razor sharp still, all experience, all proving, lies in its future. Such a finely crafted and invaluable tool, a work of art. Yet, though designed by a person, it was most likely constructed by machine. I picture a small town where everyone has an identical knife crafted by a computerized machine press, and another town with a knife maker who makes each knife individually, each with a unique style. Is there "more" art in the town with the knife maker? Is art in the modern world dying? Has everything been done? Is everything cookie-cutter?

Well, we talk about "embodied energy", but what about "embodied artistry"? The invention of the machine press and the computer resulted from highly artistic thinking. Perhaps there is less apparent creativity in each individual knife, but on the whole, factoring in the means of production, maybe everything balances out between the two towns. These days we're forced to share art, there is less opportunity for a person to own a unique object, but the creativity still exists—it has simply phase shifted. This transfer may make you sad, but don't worry about art itself, it's doing just fine. As long as humans exist, there will be art. As long as we feel love and loss and longing, and hatred, art will happen.

Toronto, Canada: My Past

Scanning my cards, I arrange them by colour and quickly realize that I'm screwed. Risk is a fun game, but when you play with five people, there's always someone who's going to be sitting out early, and it looks like tonight it'll be me. I've got five cards for Asia and Europe, none for South America, and only one for Australia. I contemplate throwing all my armies onto that one territory of Australia and trying to take the continent, but after we've claimed our land, I see that Jean Marc has the other three Aussie regions, so I'm out of luck there too. Looks like the Red Army will be defeated early tonight.

Blair has just finished rolling two ample joints, and I can't decide whether or not to partake. It's been seven months now since I last smoked, ever since that brutal weekend. I still can't believe I survived it. I've been scared to smoke again since then, but I figure this is a pretty safe atmosphere tonight, and as long as I don't go overboard, I should be all right. Life is meant to be lived, after all, and I'm not the type to run away in fear.

"Hey man, it's your turn," says Mike. Things are looking bad indeed. Not only is it my luck to have no obvious countries to go for, but also my turn is second last, and I've already been obliterated. I have nine armies remaining on four territories: Western Canada, Central America, Kamchatka and Madagascar. Jean Marc has already gotten rid of me in Australia, so I decide the only respectable thing to do is try to destroy Mike's premature monopoly of South America.

"Hmmm. Let's see, how many armies do I get?" I say sarcastically. I take my three and place them all in Central America, making it four on three in my favour. "Okay, Mike, let's go."

"Oh, you're so dead, man. Why even bother?" he taunts.

"Wasn't there a joint being rolled somewhere?" Carmen pipes up.

"Yeah man, is that to smoke or are you just practicing your technique?" says Anthony, ever the ingrate. Blair, never one to involve himself in a volley of verbal assaults, just smiles and lights first one, then the other joint, sending them around the table in opposite directions.

"Yeah, oh yeah!" says Mike, and I roll my eyes as he rolls double sixes.

"Again, with one," I say, throwing a five, which Mike tops with a five and a two.

"See, I tried to warn you. You better be careful, or your soldiers are all going to defect to the blue side."

"Great. Just what South America needs, another corrupt dictator."

"Hey, you gotta get what you can, when you can, my friend," he replies. I'm about to comment when Carmen taps me on my left shoulder and passes me the joint. I'm taking a drag as Jean Marc hands me the other one.

Two rounds later, I'm out of the game and feeling quite stoned despite my attempts to limit myself. My mind wants to drift into contemplation of the night, but I'm able to force myself to steer clear of those thoughts. I concentrate on the game and laugh at Mike's militarism and Jean Marc's prating on about how peaceful and secure life is on the beaches of his Australia. As I continue to drink, I sink further and further into my own head, leaving the battle for world domination up to the participants.

As the voices around me seem to trail off into the distance, I'm overcome by the odd sensation that someone is missing. I can't outmanoeuvre the feeling that someone has stepped out for a moment, leaving a void in the group. All five chairs are occupied, and I'm fully aware that there were five of us all along, but lurking in the back of my mind is a sense of absence. I try my best to ignore it.

Another joint is being passed around, and quite certain that a repeat of my bad trip is not in the cards, I participate freely in its demise. Everyone is becoming quite excited and animated now. Blair is looking very weak, and Carmen is plotting to deal the deathblow and steal his cards. The increased excitement and commotion makes it harder for me to relax, and the feeling of incompletion grows stronger yet. Someone is going to walk through the door and take a place at the table, restoring the balance.

Half an hour later, I look at my watch and am surprised to find that it's almost eleven. I should probably get going, so I make my excuses and get up to leave. A barrage of insults for wanting to leave so early fly at me, but I stand my ground better than I did in the game. I ask Blair if he wants to join me, but he's still holding on valiantly, so I head off alone. It's freezing tonight, and rather than reviving me, the cold air makes me feel even more stoned. After a ten-minute wait, the train comes at last, and I find myself a seat.

The car is about half full, and as we begin to move, the sensation returns once again. It's like when you leave your house and feel absolutely certain that you've left something behind. I suffer a compulsive need to monitor the doors to the other cars to see if someone is coming, but everyone is static. I look at the people around me, but there is no life, no energy. I realize it's how I've been feeling for a long time now. Perhaps it's myself that is missing from this life that I steer through every day. I'm disconnected from everyone, as though trapped inside a glass bubble that isolates me from the world and reality. I feel it growing larger, pushing everything away from me, increasing the distance and the space, stretching the bonds to the point where they snap, and I am left floating, unattached. I'm irrelevant.

Saturday, March 30th, Day 14: San Francisco harbour, U.S.A. Anchored near Point Arena, we had just completed four slower than average days—the west deciding at last to expel its long-held breath. When the wind comes from behind us, out of the north, we're able to sail an efficient course, almost directly toward our destination. Westerlies however, force us to sail a zigzag route that greatly increases the distance we must cover. Of course, this is how sailing works; you don't often get the winds you'd most prefer and are forced to make do with what you've got, and as long as you've got wind blowing from somewhere, you've got something. Since the sailing wasn't prime, we were able to shorten our days and get more rest without feeling guilty.

After four days of this, we awoke as usual in advance of the sun in order to get our early start to the day. Even so early, the air felt warm and close already. The falling barometer confirmed my suspicions that a storm was gathering up the courage to show its face. As we finished breakfast, the first of the sun's rays to cross the horizon transformed the sky from black emptiness to the shade of morning pink made infamous by the well-known sailor's proverb. The marine forecast completed the picture, informing us that bearing down on our area were strong northwesterly winds gusting up to thirty knots with a chance of thunderstorms. We were faced with a tough decision: ride out the storm and have great fun while making good time, or head for safety and wait for it to pass.

I could tell by Len's look that he'd prefer to spend a nice relaxing day sleeping and dreaming of frisbees and bones. But alas, he is not the captain, and I felt confident that *The Count* was up for it. It was time to put both boat and crew to a proper test, to see what we could handle together. The sailing up till then had felt instinctive and natural. I was in a groove and felt well-rested. It's amazing the therapeutic effect the sea has on a person, especially one with sailing in his blood. I've heard it said that for a real sailor there's only one truly undesirable place to sail a ship and that's into port. With this thought in mind, I decided once and for all that it was not our place to let this first storm cause us to go running for cover. Things don't get done that way.

I got busy making sure that the cabin was ready for heavy water and that all supplies were properly stowed away. This didn't take too long, since, like most sailors, I try to keep an orderly ship at all times. A boat must be a thoroughly neat and organized environment, just like a sailor's mind ought to be. So far the cabin had not taken on any water at all, which was very good, but this would be the real test. I stowed away the medium-sized jib I had been using and replaced it with the smallest one. I loaded the pockets of my rain shell with a good variety of snack food, as I knew I'd probably not have a chance to cook anything. After securing Len in the cabin, I battened down the hatches and raised the anchor.

The wind was already picking up, and the surface of the water had become choppy. I reefed the main sail right away. It would undoubtedly need to be done before long, and like most things, it's easiest done in light winds. The sailing was great as the wind continued to pick up, and *The Count* knifed cleanly through the rollers with hardly a notice. It carried on this way through noon with the wind climbing to force five, but the threatening weather was still keeping behind us to the northwest. I figured that with any luck, I might avoid the full brunt of the storm and simply make off like a bandit with its winds while it made landfall behind me. I was soon put in my place.

The clouds started gaining on me, and the going became difficult. I was taking wide tacks to save energy, but I had to be careful not to go out too far from shore. More seriously though, I had to avoid coming in too close. If I experienced any kind of rudder problems, the winds would grind me up against the shore in a hurry.

The sea was full of whitecaps by this point, and the spray was soaking every inch of the deck, including myself. The heads of the waves—up to six feet some of them—poured continuously over the bow. The driving rain began to sting my cheeks. Rather than regretting my decision to come out in such weather, I was feeling fantastic, invigorated and alive, laughing with pleasure at the strain and excitement. Even as the sonic booms of thunder jolted the sky and resonated through my boat and bones, I felt profound joy at experiencing Mother Nature in all her commanding grandeur.

As more time passed, I became seriously fatigued, but I was not phased, still enjoying things as the boat handled the heavy weather perfectly, and I felt as though we were flying. The wind was showing no signs of dying, however, and I wondered how long the storm might last. The shore was looking scary, so I decided to head out a bit further from land to increase my window of safety.

By four in the afternoon, my excitement was usurped by concern. The storm was as strong as ever and if anything was intensifying. I'd been sailing under strenuous conditions for ten hours; the low-pressure system had to be massive to sustain force six and seven winds for so long. The prospect of having to continue on into dark was not a pleasant one, and I would soon be getting very tired. My pockets had run out of food already, and I was feeling quite hungry. I simply had not imagined that the heavy weather would last for so long.

After two more hours, I was losing the last of the light and contemplating a heave-to in order to rest a short while when I first sensed that perhaps the wind was dying off a bit. Within half an hour, the winds had dropped off sharply to about five knots and the rain was but a drizzle. The storm had blown itself onto land behind me, and the sky was now filled with billowy cumulus clouds between which could be seen the night sky and the stars beyond. I immediately headed for shore to find somewhere to anchor.

I had to approach carefully, going mostly by my sixth sense and hoping for the best. I was too tired to do anything else. By now the winds were basically gone and the crescent moon was providing enough light for me to see that at least there was no water breaking anywhere other than on the rocks of the shore itself. About two hundred and fifty metres from land, I attempted to set the anchor, and on my second try managed to stick it. I let out a five to one scope and decided that I'd spend the night in the cockpit, just in case. It was a less than ideal situation, but it was all I could do; I was just too tired, and there really was no other option. I let a stressed Len out of the cabin and leashed him up in the cockpit with me for the night.

The next morning, I awoke to the warm sun and dead calm. I had slept twelve hours and woken up starving. After having breakfast and hanging all the wet bedding out to dry, I finally had time to consult my charts. We were only fifteen knots from San Francisco. With the help of the storm, we had sailed about 125 knots—not much really. Strong winds increase your speed only up to a point. After that they slow you down as they overpower your boat and kick up waves that knock you about. There is also the fact that I'm far from a master sailor—I was glad just to have made it through the strenuous day. The wind made itself scarce for the rest of the day, but we managed to make it to San Francisco, which is where we're docked now. Standing on land was quite hard at first, and Len was tentative. I laughed at him, and he didn't look impressed.

"It's better than the pound, is it not?" I asked him but received no reply.

THE HARD

In the forest, Norway: My Past

It's Kira's birthday this weekend, and we both agreed that there was no better way to celebrate than to go camping for a few days in the deep forest. This morning we drove about two hours northeast of Namsos along a dark ribbon of pavement winding its way through the trees and rock like a neatly-healed scar. This is where she used to come with her family when they were young, before everyone became too busy for such things. She's the local, so I left all the planning and preparing to her, and she was more than happy to take on the task. I'm simply along for the trip, and she enjoys being in charge, guiding me around and showing me the things and places that have made her what she is.

We could have driven closer in to the lake, but Kira really wanted to take me on this hiking path that we're trekking along now. After parking the car on the side of the road, we donned our packs and headed off down the trail. It was quite cool this morning when we set off, but now that the sun is overhead, we've shed our outer layers and are comfortable in shorts and T-shirts. The temperature this far north only averages about fifteen degrees in June, but it's refreshing and pleasant. The blue sky is littered with small puffy clouds incapable of stealing away with our shadows for more than a minute before returning them guiltily.

The entire time we walk, Kira is telling me the names of the various flowers and trees that we happen across, and I'm ashamed of my ignorance of flora and fauna, particularly since I consider myself a nature lover. I've just never been one for remembering names. What's in a name, after all? I am, however, able to recognize the abundant pine and spruce trees, as well as the occasional maple tree, Canada's national emblem and icon.

"You should see the maple trees in Japan," I tell her, trying to add something to the pool of knowledge. "The leaves are tiny, maybe three centimetres across. I couldn't believe it the first time I saw them. It was just such a perfect representation of the difference between Canada and Japan. On the one hand you've got Canada: big and bold, sparse and spacious, with energy and resources to burn. Then you've got Japan: efficient and compact, gracious and unassuming. It was uncanny, and when I got some dried maple leaves sent from home, my Japanese students were suitably impressed by them. The Japanese trees are every bit as beautiful though, if not more so for their daintiness. In the fall they turn the same colours."

"I think I'd like to go to Japan someday," Kira says.

"Well, I'll tell you, from what I've seen, it's a world of its own. I don't know how much of it you could really absorb in a short trip though. It'd probably be hard to get a real feel for its charms without spending a lot of time getting underneath the superficialities."

"Well, maybe I'll teach English there someday. I do have a degree, after all."

As we continue along, listening to the calls of peace from the birds and the fluttering of the leaves in the wind, I revel in the deliciously fresh air. Nothing can make me feel more at peace than feeling accepted in an unspoilt and timeless environment.

"Look up there," Kira whispers, her finger pointing up ahead. "It's a wolverine." Lumbering clumsily up the trail I see an animal about the size of a small dog, but much stockier. It looks like a cross between a skunk and a bear, quite cute actually, with fur sticking out haphazardly all over its body as though it has just wakened from a long sleep.

"Is it dangerous?" I ask.

"No, no. They only hunt small animals like lemmings, or I think maybe even foxes sometimes. They'll eat deer or bear if they happen to come across one that's already dead. Everyone likes a free lunch, right? If you scare them, they'll snarl and growl a bit, but that's about it."

"It does look like a skunk," I tell her. Just then it notices us, as though insulted by the comparison, and turns its head to size us up. Weighing all the available information, it eventually decides that we pose sufficient enough threat to justify leaving the trail, but not enough to necessitate hurrying. We continue along where it left off.

In Norway there exists the egalitarian "Everyman's Rule", which allows you to legally camp for free anywhere in the country for two nights, as long as it's 150 metres from the nearest home or cabin. Norway is a fantastically expensive country, and this generous policy has allowed many a traveller to see this incredible part of the world without going broke. I marvel at this rule and the fact that it's been in effect for over one thousand years.

After seven hours of hiking, broken by an hour for lunch, we reach the lake where we'll camp. We gratefully unburden ourselves of our packs and sit down on the beach, feeling exhausted by the long day. "We used to call this 'our beach' when we were young," Kira says. "Whenever we came here, there were never any other people, and I remember that my brothers and I were convinced that we actually owned this beach, and even the lake. I remember my dad always used to let me help him with the fire, saying that it was the most important job and that it couldn't be left up to my brothers. He always used to tell me stuff like that. I guess he was worried about me feeling overshadowed by them." She points to a rock protruding from the surface of the lake, about a kilometre from the shore.

"You see that rock? My dad used to tell us that an optical illusion made it look like a small rock close to the shore, but that it was actually an island ten kilometres away. He said that a family of trolls lived on it and had been there for hundreds of years. He warned me to be careful and never look at it too closely, because anyone who caught a glimpse of a troll would instantly be turned into a pile of rocks. He told me that most of the rocks on the shore of our beach came about this way. You wouldn't believe how much I wanted to see one of those trolls and find out if they looked how I imagined. But I never allowed myself to look too hard. The last thing I wanted was to be turned into a pile of rocks that no one would even know had been me. I used to imagine that maybe the rocks were still alive. I wondered if maybe they could still think and even feel pain. I was always very careful of where I stepped, and I used to get mad at my brothers when they would skip rocks into the lake. As I got older and we stopped coming so often, I forgot about the story. I came canoeing out here with a friend when I was a teenager, and we rowed past that rock. I felt bereaved as I finally saw that all along it was not more than a kilometre from shore, and not even home to a colony of ants, never mind a family of trolls."

Friday, April 5th, Day 20: Santa Monica, U.S.A.

We arrived at Del Ray marina yesterday evening at six thirty—later than I usually like to keep at it, but I really wanted to make it here. The sail from San Francisco was uneventful, just the usual serene beauty and peace of being on the ocean. I think I could do this forever.

Del Ray is supposedly the largest man-made harbour in the world, and conveniently for us, it has guest docking for up to seven days. We spent the night on the boat as usual and slept in until seven a.m., a nice treat for the both of us. Leaving Len on the boat, I registered at the office and set off to find a rental car.

A nice warm morning meal of eggs and sausages was a welcome change after almost three weeks of boat food. Now, driving this convertible back to the marina with the warm California sun gently caressing my head and shoulders, I feel flush with excitement and anticipation. Why, I cannot quite say, but the feeling is overpowering.

I haven't decided how extensive of a side trip this will be. As with most things in my life nowadays, I'm allowing the current of fate to lead me where it will. For now, it has lead me off the boat and back onto dry land. The desert calls, and I must find out why.

I lead Len along the dock, and he runs circles around me, making maximum use of the entire length of his leash. He leaps willingly into the back seat and gives me a look as though questioning the validity of a car with no lid. He's lived a sheltered life, and I imagine that never in his wildest tongue-wagging-in-the-wind fantasies did he imagine there was such a thing as a car that was all windows. I'm happy to see that my first mate seems to so eagerly support my decision to explore land for a while. My only demand of him is that he stay in the back seat.

I bought a road atlas from the car rental place, but for now I'm not bothering to look at it. I drive along Venice Boulevard then through Beverly Hills, populated by expensive cars driven by even more expensive faces. All I want to do is get the hell out of here, this cesspool of the worst compulsions and drives of the human race.

Once on the Santa Monica Freeway, it's easier to tune out the money. I pass through downtown LA, the skyline dominated by the First Interstate World Centre and the Gas Control Tower, made distinctly unimpressive by even the slightest recollection one might have of the Manhattan skyline. The differences between these two cities are strikingly similar to those between Toronto and Vancouver in Canada, though you can hardly compare the American cities to their Canadian counterparts. In Canada I would rather live in the Western half of the pair, but in America, I'd shoot myself if I had to live in LA.

Soon enough we're wheeling our way out of town on the number ten San Bernardino Highway, aiming for the mountains lurking behind the haze. They grow in size, and as their texture clarifies, so do my thoughts.

Beyond the general knowledge that I'll likely end up in the desert somewhere, I still have no idea what my destination is. I have a sleeping bag and tent, so it's possible for me to sleep anywhere—even the back seat of the car would be fine. I've just passed San Bernardino and turned north onto the 215, which will take me straight to and through Las Vegas if I stay on it long enough. Perhaps I'll head for the Grand Canyon. It's a cliché, but for good reason.

I can still clearly remember my first time seeing it. I was taken aback, standing in awe of the enormity of scale and the grandeur. Someone once said the Grand Canyon is more stunning than any mountain on earth, because with mountains, you can see them from afar, watching them grow in size as you approach; you're prepared to some extent. With the Grand Canyon, you see nothing of it until you arrive at the edge and peer down into it; the full vista hits you all at once and takes your breath away. It's like standing on the edge of the world. It's like a punch in the face you never saw coming.

Though I drive fast, I'm really in no rush to get anywhere. I love this corner of the world: the crisp dry air, the crystal-sharp colour of the scorched sands and azure skies—and the emptiness. Passing through Barstow, I decide to change tacks and head onto the 40, east to Needles—a smile comes to my face as that word reminds me of Snoopy's ossified cousin—then on to Kingman and Flagstaff. I can head north on this road then turn onto the 64 after Williams. From there it's only a short stretch to the canyon.

It's now noon, and I feel a distinct emptiness in the pit of my stomach. Damn! I forgot to bring Len's dog food! He hasn't made it obvious that he's noticed, but I'm most certain that he must have.

"Sorry old buddy, if only you could speak English, eh? Don't worry. I'm sure there are other dogs around here, which means there must be dog food, right? Maybe we can find you some spicy Tex-Mex stuff, huh. What do you think? Huh?" As usual I get nothing in reply other than a slight shifting of the eyes. Old Len is none too talkative. I guess I deserve it this time though.

About an hour out of Barstow, we approach a small gas station and grocery store in the middle of nowhere. Three old relic cars convene amongst the dust and dirt alongside the building like old men discussing the unchanging weather. I pull into the parking lot and ease to a stop. Killing the engine pulls the cover off our private world, and the silence of the surroundings invades the car, sucking us into it. A car whizzes past, ignoring the token "slow down" signs. Its sound chases along after it, and all is quiet again. There is no one to be seen anywhere, and other than the "open" sign on the door, there's really no good reason to believe that this building actually harbours any humans.

Letting Len out of the car, I make my way to the door as he initiates an olfactory inspection of the local terrain. The loose pebbles and dirt crunch under my feet, and I feel as though I'm being unreasonably noisy. Stopping to look around, I reinstate the silence and observe the hard blue sky. The air is bone dry; not even the suggestion of a cloud can survive in this desert. I feel reassured being in such a decisive climate.

I reach the screen door and pull it open, surprised by its heaviness and offended by its cantankerous squeak, which renders superfluous the tinkling bells intended to warn the attendant that a potential thief is entering. The door closes behind me, and the dry, cracked tile floor groans beneath my feet. I can see no other customers, and no employees for that matter. Strolling through the aisles all alone my eyes scan the wares: chocolate bars, crackers, cans of soup, high priced batteries, cookies, an assortment of toiletries. Thankfully there's also dog food. I bring a two-pound bag up to the counter and continue on my shopping spree, having yet to arouse anyone's attention. Looking for anything that might serve to erase my own hunger, I finally decide on what really is the only choice for a road trip: chocolate bars and potato chips. At the back of the store are the fridges containing beer, pop, juices and milks. I finish my shopping by grabbing some chocolate milk and a gallon jug bottle of water. Then I reconsider, put the milk back, and take three bottles of beer instead.

Standing once again at the counter, it doesn't take long for me to realize that unless I get proactive, no one is going to come. On the counter sits an old-fashioned ring-for-service bell resting behind a sign suggesting that I please "Ring For Service". I give it one hard tap, and the resonating metal on metal rings bright and true throughout the store as if professionally tuned, an E perhaps. For my bravery I'm rewarded with the sound of movement in the back room off to the side. For a moment I feel nervous, as though I've foolishly wakened the hibernating bear. The sound of footsteps is soon followed by the emergence of the clerk, her appearance absurdly inconsistent with the surroundings and my expectations.

A girl of maybe fifteen, with silky blonde hair coaxed into twin pigtails and wearing a long sleeved Beastie Boys shirt, approaches the counter with an honest and endearing smile draped gracefully across her face. A plastic nametag, covering the "Bo" of Beastie Boys, tells me her name is Liz.

"How you doing?" she says in the soft voice of a carefree nature that reminds me how old I've gotten in the past few months.

"Great, fine. And you?"

"Oh, pretty good I guess. Sorry I didn't hear you come in, I was playing Playstation with my friend back there."

"Oh, no problem, Liz. It's always nice to be able to shop in a low-pressure environment."

She looks at me a little strangely at the mention of her name until I point to her nametag.

"Oh yeah, right." She smiles and reveals two rows of perfect teeth. "So where you off to?" she asks, as though the only people she ever encounters in her existence on this planet are those on their way somewhere else.

"Ah, you know, the usual tourist stuff—Grand Canyon, Hoover Dam, stuff like that," I say.

"Well, you sound excited to be here." I don't quite know how to respond, so I don't. "Anything else then, sir?" she asks, and I cringe at the last word for some reason.

"Yeah, give me a couple packs of Marleys, please, regular."

"Okay...that'll be...twenty-four forty-seven, please."

Handing her the money, I ask, "So what concert was that?"

She seems taken aback at first that an old guy like myself would notice. "Oh, it was San Francisco last year, great show."

"Yeah, I guess," I reply.

"You like the Beastie Boys?" she asks doubtfully.

"Seen them three times," I tell her.

"Cool, man," she says, looking me straight in the eyes, a novelty. I remember what I used to think of thirty-year-olds when I was fifteen. "That guy's been on this planet *twice* as long as me!"

She hands me the change, and I ask her, "So, any recommendations for an itinerary? Any inside information?"

She appears to turn the question over in her head for a moment then says, "No...not really. This whole area is pretty boring, if you ask me. All we've got are poser hippies, stud mountain bikers from the city, and old stiffs going to Vegas. I guess all I can recommend if you want to see cool stuff is to stay away from any people you see."

I think for a moment about how much she probably wants to get the hell out of here. Unable to think of a good reply, I tell her, "Well, thanks for that, then." I pick up the bag and head for the door.

As I grasp the handle I hear her say, "Drive safely!" I casually raise my hand to her without turning to look, and fancy that there was some extra sincerity in her voice.

I step out into the light feeling invigorated and refreshed. I'm filled with a sense of hope, having encountered such a seemingly well-adjusted teenager in a place where the elements conspire wholeheartedly against such a thing. I reach the car and deposit the bag on the trunk. Leaning over the side, I wonder what to put the dog food in. "Oh well, that's what rentals are for," I say to Len, pouring the contents of the bag onto the floor behind the passenger seat. "Looks like we're still roughing it. At least *your* food has some nutritional value," I add, tossing the chocolate, beer and chips onto the passenger seat.

Before I let him into the back seat, I take the empty plastic bag, fill it with water, tear a hole in the corner and feed him like a little baby. He drinks almost the whole bag before giving up and looking at me as though to tell me he knows what's what and that I had better produce the eatables, or he's off. So I let him leap into the back and onto the food-covered floor.

Turning the key in the ignition, I give it some gas, and the engine revs high, a polite reminder that such coaxing is unnecessary. I steer back onto the highway, gunning the gas solid until I'm at highway speeds and once again cocooned within the isolation of the sound of the wind rushing over the windshield. I wish I had a manual, but they're few and far between in the car rental industry. No one really wants to drive any more.

Driving south of the Mojave National Preserve, we cross the Colorado River, and I imagine the ancient history of this aged stream of water that carved the grandest canyon in the whole world. How many thousands of years has this river found its way through the world? How different did this world look and smell, before the destructive ways of man had tarnished the landscape? Of course, this area is one of the least bastardized places on earth, though the signs are there: the odd building, the power lines, the airplanes passing overhead, and of course the road and the cars, my car.

I'm amazed that the road is so barren. I suppose most of the tourists wait until deeper into summer to head off on their excursions. I had assumed there would be a steady stream of cars from California wanting to escape the cities. I guess there's work to be done. That suits me just fine. As long as there are empty places such as this to escape to, mankind has a chance of retaining its sanity.

In my nightmares I imagine a world where there is no longer a piece of plain or fragment of forest devoid of human habitation. Imagine never being able to escape to nature, never being able to isolate yourself within the great outdoors. Picturing the scenario makes me feel as though I'm in the psychic version of those massive crushers that turn cars into paperweights. But it seems like this is where we're heading. It makes me want to cry thinking about it.

Passing through Kingman I see a water tower serving double duty sporting a large sign welcoming me to Kingman and pronouncing "Historic Route 66". I get on the old highway and follow it for a while. As I pass along this worn and deserted bridge to the past, I feel as though I'm callously driving over a graveyard. It seems wrong that a road with such a busy history should be cast off in such a manner. There is no dignity in this. It's as though the cracked pieces of asphalt are the sun-bleached bones of a buffalo, half buried in the desert sand, picked clean by scavengers a lifetime ago. Everyone from unborn actors chasing dreams of immortality to failed farmers escaping the dust bowl of the thirties used this road, hoping a new backdrop

for their lives might also force a change in plot. And now here
it lies, a road through the past, forlorn and forsaken, like an
unmarked grave. From the cracks, tufts of dry grass grasp at the
hot air like fingers, and the wind howls the calls of those that
ages past came and went. I'm wrapped in the gaze of departed
souls, watchful and wary. I feel tense, unwelcome. Maybe it's
the fact that I'm driving in the wrong direction—this road was
originally created to serve the westward wanderers. You'd think
the ghosts would be happy to see someone, but I suppose time
has created an unbridgeable gap.

After about forty-five minutes of this, I can take no more and
decide to stop in a place with the idyllic name of Peach Springs.
I think I'll call it a day. Tomorrow I'll head for the spiritual
scenery of the canyon and see if I can't find whatever it is I'm
looking for. A while back I passed a sign telling me that I was
entering the Hualapai Indian Reservation, which I assume
I'm allowed to be on as there was no subsequent sign warning
me away. Soon I pass another sign reminding me that I'm still
on Route 66, and that in seven minutes I'll hit the Hualapai
Mountain Lodge.

I pass right through Peach Springs, nothing more than an
old gas station, a new gas station, a general store and an all-
you-can-eat restaurant, then find the turn off for the lodge just
outside of town. A few bends in the rising road later, I'm there.
I park the car and step out, followed closely by Len, anxious to
locate the facilities. The lodge is a rather fancy affair, poised and
modern, and its elaboration stands starkly incongruous with
the sandy surroundings. There is, however, a touch of genius
in the architecture, as the lissome lines of the windows and
roof give the building an organic shape, allowing it to exist in
harmony with the rocky outcroppings and flowing dunes of the
landscape it sits upon. The effect is highlighted by the paved

plane of the parking lot, utterly devoid of cars and appearing to be one with the barren expanses of the surrounding desert.

It's beautiful, and I wonder why such a hotel would be in such a place. It looks closed. Fully expecting to meet mechanical resistance, I grasp the handle of the farthest right door and pull. The door eases open gracefully and with smooth weight, providing me with that ever familiar feeling one gets when the grocery, beer, or drug store is found to be open and offering its wares despite all external appearances. I step into a bright, airy lobby. The smell is pleasant, dominated by the ample wood surfaces and the flowers and plants. An energetic sun drops charitable donations through the generous skylights, illuminating an assortment of expertly rendered native artwork.

My gaze fixes on a vivid canvas painted in my favourite aboriginal style. It's certainly rare to see a Woodlands piece this far away from its home in the region around the greatest lake in the world, the icy blue Lake Superior. As I approach the painting, I'm even more surprised when I read the card posted below the frame:

Mark Anthony Jacobson
Sleeping Giant, 1989
Acrylic on canvas

This is a fantastically well-crafted work, and I've even seen for myself the landscape depicted. There is something about the Woodlands style that speaks to me: the sensual lines, the deliberate colours standing proudly in such brave contrast, bold and self-assured yet accepting and complementing one another. It's an illustration, a microcosm, of the universe, particularly our own world and the borders and interconnections within it. It strikes me as a good omen that I should run into such a thing here.

And as I look into this painting devoid of humanity but for the human who held the brush that created it, I realize exactly why it is that whatever within me drove me here did so. An elation fills me, a fear, the beguiling call of a moment of truth and the consequences of it—absolute success or failure, reality or falsehood, proof or refutation of one's self.

A creaking breaks my reverie. I look across the expansive lobby and see the reception counter on the far side. No one is there. I make my way across the stone floor, stepping silently through warming shafts of sunlight, and as I reach the counter, a man steps out from behind the wall. I get the feeling that he was aware of me all along, as though his time is so precious, he wished to waste none waiting for me while I bridged the distance between the door and the counter. Or, he did not wish to waste any of mine.

A frank smile dominates his strong native features, accentuated by a full head of long silver hair pulled into a braid. His deep-set eyes are grey and remind me of a Viking shield, perhaps protecting him from the sights in the world that would harm his soul. His countenance goes a long way toward dispelling any unease I might have felt in this foreign environment. He's extremely tall and thin, much more so than myself, almost waif-like, but he looks healthy. Like a wild animal.

"And how are you today, sir?" he states in a soothing bass voice that seems to wind its way into my being like a serpent trying to consume me from the inside out. The fact that such a resonant sound could emanate from his thin frame only adds to the half-real, half-imagined surrealism I sense in this desert oasis, so far removed from the wet world I have made my home.

"Well, it's hard to be anything less than great on a day like this," I say, trying my best to match his pleasant demeanour.

"Most days are like this in these parts, sir. We are most fortunate."

"I'll say."

"And how is the weather in the part of the world you call home? May I take a guess and say Canada? Ontario, perhaps?"

I'm impressed, but if he saw me looking at the Jacobson piece, it wouldn't be too large of a leap of faith to assume that I'm Canadian.

"That's a pretty good guess," I give him.

"If you have come to escape the snow, you need proceed no further."

"Actually, I've come to escape a lot more than that," I say. "But escaping the snow is good enough for now. I trust that despite appearances, you are indeed open?"

"That we are, sir. However, you have come on a particularly unpopular day in a particularly unpopular season, so I am happy to offer you the benefit of your choice of room and freshly cooked food," he says, playing well the role of gracious host.

"Sounds good to me. How about giving me the room with the best view?"

"That would be one of the north facing rooms on the third floor. I'll make the arrangements. All I need is a credit card." Upon receiving it, he embarks upon the formalities of making me an official guest.

"If you don't mind, I must ask—how does such a fancy hotel come to find itself in a neck of the woods such as this?"

He stops what he is doing and walks back to me, planting his feet firmly on the floor before beginning. "Well sir, as you must know, you are now standing on the land of the Hualapai Tribal Nation. This reservation was formed by government executive order in 1883, and has been our home ever since then. Of course this land was our home long before that, but it is nice to have official documentation in this day and age, if you know what I mean." He gives me a wink, and I nod in understanding. "This lodge is owned and run by my people, and we are fortunate to do a brisk tourist trade. People are attracted by our culture, as well as the fact that the National Parks are so crowded these days. We are very close to the Canyon here, and we have the only drive-in access in the area. In fact, we are the only native-run tourist operation in the entire park. You see, our people have been here a long time, much longer than the competition," he says with a smile. The oratory could be swallowed as promotional hype, but his method of delivery is flavoured with equal parts pride and affection, as though he's telling historical fact. I feel as though I could listen to him speak for hours.

"Well, I'm certainly happy to have happened upon you," I tell him.

"And we are most pleased to have you as our guest. Your room is number three-zero-two. Go down this hallway to the end, take the stairs up to the third floor, and follow the brass numbers on the doors."

"All right. Thanks a lot," I say, hesitate then turn away toward the door. After a few steps I realize that I forgot to ask about Len. Turning around, I see that the man has already disappeared. "Excuse me," I say, and five seconds later, he reappears. Again I'm struck by the odd familiarity I feel in his presence. "I'm so sorry for not asking before we went through all the motions, but is it all right for me to bring my dog into the room?"

"That depends. Is he a nice dog?" he says with mock seriousness.

"The nicest you could hope to meet and then some."

He feigns surprise and tells me, "I suppose he can stay then. I look forward to meeting that animal."

"He appreciates it a lot," I reply and walk out into the blinding desert light.

I retrieve Len and our meagre provisions, and we make our way to our room, but not before I warn him that he has a high standard to live up to. The room is of the same spartan style as the rest of the hotel. What furniture there is appears to be handmade and unfinished, beautiful in its simplicity and functionality. Covering the bed is a striped quilt in vibrant colours that match the painting hanging over the bedstead. The piece is yet another Woodlands original. I don't recognize the name of the artist, or the word "Bebaminoomat", but the piece itself is sublime.

A man and a woman stand before a small fire on the banks of a calm river, and branches of trees devoid of leaves reach up to the sky. The exaggerated height and rigidity of form lends each figure an air of wisdom and experience, solidity. Both wear their grey hair in lengthy braids, symbolizing oneness of spirit, of soul. The woman leans slightly forward and into the man, her right hand reaches out to him as she looks up at his face, their gazes connected, cemented to a shared vision. It's an image of undying love, the simplest, purest and rarest fulfillment.

Brushing a solitary tear from my eye, I turn my attention to the large triple window that dominates the wall opposite the bed. An unobstructed view of the desert fans out in front of me, and it's as though I'm hovering above it like a cloud, or a departed soul. I see the odd piece of greenery here and there and mountains off in the distance, but mostly all I see are cacti, sand and rocks. The sun is low on the horizon and will set soon, though I don't expect too much of a show given the dry air and lack of clouds.

After a shower I'm feeling good, but exhaustion overcomes me. Len is already sound asleep on the wooden chair in the corner. Taking his cue, I settle down on the firm bed and give in to a much-needed session of shut-eye.

IN IRONS

In the forest, Norway: My Past

I can hear Kira whistling as she gathers wood for the fire while I go about setting up the tent and preparing our living quarters. It's nine in the evening, and the sun is still in the sky; even after we've finished eating, it's still perfectly light out and will remain so all night. This far north, the sun never really sets in the summer—it does sink below the horizon, but the sky remains bright. It looks like pre-dawn all night until the sun shows itself once again in person after a couple hours off the stage. It's amazing the effect this permanent daylight has on your psyche.

I feel willing and energetic all the time. I'm only sleeping five hours each day, and even these are interrupted. I am continually happy, and there is no question that the usual chemical balance in my brain is being disrupted. Kira tells me it's simply because I'm so happy to be with her, and that is definitely part of it, but I think there's something even deeper going on. It would be interesting to see how I would fare through the long, dark winter. Many people in the far northern regions of the world suffer through depression when deprived of the sun for weeks on end as the winter drags itself lazily along. It's not hard to imagine.

As we sit arm in arm sharing our wine, I look out on the lake hemmed in by hills and forests, and it makes me think of home. "You know, someday we'll have to do a trip around Lake Superior. I did it once by bike."

"Just tell me when," she replies.

"It's the biggest lake in the world and well-named," I continue. "You can't see any land on the other side. It's like looking out on the ocean. In terms of its size and behaviour, it's probably more accurate to think of it as a small ocean. The storms that blow up on that lake have sunk ocean liners."

"Well, I guess if you have to drown, it's probably more pleasant in fresh water," she says, and I can't tell if she's making a joke or being serious.

"And you've never seen a blue to compare with the water of Lake Superior, it's so deep it makes the sky jealous."

"It sounds beautiful," she says.

The thought of sharing such a trip with her is thrilling, and I have to shake my head once again as I think of how lucky I am. Glancing at my watch, I'm surprised to see that it's somehow already three minutes past midnight. It's certainly a challenge to keep track of the time in this unchanging light. Pulling Kira around to face me, I give her a great big kiss followed by a generous hug.

"Happy birthday," I whisper in her ear. It's our first shared birthday. "I hope we can spend the rest just like this," I continue, and I hear her sigh. "And I've got something for you," I say, getting up and going over to my pack. Fishing around in the top pocket, I locate my Mp3 player and sit back down beside her.

"You know I'll love anything you give me," she says, "but, a used walkman?"

"It's not the walkman, dummy," I say, placing the headphones gently on her head.

"Not too loud, okay?" she says, concerned. I know.

"Close your eyes," I tell her, then press the play button. I sit and watch her beautiful face as she listens, and after about three minutes, I see a tear trailing its way down her left cheek. She wipes it away with her shoulder. A moment later, she takes the headphones off and opens her eyes to me; they are damp and searching.

"You wrote that for me?"

I'm embarrassed and shy. I have never written a song for anyone before. "Yes."

Her face takes on a pained expression, and she starts to cry, for real now. She reaches out to me and pulls me into her, burying her face in my shoulder. "I, I can't believe it...it's absolutely beautiful," she says, her voice muffled as she speaks into my fleece sweater. "I can't even...it's perfect. It's all so perfect, everything. I love it, I love it so..."

She pulls back from me enough to look into my eyes then whispers, "I love you." It is the first time these words have been said; they seemed so unnecessary, until now. As they flow from her soul and into mine, they cement a bridge between us—a coalescing, a union and divine convergence. I'm in another universe, one without beginning or end, start or finish, life or death. Just now. Everything exists in this moment. Everything is one and reality, peace and truth. I have never been here before, and I wonder if this might not be the end of life as I knew it. Sitting here in this perpetual light, I see there are no more shadows or blackened corners, darkness no longer.

~~~~~

Upon waking from a nap in my hotel room, I have a hard time at first deciphering my surroundings, but after a few moments I'm able to recognize which dream I'm in. I've always found it disconcerting to wake up from a dreamless sleep, as though time has been stolen from me, the laws of energy conservation distorted for some inexplicable reason. As if I truly ceased to exist. Thankfully, I'm able to bridge the gap of time and remember how I got here, if not precisely why. Who can ever tell you why?

I wake up hungry. Looking at Len, it doesn't require too much insight to see that he's in the same boat. Assuring him that his best interests are first and foremost in my thoughts, I leave him behind in the room and head off for the restaurant I saw off the lobby when I came in.

Entering said lobby, I pause, taking in all the angles, and see the man standing in the far corner, still as a bowl of dusty plastic fruit, watching me expectantly. Something tells me this enigmatic man knows what I need even better than I do. "I wonder if you have anything…" I say, unsure of how to put it into words.

"Of course, sir," he says, stepping out into the open and gesturing to the opposite corner of the space, where a pair of wooden chairs face one another in a nook of windows that look onto an interior enclosure of bamboo shoots growing out of the centre of a rock garden with sections of sand raked into circles like a Zen garden. I sit in the chair on the left, which gives to accept my weight but does not groan.

As if he had it waiting for me, he hands me a heavy ceramic teacup half-full of a light brown liquid. He says nothing as I take its warmth into my hands, then bows and walks away. Not wanting to allow second guesses to seep in, I put it to my lips and dump its lukewarm acidic contents into my mouth, guzzling and not thinking. The taste is bitter but quickly dissipates and becomes nothing. I sit as if nothing happened and wonder if anything did. I look into the garden and wait for the stones to move. They don't. Not even a wind stirs the air.

I wait a few minutes and feel nothing. I get up and walk to the entrance of the restaurant. I look through the tinted glass door, which betrays no hint as to whether the restaurant is open or not. Assuming everything here is a possibility, I pull on the door, and it concedes defeat easily. The room is completely empty, though all the tables appear to be set, and a dim light leaks through the circular window in the door at the back, which I assume leads to the kitchen. The room is unlit save for the bluish light emanating from the wall of ceiling to floor windows looking onto the desert at the front of the restaurant. Of the tables arranged along these windows, the centre one, set for two, contains a white candle illuminating a stylized white celadon vase. The vase contains a solitary chrysanthemum glowing an impossible virgin white, surrounding like a halo a field of verdure in the centre. I take it as nothing more than a coincidence that my favourite flower is placed on the table, inviting me with a silent voice. I take my place in the right-hand chair, and as my eyes adjust to the brightness of the candle, the restaurant disappears into the surrounding blackness. My table is an island of light within the otherworldly glow of the moonlit landscape imposing itself on me through the wall of windows. I'm sitting at a table all alone in the open desert.

The sun has completely set, but a full moon hangs low on the horizon, sharing enough of its light to provide all the features of the terrain with a translucent glow. I have never seen or even imagined the desert in such a type of light; it looks unearthly, sinister. I give up trying to distinguish between real and not, assuming I'll know truth when I see it.

No sooner have I sat down and noticed all this than the man is standing over me, placing a large glass of ice water onto the table.

"A man of many talents," I say.

"We have to wear a number of different coats around here in this season. More than you would likely imagine," he says, leaning over and lighting another candle he has placed beside the first one. Rather than add to it, this second flame serves only to decrease my circle of visibility.

"Please, don't go through all this trouble just for me," I tell him.

"Whom else would I do it for, if not you?"

"Well, if you must. I suppose I can live with being fed a good meal for once."

"It's my pleasure sir. It can get quite dull around here this time of year; I appreciate the opportunity to work. So what would you like?"

I haven't had a chance to look at the menu yet, as he must know, so I choose something easy. "How about…a club sandwich with fries? Really, anything is fine."

"Might I suggest the house special?" he says.

"Like I said, whatever is easiest."

"Regardless of the difficulties involved in the preparation, I happen to find it infinitely easier to serve a customer good food rather than bad. So if you leave it up to me, I would suggest serving you the special."

"Well then, let it be," I say, perhaps melodramatically, but it seems to suit the atmosphere.

"Fine," he says. "But I'm afraid I dare not tell you what it is. Is that acceptable to you?"

"Sounds intriguing. Not even a hint?"

"I'm afraid not," he replies, seriously. "But I can tell you that included with the special is a bottle of our house wine. Would you prefer white or red?"

"Well, that of course would depend on the meal, wouldn't it?"

"Quite right," he says. "I'll be back in a moment." With that he steps away and fades into the darkness. I'm left once more in my own little orb of existence. Every so often I sense movement in the corner of my eyes, but when I try to focus on it, nothing more than black stillness reveals itself.

A moment later my stealthy server is back by my side. I don't see or hear him approach, and I'm overcome by the sensation that he has been standing there all along. In his hands he holds an unlabelled bottle of red wine along with a glass. Without saying a word he places the glass on the table and proceeds to open the bottle effortlessly. The wine glass is formed into a simple yet exquisitely graceful shape, tall and slender, the glass so thin that in places it seems to disappear; the curves are soothing and sensual.

Watching the crimson fluid flow lasciviously into the glass, I'm enthralled. He stops short to allow me to sample the bottle. As I cradle the elegant glass between my fingers, it feels weightless, smooth and soft, like the supple skin of a young woman. Bringing it up to my nose, I inhale lightly, and a moment later a wondrous assortment of aromas enters my body. The harmony of sweet, flowery and earthy scents dazes me, and I almost forget that I must drink the wine. While the magical scent lingers in my nose and brain, I put the cool glass to my lips and tilt it, allowing the liquid to flow over my tongue. It's heaven. I know it's wine, but it tastes so different, so extraordinary, that it seems a disservice to call it by such a name. I'm made speechless, and as it eases down my throat and into my stomach, I'm enveloped in a warmth and wellbeing of a sort that I assumed had deserted my life for good. The mysterious man fills my glass and gently sets the bottle down on the table, then is gone. He does not wait for my comments, as though he knows full well the pointlessness of words in this ritual he is performing.

Suddenly, breaking out of my trance, I become hyper-aware of my surroundings, as though waking up from a dream or a coma, having almost forgotten where I am and why. I take another sip, which tastes even better than the first, but I'm expecting it this time, so I'm able to stay on top of myself. After a third sip, I decide I'd better stop for a while.

Turning my attention to the window, I observe no change other than that the moon has risen higher and brighter. The glare prevents me from being able to make out the full features of its surface, and I wonder if it's intentional. What's going on up there that I'm not supposed to see? The brightness does allow me to better see the vaguely earth-like environs laid out before me. Never have I seen such a strange land, and I'm glad that I'm on this side of the window. Something is happening within me. I can't put my finger on it, but I'm feeling very… alive. What would it be like to feel life for the first time?

Taking another sip of wine, I close my eyes and revel once

again in the amorphous maze of pleasure it brings. It's almost too much to handle. Opening my eyes, I notice my purveyor of pleasure standing once again by my side. In front of me he places an ink-black plate containing nothing more than a gleaming silver cocktail spoon and a small portion of something that closely resembles caviar placed neatly in the centre.

"Your appetizer, sir. Enjoy," he says, and is gone again.

Before I try this intriguing course, I study it. The plate is a shade of black deeper than any I've ever known. It deserves the more accurate description of an absence of light, as indeed its most obvious quality seems to be its lack thereof. The food itself looks like a soap-bubble universe of tiny, polished bowling balls. Each glossy sphere mirrors the flame of the candles and I'm seeing a million points of light created out of darkness. A universe of stars is laid out in front of me, surrounded by a void.

I take the silver spoon in my right hand and feel its cold smoothness against my skin. I coax some of the mystery away and feel a tinge of sadness over the destruction of form. As it nears my mouth, I feel the force of a magnetic attraction, and making contact with my tongue, it creates electrical impulses that emanate throughout my body. I'm immobilized by the sensation as my brain focuses all its energy and attention on its hyperactive pleasure centres. Strange things happening here, no question.

Soon though, the feeling fades, and I'm overwhelmed by a deep urge to replace it immediately. I take another spoonful, and another, until all that is left is a memory unlike any other. It would be inaccurate to describe a taste per se, but the sensation is like that of the wine, perhaps even more intense, but different. It's impossible to explain. Of all the words in an English dictionary, there might be a select number that could be placed side by side in such a combination as to form the perfect description, but that task is beyond me. Truly.

I take another sip of wine, refill the glass, and wonder what the hell is going on. I feel perfectly lucid and in control, although that could be nothing more than an illusion. I know that I'll sit in this chair and do what this man tells me for as long as he wills it. The moon has risen further still, more than it should have for the amount of time that has elapsed, or so it seems anyway. Flashes of light appear intermittently throughout the sky like some kind of pointillist northern lights. They seem to grow closer and larger, but more faint as I attempt to focus on them. It's as though invisible searchlights probe the dark sky, reflecting off small, scattered clouds. But there are no clouds and only the ground reflects the moon's light. Once again my ever-present host distracts me from my thoughts.

"Your main course, sir," he says, placing another, larger, black plate in front of me. Arranged symmetrically on it are parsimonious portions of various foods I'm at a loss to recognize.

"Finish your wine, sir, there is plenty more where that came from," he tells me, smiling cunningly before he once more recedes into the surrounding blackness like a hallucination.

Looking at the newly arrived plate, I take stock of its contents, but not until I have taken another sip of the wine. There are three items. One is a formless cluster of material similar to the appetizer, only this is pure white. Alongside it is a gathering of shining tubes that glisten under the flickering light of the candles, somehow a deeper black than any yet. Teasing both of these items is a small piece of what appears to be extremely rare red meat of some sort. Nothing on this plate is visually tempting in the normal way of food, but given the lead up I have received, there's no reason to believe that this assortment will be any less spectacular than I imagine. Whatever it is that's happening here, I'm powerless to resist. I know that should frighten me.

I start with the black tubes, which make me think of the hypothetical wormholes in the space-time continuum. Is it possible to eat a hole? Resounding waves of pleasure pulsate through my cerebral cortex, causing me to drop my fork onto the plate as my fingers release their grip, my brain having let go of their leashes. My mind quickly reorients itself and locating the fork once again, I manage to manoeuvre more of the food into my mouth with the same results.

Each successive mouthful yields the same feeling, the only difference between each food being the colour of the aura it creates.

The meat is a warm passionate sensation, which stirs the embers in my heart to a roaring flame that causes sweat to form on my brow.

The white substance counters this fire with a brisk, refreshing, life-affirming blue that gives me a feeling of imperviousness to the world and all its torments.

The black-hole tubes create a vibrant, ecstatic orange glow that pulsates and throbs deep within me, making me want to scream out in happiness and ecstasy.

A glutton, I'm unable to stop until the plate is left a void once again, which suddenly liquefies and seeps into the blackness beyond the reach of the candle's light. This doesn't faze me as it normally would. I'm experiencing every conceivable pleasure of life here in this one sitting. What else could there possibly be? What else could possibly matter?

Faced with the end, however, I'm not sad or wanting more. I'm satiated, invigorated and contented. I feel no urges, nothing more than a desire to lie back and wait to do it all again. Looking out the window now, I see that the flashes of light have grown in intensity and now fill the sky like a thousand syncopating supernovas. Intuitively I'm aware that I'm entirely too far south for the northern lights phenomena, but who's to know what rules rule?

Unlike the northern lights and their smoke-like transitions between light and darkness, this is more like a sporadic twinkling of light flashes, more akin to fireworks. They are set to a tribal drumbeat that I do not so much hear, as feel, in my soul.

It's safe to say I've never before experienced anything like this in my life. I wonder for a moment if I did not in fact get killed in a car accident on the way here. Abruptly however, the lights are extinguished along with all sound, and I feel as though I've just been silently slapped across the face.

Turning my attention again to the indoor surroundings, my eyes immediately fix on the countenance of a woman sitting across from me. The table has been cleared of all but the bottle of wine, a single candle, and the chrysanthemum. She is sipping from my glass as she gazes at me.

"I hope you don't mind my joining you," she says, in an enigmatic, exquisitely feminine voice.

I'm taken aback, but manage to utter, "No, no…of course not."

She turns her eyes away for a moment, and as though on cue, divine orchestral music begins to permeate the room. The sound is as clear as a bitter winter night, like breath crystallized on glass. Twin twelve-piece orchestras are playing into each of my ears. It's not a piece I've ever heard before. Somehow it evokes in me every possible emotion, simultaneously, like pressing all the keys of a piano at the same time and hearing every piece of musical magic that has ever been created, contained within one moment of sound. I immediately understand that anything less than perfection could not exist in this woman's surroundings.

"Did you enjoy your dinner?" she says softly, insinuating.

She is astoundingly beautiful, with the type of face you dare not take your eyes off of for fear that it will be gone when you look back, loathe to squander a second of its presence. Two dark braids of hair hang down behind each meticulously carved ear. I notice a distinct resemblance to the man who has been serving me all night. Could this perhaps be his daughter? But there is something more; I feel a definite association, a familiarity. Then it hits me—the girl from the bus. Not exactly though, the woman sitting across from me now is older and looks very different, but most definitely they are the same soul.

"Would you like some dessert?" she asks, her prurient lips massaging the airwaves such that upon entering my ears, they render me speechless. She waits a moment, then, calmly, as though she anticipated the necessity, repeats her offer.

"I don't know. What do you have?" I reply, surprised and impressed by how solid and unaffected my voice sounds—an automaton. Someday we all impress ourselves. It's only then that I realize she is wearing nothing. My heart skips a beat, then another.

Her proud shoulders round out and give way to perfectly formed arms, which hang by her side, bracketing regions that I can only imagine, hidden by the table. Her strong neck muscles attach to rigorously defined collarbones, which in turn support flawlessly conceived skin flickering here and there with the reflection of the candle flame. This skin gradually rises and forms the firm swelling of each breast, hanging delicately, upturned, floating impossibly as though even gravity is reduced to a useless, blubbering fool under her influence. Each milky globe revolves around an erect nipple, the eye of the storm, standing rigid and defiant. I feel a longing inside, so primitive and animalistic that I imagine I haven't felt it since I was a hungry infant longing for my mother's milk.

She seems to attract even the candlelight; it causes her to glow luminously. The surroundings drop away into non-existence in the face of such an assault of pure essence. What right do they have? I am incapable of speaking, moving, or even breathing.

"I'm sure you want dessert," she advises. The words pierce my ears as though they are the first I have ever heard. Were it not for her gentle serenity, my eardrums would surely snap under the tension.

She stands up gracefully and makes her way over to my chair, wine glass in hand. I'm transfixed by the effect of her steps on her magically weightless breasts, hovering. With the ease of a gymnast, she lifts one leg over me and straddles me as though

I'm a horse, or a foe to be destroyed.

She is shadow now, as the candles are behind her but still remnants of the glow persist. Even the light rays bend to her will. I know she is completely naked, but I cannot turn my eyes any lower than her breasts for genuine fear that I will disintegrate into a million particles of light, which in turn would be sucked in and consumed by her immense gravity, like a black hole. I can't imagine a more pleasurable fate. Perhaps she is the cause of all those dancing lights I have seen in the sky tonight. They are the disembodied remnants of her former admirers.

She puts the glass to my lips and spills some wine into my mouth. It still tastes good, but its effect is muted, overwhelmed by her radiant visage like a flame held in front of the sun. One or two drops of wine fail to make it into my mouth, and I feel them running down my chin. She leans over and licks them away with her tongue. The skin left in its wake feels as though it has achieved its only goal in life and gone on to somewhere better. She then licks a drop of sweat that had been tracking its way down my cheekbone from my forehead. It seems to evaporate from the searing heat before her tongue even makes contact. As she does this, her stony nipples brush lightly against my chest, which I'm not surprised to find is bare also, though I have no recollection of having removed my clothes.

She moves her tongue up my chin and over my mouth, her hair tickling my shoulders. She pushes between my lips, and I allow her entry. It is as though a million volts of photoelectric energy have passed through my body, energizing and reviving me. I'm blinded, and invigorated. I have just touched—no— *kissed* lightning. An urgent desire tears through me, and I am no longer in control of myself.

I raise her off me and onto the table, placing her on her back. The candle falls over and goes out, but the moonlight coming in through the windows bathes her body in the blue light, lending her form the divinity of an angel, the tumescence of a dream. Her slender muscular legs splay out before me like the gates of heaven, and I fall onto her, kissing her violently. Her legs wrap around me, and I feel the rise of her pelvic bone grinding against me. I wonder for a moment who is using who. But only for a moment. I clasp her firm, full breasts, each nipple pinched between two fingers, squeezing hard, grasping at a response. Pulling my face away from her lips, I look into her eyes. She is smiling with a confidence that shocks me. I realize that it's she who is in control, absolute. The violins rise, nearing their climax.

In desperation, I press hard into her. She does not resist and yields easily; it's what she wants. Reaching fully inside her, seeing the whites of her eyes as she moans, it's as though the lights have been turned on, and now I see what is happening. I try to pull out of her, but her legs are a vise, tightening, pulling me in, deeper, deeper, trying to get the whole of me inside, where there will be no more light, no escape. I reach behind and grasp her ankles, try to pry her legs apart, but she is too strong, I am locked in place. She curls up off the table and wraps her arms around me. I stand and she comes with me, grinding herself against me, still holding me inside. She's still moaning, and I grasp her armpits, trying to press her away, but she only holds on tighter. I think of giving in, as if to drowning.

I refuse to! "I won't!" I scream and step back, pushing with everything in me against her, but she only pulls in tighter. Something catches my foot, and I fall back, flat on my back, winded, choking, lights fading. She writhes upon me, refusing to let go, and I feel faint, knowing what she is doing, what she is trying to take from me. I gather all my resources, every vein of power and every last vestige of will, and I thrust violently up and into her, trying to either throw her off or kill her from the inside out.

Like a car lifted off, her weight is gloriously gone. I feel nothing but the atmosphere pressing upon me, I am free again, I am floating, levitating. I have won, but it doesn't feel like victory. I roll over onto my side and feel a tingling through my body that becomes a burning, then a corrosive sear which gathers and intensifies, causes me to wretch violently. Over and over, until I don't care whether I live or die. I shall die, I will die, I am dying, I am dead. I am dead, and dead is all there is. Dead is all there ever was.

A woman is kneeling over me, naked and flushed, her hand on my head.

I leap to my feet and run out of the room. Sprinting down the hallway and up the stairs, I somehow know where I'm going. I can hear Len barking madly as though he knows better than I what is happening. Throwing open the door of my room I turn on the light and quickly put on some clothes. The hotel has taken on an air now of terror, disease, a virus that seeps and pours and flows into any unsuspecting and unprepared body. Evolution. I feel as though I'm inside a living entity, a creature intent on destroying me, making or proving me crazy. I must get back to the boat, as far from here as I can get. It was a mistake to leave it in the first place.

I run out of the room, Len following after me. Flying down the stairs four at a time, I feel as though I'm wallowing in quicksand. I see the man standing in the lobby; his mouth is moving, but I can't hear anything over my breathing and Len's furious barking. It's as though I'm running through someone else's dream, or another wavelength. I burst through the front door, and running toward the car, frantically pull the keys out of my front pocket. Len jumps in, and turning the key in the ignition, I skid out of the parking lot. On the highway once again, I watch the speedometer climb.

150.
160.
170.

Not fast enough. The time, somehow, is 4:08 a.m.

What? The?

It could be worse. It can always be worse.
No.
Not always.

I am not scared. I am no longer scared. When the worst has been done, there is no longer anything to fear.

Ha ha ha ha ha ahhhhh. Ahhhh. Ha!

It comes. It always does.
Like walking after crawling, for those with the strength and the courage to see from a higher place, to give up what is safe and comfortable to achieve something greater.

These waves. These bottles. This maddening sphere. This ink blot sky and no light. This glow from within. This birth of confidence. This proving. This power. This control. This Will.

Apollo and Dionysius are *one!* We've just separated them out of mistaken assumption that to divide is to conquer. I don't understand, but I know. Words can only say so much. Language compartmentalizes what is whole. The Holon. The animal nature that consciousness obscures.

SPACE

CHARTED

I regret that I couldn't have been there when the inexorable force of a thousand iron wills at last coaxed the Berlin wall down to the ground. What a moment. Perhaps no single event in my lifetime has symbolized so much. The legacy of a vicious war and the enduring visual image of a cold one, the wall divided Germany into a country with a split personality. Regardless of what side came out victorious, you knew the situation couldn't endure forever. A standoff only lasts until one person blinks, and when that blink finally came, like a master samurai exploiting an opponent's weakness, the people knew instinctively what to do. The euphoria was palpable; could it be that peace would win and that godawful war would finally be placed in the past?

I remember being in Amsterdam, thinking about how it had fallen so quickly during the war to Hitler. The canals and streets are still lined with the imposing row houses that existed through the war and seem to huddle together, comforting one another. They whisper to each other. Things not for my ears. They remember all the people rounded up and taken away before they had any idea what lay in wait. I recall my visit to Anne Frank's house, a disturbing journey into a present that occurred years ago. The same map hangs on the wall still, a faded and desiccated time traveller. Climbing the secret pathway leading up to their hideaway, I stood and listened. I could hear the pen scratching on paper, all the murmurs and hushed tones. And fear.

I hurried past the room with the televisions showing the conveyor belts efficiently carrying emaciated board-stiff bodies to their unholy graves; the bulldozers groaning and whining in remonstration as their crushing weight is steered over the cadavers, arranging them into neat piles. Who can stand to watch as those bodies reluctantly give way to each other, limbs whirling about, like a pile of twigs, arms and hands obdurately reaching for the indifferent sky?

In the sixties, before effective codes of ethics were written, it was demonstrated that, when commanded to do so under duress, the majority of people off the street would follow instructions to administer lethal shocks to strangers. Another famous experiment had student volunteers take on roles as prisoners and guards in a simulated jail. The behaviour they observed was so shocking that it had to be called off after only a few days. Those randomly selected to be "prisoners" were being beaten and starved by those randomly selected to be "guards". Years later, the subjects of these experiments stated that they had experienced extreme psychological suffering and damage, all resulting from the actions of everyday human beings. They were upset to learn how similar all of us really are.

I truly believe Hitler and his cronies could have turned out differently. I must.

Berlin, Germany: My Past

The wires of the chain-link fence embrace each other closely in fear as I peer through them, out onto the field under which they say lies the bunker in which Hitler killed himself in; his body perhaps still buried there somewhere. Being this close to where his physical presence may reside stirs in me a faint nausea. I summon all my powers of imagination and recreate the scene. Ninety per cent of all the buildings have been razed by daily Allied bombing runs. Skeleton shapes of buildings longing for safer days stand

rigid and stubborn, black against a protesting sky. Madness reigns
as soldiers and civilians scurry around the smouldering rubble like
ants escaping the boot, aware that the end is near. Destroyed cars,
trucks and tanks find scant space to lie down and die amongst the
chaos. The acrid stench of smoke, gasoline and gunpowder fill my
nostrils with the smell of wanton death and doleful waste. And
the bodies, never forget the bodies, lying everywhere. It's hard to
believe they were ever alive, real men.

Hitler's generals have told him that all is lost. They are
finished. The Third Reich is dead. Like the commander of a
destroyed army, he looks small now, emasculated and gaunt, a
cheated God. He tells them to leave and, defiant to the end, the
last thing to pass through his mind is a bullet as he ends along
with himself another heart-wrenching phase in Europe's long
history of war. Tragic. What led to this moment? A mockery of
death, humanity gone mad.

The main reason I came is to feel these things. It's why I
have felt sick the whole time I've been here. Yesterday I found
a long stretch of the wall, almost indistinguishable from any
other given the lack of fanfare around it: no guards and no
tourists. At first I wondered if I was in the right place, but there
was no mistaking the aura emanating from the graffiti-covered
concrete slabs like steam from a winter hot spring. These walls
can talk. I sat down with my back to the now benign barricade,
leaning against it, picturing the different view that would have
greeted my eyes if I had been here twenty years ago: gun towers,
spotlights, barbed wire, dogs, guns, fear. I grew up in a city
where nothing ever happened. What would it have been like
to grow up here, alongside this wall, at the age when a child's
imagination is so strong? Instead of imagining the dinosaurs,
imaginations here were ruled by war and death.

I pass by the Brandenburg Gate, finally free of the shadow
of the wall, and arrive at the Reichstag. The building itself
was virtually destroyed during the war. Only the front façade

remained intact to stand determined and dignified through the intervening years. The entire building has now been rebuilt behind this original frontage and will once again become the seat of official power. The Federal Government designated this, the tenth anniversary of re-unification, as the year that they will move back to Berlin from their temporary home in Bonn.

I go inside amongst a clamouring gust of tourists, and we head to the top floor, where a simple museum has been created. It is on the roof, enclosed by a glass dome resembling a beehive. A massive spiral staircase winds around the circumference of the dome and leads up to an observation platform. From this position I'm afforded an amazing panorama of the surrounding area. This part of the city was cleared of rubble and bones after the war and became nothing more than barren fields, full of memories and regret. Since 1990, despite the removal of the wall, the East and West have remained two geographically separated cities.

From up here you can see that the whole area where the wall bisected the city is only now being rebuilt in earnest. Moving the government back to its home spurred on a massive growth of development, each project born simultaneously. A corps of construction cranes meets the gaze of anyone with a bird's eye view of this no-man's land. All this leaves me with the distinct impression that I have been transported back in time. Over fifty years have passed, but I'm easily able to make the leap as though it were only yesterday. I'm standing in a Berlin that has only narrowly survived a recent war, at the beginning of the rebuilding process. But there are no buildings of note yet, only a sea of intentions.

As I look around me, I notice two small boys running around chasing each other. One is perhaps five and the other maybe three. Their squeals of delight pierce the heavy atmosphere like a ray of light in a dark room. The older boy stands still for a moment, and just as his brother is about to latch onto him, takes off again, hiding behind a photo display of a bombed out Berlin. My heart feels light, and heavy at the same time.

FATHOM

Thursday, April 11th, Day 26: Punta Eugenia, Mexico
Noon finds the searing rays of the high Mexican sun beating
down relentlessly on the sparkling ocean and this small boat
bobbing gently upon its undulating surface. I awoke less than
an hour ago to Len's hungry tongue licking my face in the hopes
of provoking me to provide food. The truth is, I'm not sure of
the last time he ate. I'm not too worried, as he doesn't seem
any worse for wear, but it is disconcerting. I suspect I've been
sleeping for perhaps two days, a smothering, dreamless, death-
like sleep reserved only for those souls that have been strained
to their limits and are at risk of imminent self-destruction. It's
quite spectacular the myriad ways a mind finds to escape itself. I
recall not one cursed word or weightless step, not a single wrong
turn or fearful moment. I can only piece together the events
of the last few days by what I see around me, the few words I
wrote, and what I feel within me.

I'm painfully aware of every muscle fibre in my body, leading
me to the conclusion that I have undertaken some kind of
extended physical exertion, most likely prolonged sailing of
the boat. There's also the GPS, which tells me I'm near Punta
Eugenia in Mexico, about six hundred kilometres south of
the border. I have no idea how I got here; the entire trip since
California is whitewashed from my memory. It doesn't feel as
though it's something I've forgotten though. It seems it would

be more accurate to say that the passed time and events simply made no mark on my brain—there was nothing to forget because it never became a part of me in the first place. Perhaps I was in a daze the entire time, my brain and body simply running on autopilot as my mind stepped out for a rest.

The boat is a mess, but not overly so. One thing is very strange though—all my booze is gone. Every last drop has disappeared into thirsty air. Perhaps I drank it—but the bottles themselves are nowhere to be found, and other than my sore muscles, I feel fine. It would be accurate to say I feel refreshed, revitalized, reborn even. Whatever has transpired within me over the last few days has served as a refocusing, an affirmation of the task which lies ahead. Somehow I survived, and now I'm more certain than ever of my duty, and my ability. Everything that's happened has gotten me this far.

We'll not sail today. This day will be about relaxation and reorganization. I shall inspect the boat and set everything in proper order in preparation for the resumption of our journey.

~~~~~

Have you ever had one of those moments, one of those sparks of cognitive conception, when a brilliant idea coalesces in the shapeless ether of your subconscious, dragging itself up to impose itself upon your thoughts as though from out of nowhere? Or have you ever tried to force yourself to stop ruminating over a lost lover, or a disastrous decision, trying to dam up the rapid-fire flow of thoughts and ultimately failing? Can you exert physical control over your own thoughts and mental functioning? Is there even any point to this question?

When someone dies unexpectedly, many people comfort themselves and others by saying that it was their time, it was fate, it was meant to happen. My dad died yesterday in a car crash, but it was his time. If I believe this, does it mean that at exactly 10:47 p.m. last night, he was destined to die regardless of circumstance? If he'd gotten off work earlier, he would have instead died at the dinner table, or working on the car in the garage? Or is it a more exacting process? Was he destined to be in his car at that precise coordinate in space-time? If we accept the former, then we're discussing an issue specific to the timing of death, and there are no meaningful implications that I can see for our subjective contemplation of life. But with the latter situation, there are many interesting ramifications.

If the exact conditions of my dad's death were fated to exist, do we have any freedom whatsoever to control and influence our own lives? If the accident involved another person in another car, this means that that person was also destined, or dare I say, directed, to be where he or she was. Now we have two people meeting not by chance, but by design, which is what one implies when they say it was someone's time. Of course, the only way for each of them to have gotten to their proper places at the proper time was for every event that preceded the crash to happen exactly as it did. This is the age-old question of free will versus determinism. In the case of my father, how could we attribute any free will to his situation—or by extension yours and mine—if there was no option for him other than to go through all the motions that would eventually lead him up to the moment of his timely death? Many people have trouble dealing with the concept of arbitrary or avoidable death, but the alternative is a harsh reality as well. In essence, if you're saying it was his time, are you not saying that his life could have been nothing other than what it was, that he had no control over events, any events? Many people reject this idea as preposterous, yet, when a loved one dies, they believe there must have been a reason, that it could not have been avoided, for that would be such a...waste?

When you ask them, it seems most people will not hesitate to tell you that they most certainly are in control of their minds and that yes, of course they have free will. When asked to explain how they know this, the certainty is shown to rest on tenuous foundations. Putting aside all religious arguments, which render pointless any discussion on logic, one is faced with a dearth of reasonable explanations. Most people will call upon their strength of perception and say "I know it because that is how it feels in my head; I perceive free will, therefore I must have it." Many people will give examples of how they're often able to overpower that inner voice that says "just one more beer," or, "no doesn't always mean no." But what does saying that "in an internal struggle over two courses of action, I chose one," really say about our possessing free will?

Thursday, April 18th, Day 33: San Lucas, Mexico
The weather has been beautiful but characterized mainly by light winds. Our average speed is down as a result, but we're taking the opportunity to relax and bask in the pleasure of being on the ocean in a sailboat. We're now at the southern tip of the Baja Peninsula, and tomorrow we shall head directly east, traverse the mouth of the Gulf of California, and hopefully make it across to Mazatlan, more than 350 kilometres away. This is the largest stretch of open water we'll have to negotiate on this trip, taking us out of sight of land for much of the distance. I feel a tinge of apprehension, especially as this leg will require more than a day of straight sailing. We'll head off tomorrow, later than usual at ten a.m. This will allow me to get topped up on sleep, and it should have us hitting land in daylight on Saturday after sailing through the night. This should prove to be the hardest leg of the trip, but after a month on the water I feel up to the strain.

Namsos, Norway: My Past
I'm watching some unintelligible Norwegian drama on television when Kira comes in and sits down on the couch

beside me. She's been helping her mother in the garden, and strands of her hair hang playfully about her face, having escaped her ponytail.

"I just love getting my hands dirty," she says as she leans into me, resting her head against my chest. "There's definitely something spiritual about planting seeds in the earth and seeing them come to life. It's almost as though without you, the world would be a different place."

"Sure, you're basically playing God."

She squeezes into me and I place my arms around her, revelling in the perfect fit of our bodies and minds.

"This is my favourite place in the whole world," she says softly.

"What, your couch?"

"Right here," she replies, giving me a hard squeeze. "My body against yours."

I think about it for a moment then feel a sharp stinging in my eyes, the ripples from a stab of pain in my heart. It hits me that someday, with my own death, I shall be responsible for taking this all away. I will nail shut the door to her home, douse it in gasoline, burn it down then bury the smouldering remains six feet below the earth. I picture her abandoned form slumped on the ground, her hands and forehead pressed into the dirt, trying to bring it back to life without a seed and only the salty water of her tears. The only thing that will grow will be her sadness and misery; the only thing that will come to pass will be her own life.

Who could have the heart to tear a soother from a child's mouth, or the safety blanket from his clutching hands? How can I bear the thought of doing this to my Kira? I'm overcome and overwhelmed by guilt and fear for having created such a situation. I hope she goes first, at least then I'll know she isn't suffering.

Monday, April 22nd, Day 37: Cabo Corrientes, Mexico
When sailing in sight of land, you have the convenience of

knowing where you are all the time, as well as the comfort of safety. But on open water, you truly become one with the ocean, sky and stars. In the thrill of the isolation and solitude you commune with the dark blue depths above and below you, for there is nothing else. When I was younger, I made a promise to myself that I would sail around the world someday; what a feat that would be. This more modest trip is giving me a good sense of what it would have been like.

Thirty-seven days into the sail, I'm feeling good, but similar to how I felt as I neared the end of the bus ride, anxiety and restlessness are surfacing. I'm nearing my goal, and the meanderings of anticipation can be felt. It has been a long journey, and now it's almost at an end. I must be careful not to get ahead of myself, however. There is still much water to pass under the hull, but the goal is certainly in sight. This is the easy part.

I look to land again, the palm trees, which always look like plastic plants to me. Growing up in Canada, trees were a part of my everyday life, a constant backdrop against which life was lived, like the blue sky and green grass. Palm trees, with their impossibly large fronds and eccentric, shingled trunks glossed over by the softness of the magazine paper, seemed like creatures from another planet. Looking at them now here in front of me, my strongest association is with movies about the Vietnam War. I half expect to see a pair of F-16s streak toward me silently as they outmuscle their sound and light up the forest with incendiaries. The fire would paint the sky behind the trees with a red glow like a beautiful sunset. How would my feelings be different here and now, if I had real-life memories of that war to fall back on?

It's still evening in the bay, and the tepid weather creates an anxious tranquillity, reflecting my temperament. It always seems that when the ocean is still, one gets an uneasy feeling, the calm before the storm. It's like watching someone sleep— you begin to feel as though any moment they are going to jump up and scare the life out of you. Or maybe it will be something less obvious, but more sinister, like a single eyelid rising slowly, uncovering something deep in the soul, hidden from the owner's consciousness and not meant to be seen.

In an attempt to calm myself, I've just finished serenading Len. I think he surprised himself when he started howling along, a voice pulled out of him by the music itself pressing a button for a reaction hardwired into his species. Such a mystical sound. It seemed to embarrass him, and he eventually went down into the cabin and hid himself away. So I played on on my own. Here in this heavy silence, my music seems abrupt and aggressive, it feels out of time and out of place. This is a foreign world, a foreign existence—my future, not ready for me yet. The music is an intruder from a lost age. It grows more distant each day. There isn't much music left in my soul. Just one more overture.

Sunday, April 28th, Day 43: Acapulco, Mexico

We're moored to a buoy, just off the resort town of Acapulco. Reflected off the dark waters like smudgy shimmering stars, the lights of this tourist mecca portend beaches, drinks and women—diversions I know I'm beyond; I don't even need to be tied to the mast. Still though, the fact that we're getting quite low on food supplies makes it even more tempting. Len is doing fine, but my personal menu has become quite limited. How easy it would be to pack it all in and run away. I would never be able to live with myself.

The last two days of sailing have been damn lousy and make up for the previous week of fine weather. This is the latitude where the cool, south flowing California Current meets up with and sinks below, the warm, north flowing Equatorial Counter Current. It all operates just like the plates of the earth's crust at the subduction zones, except instead of volcanoes and earthquakes, this oceanic process results in the abundant rain and thunderstorms we've been sailing through for the last forty-eight hours. It's some serious bad luck to get so much rain at this time of the year, though. It appears our parade shall become soggier yet; the forecast calls for rain tomorrow as well. On top of all this, or rather beneath it, the change in current has also slowed down our speeds, as we're now sailing against the flow of the water.

The good news is that the cabin has remained dry and the boat is holding up fine. Only the normal amounts of sweat have breached the hull, the bilge pump making short work of it. *The Count* was certainly a good purchase, perfect for my needs and a pleasure to be aboard. It will be a shame to let her go.

I imagine again the luxury mere kilometres away and drive the thought from my head. Looking at the painting on the wall across from me, I think of that train. Strong now, powerful, assiduous. This machine has chosen a track, and having made its decision, betrays no hint of regret or second-guessing, just full steam ahead, an inspiration.

Namsos, Norway: My Past

I'd never imagined that it would actually happen, but I'd thought about it, finding a life partner that is. Faced with the situation now, I feel like most people do when they think they've pulled a fast one over on the powers that be: ecstatic, but nervous, waiting for the other shoe to drop. This results in no way from anything at all to do with Kira, or my feelings for her. Our love is absolute, and I trust it to the ends of the earth. I have no fear of her ever leaving or betraying me. But despite all this—or maybe because of it—a part of my heart is filled with fear and doubt that I cannot tuck away under the rug of my happiness.

The problem is related to my overactive mind or more specifically, my inability to be content within a moment. By all external lifestyle standards I'm a poster boy for the "live for the day" mentality of the modern era, but in many ways it's a sham. I do what I want to do and follow the vagaries of my heart wherever they may lead me, but in my mind I live a much more holistic existence. In my head I live within a continuum, I see an unfolded chart on the wall with my complete trip plotted out. I'm stuck in a static contemplation of my life in its entirety, encompassing all my past days as well as those yet unlived. This often has a detrimental affect on my experience of the here and now.

I wonder. How can any of us really enjoy these lives each of us is living without adopting some sort of delusion as a foundation? Happiness is ephemeral, seemingly merely a transition phase between sadnesses. One minute you're standing at the altar staring into the twinkling eyes of the love of your life, the next moment you're surrounded by crying people all dressed in black, staring at a polished wooden box containing said love of your life. One moment you're ecstatically holding your newborn son in your arms, the next minute you're holding his hand as he lies in a hospital bed in a drug-induced coma. Sadness, in such forms, surrounds us on all sides, and I'm unable to adjust my scent to tune it out. It forms burning brackets around each happy moment, outstretched arms beckoning our lives into the embers of its smouldering embrace.

It has always seemed to me that the only way to avoid all this gut-wrenching pain is to shut out all potential sources. Maybe it's cold and desolate growing old all alone, but at least you don't have to occupy every waking thought with the knowledge that your most treasured love, the most important thing in your whole existence, is going to knock off as well. And how can parents not live a life of constant fear, frightened to death that something terrible will happen to their children, ushering the rest of their lives into the most profound sadness any living thing can experience. Sure, a lot of people use religion to combat all this risk, saying it all happens for a reason and there's no sense losing any sleep over any of it, but talk about blind faith!

And now here I am, setting myself up for the very thing I have always felt it imperative to avoid. Will I actually be able to sit by Kira's deathbed someday and still be thankful for this? Will I consider such insufferable pain to be worth the extra happiness I derived from a life shared with her? Could we still joke about things, still be happy? You cannot even begin to contemplate true sadness until you've felt love, true and crushing love.

I used to enjoy watching and reading all manner of creative entertainment. If a movie had a sad part, I would feel the hurt, but I could still enjoy watching it. I was even happy to see a sad ending, thankful for the deviation from the standard "happily ever after" ideal. But now I feel the grief so intensely, so thoroughly, that I tear up and wind up depressed for the rest of the day. I'm imagining Kira and me in the place of the decimated characters, and I want to cry. Any little thing can set me off now, and it's because I already know in my head what it will be like. I know as sure as I know my name. And I dread.

The only hope is that perhaps before too advanced of an age, we'll die together somehow, instantly, with no time to contemplate: a head on collision, or in our sleep—the only painless way to end our existences. If she goes before me, I will be lost, snapped, there's no way in hell I could go on. So now I'm reduced to hoping that we die together while still young as our only salvation.

I can no longer live without her; she is now my life impulse. I could force myself to stop breathing easier than I could stand to be without her. And as I look at her, sitting at the kitchen table reading, the smooth sensuous lines of her lightly tanned legs flowing up and under the soft white cloth of her boxer shorts, I know my very existence is tied to hers now. I wish I truly could just live for today, but more than that, I wish I could live only today.

Friday, May 3rd, Day 48: Salina Cruz, Mexico

After a month and a half of relatively smooth sailing, the last week has been miserable, and yesterday was our first real brush with disaster.

From Acapulco we had two straight days of rain and strong

winds as vicious as thirty knots at some points. The going was strenuous, but we managed to find a sheltered bay for the night between the dodgy days. The rains remained intermittent until yesterday, and I simply can't believe that the weather can be so terrible at this time of year in this part of the world. The front desks of the tourist resorts must be crammed with pasty-skinned foreigners demanding refunds.

This time the cabin did not prove as airtight as in the past, and below decks took on water. Nothing serious, but Len has only just now dried off and looks none too happy with me. I myself am still damp as I write this, and tonight shall be another wet one in the moist cabin. It is a test. Yesterday, however, the problems were a little more serious than worries over wetness.

Moderate east-south-easterly winds were allowing us to keep a direct heading on nice and tight, close-hauled tacks. Things were looking good around noon; the rain had died and the sky was blue with high cirrus clouds. We were on a port tack in winds about ten knots, when out of nowhere the windward shroud snapped. The sound was like a gigantic bass string being cut under tension as the wire flicked itself up violently into the air, thankfully at neither Len's head nor mine.

I immediately dropped the main to ease the pressure on the mast, spooled the jib, and started the engine to steer us toward shore, all the while thanking the heavens the mast hadn't folded. The chart showed a sheltered bay about five kilometres away, and I headed for that, my heart in my mouth, praying the mast would hold. It was angled a few degrees to starboard, and I knew I had to fix it soon. I was lucky it wasn't the outside shroud that had snapped, but I was very worried that any extra stress might be enough to buckle the mast and render the boat un-sailable. To lose the mast would mean disaster for the trip, and maybe even worse.

The cause of the problem was readily apparent, as I could see that the fixing bolt had somehow given out. How the hell was I going to jury-rig this? Reaching the bay, I set the anchor and retrieved my tools and supplies. I had replacement hardware, but simply having the spare hardware is only half the battle in these situations. Somehow I would need to get sufficient weight onto the shroud wire in order to create enough slack to reconnect it.

My first thought was the anchor, but it would never be heavy enough. Another possibility would be to detach the anchor rode from the boat and attach it to the shroud. Then I could set the anchor and let the boat drift, slowly allowing the weight of the boat to pull the shroud. After tossing this idea around in my head, I finally decided it would be impossible to cut the angle enough to reconnect the shroud, and the whole plan was just too risky, as the boat would most likely end up capsized. I thought of all the weight I had on the boat, and none of it would be enough to tension the shroud sufficiently.

I was thinking about how I might use the winch to indirectly tension the shroud when a gracefully simple solution came to me. I would use the sailor's best friend—the wind, of course! If I set the rudder to hold course on a starboard reach, the force of the wind on the mainsail would angle the mast over to port and maybe, just maybe, the wind-induced slack would be enough, such that combined with the force of my body weight, I could reattach it. It was risky, because I would be out in the wind again, and if it suddenly changed directions, the boom might jibe on its own over to starboard, and that would likely be enough to pull out the other remaining shroud and topple the mast. Most sailors would deem the potential for disaster of going back out into the wind too high, but I just loved the simplicity of this idea.

I put Len below deck and connected a lifeline for myself, then fastened the vice grips securely onto the end of the shroud, so that I'd be able to pull it into place. I made sure to clamp them as tightly as I possibly could; I would have to put a lot of my own weight on them, and if they slipped off, Len would finally get his wish for a promotion to captain of *The Count*.

Mercifully, the headwind was constant motoring out of the bay, and as I raised the mainsail, it filled with air, and we began to heel. I would need the sail to carry as much wind as possible to weight the mast sufficiently. It was going to be close at best. I watched and waited with great anticipation and intense worry as our speed steadily increased. We heeled steadily over to twenty degrees, then twenty-five, then finally topped out at thirty. Setting the rudder, I took a deep breath and prayed for the wind to hold. Scrambling over to the mount for the shroud and bracing my feet against the guardrail, I pulled with all my weight on the vice grips. With the severe angle of the deck, I was so close to the water, it felt as though I was sitting right in it. After three so-close attempts, I put all my strength and the full weight of my determination on the line, and with no room to give away, I was finally able to attach the new hardware and secure the shroud. I stared at my handiwork for a moment, almost unable to believe my eyes receiving the vision of the reattached shroud. I couldn't believe it, success was mine! After letting out a holler, I spared no time in removing the vice grips and scrambled back into the cockpit to regain control of the boat. I was glowing as endorphins and pride circulated around my brain in a victory parade. There are few satisfactions like that derived from a successful jury rig. Our first real technical challenge had been faced and met with success.

Only after I had succeeded did I let myself ponder the size of the risk I had taken. But my instincts had been correct, and gently working the helm of my boat, I felt comfortable, assured and content. No longer a newcomer on this boat, I'd staked my claim as a deserving and worthy captain. *The Count* no longer needed to fear me and would place her every confidence in me from this point onward. We sailed together in the soothing peace of the wind and sea as I dreamed of impossible things.

Toronto, Canada: My Past
Something's got to give. My life is becoming a void, a non-event.

Time itself has become a depressant, smothering my mind under its weight. I don't know what the purpose of all this is, but I have a feeling I know what it isn't. It isn't this. I wake up each day and open my eyes to a staring contest with futility and always blink first. My one wish is for something desperate, complete and whole, a sign. There's something going on just beyond the reach of my senses, and I can no longer ignore it.

Perhaps I need to get away, leave all this behind. I need to become a man of action, get proactive. It's just so hard when all the books have the same cover and the signs all point in the same wrong direction. I'm like a marble perfectly balanced on the tip of a pencil. I can go in any direction I please, all that's required is a shift of weight. But all paths lead to the same place—down. I want to go up! How do I get there, how do I do it? I can balance here no longer, but I refuse to move simply for the sake of movement.

And at the back of my mind there is a voice. The voice of myself; the voice of truth. I can't listen. To do so would mean the end.

Sunday, May 5th, Day 50: Tonala, Mexico

Smooth sailing now. I expect two more days lie in wait, then I shall be saying goodbye to the ocean green. We're so close that the very air is beginning to make my pulse quicken and cause my hair to stand on end. Len is sensing these changes and is keeping to himself a bit more than usual, perhaps afraid of what is happening. I guess it's the same way animals can sense the atmospheric changes when an earthquake or hurricane is imminent. I'm trying to remain calm, but it's virtually impossible. I am hyper-alert, every slight change in wind speed and direction is registered deep within, and my body reacts unconsciously. I'm feeling no doubt or reservation; it could have been no other way. Still though, being so close makes me sick to my stomach.

DEAD RECKONING

Namsos, Norway: My Past

This small room, with its firm double bed pressed square against the large window looking out onto the Norwegian landscape, has become for me nothing less than a chamber of mental torture. This unlikely scenario results from the unending conflagration that plays itself out in my head, day in and day out. Being here with Kira, in a room that lives and breathes her existence, is absolute contentment, perfection. I know the impossibility of such things, but I wrap myself up in them anyway. I run away from my infernal fear of the future and all that is hiding in its shadows. But the thoughts seep in through the cracks like water into a sinking ship. One moment I'm receiving a phone call informing me that Kira has been killed in a car accident, the next I'm holding onto her stiff, cold, drowned form as we drift in a life raft on a heartless ocean. Whatever the exact circumstances, the outcome is always the same.

I'm sure everyone experiences these feelings when they find their true love, but there is a difference between those people and myself: they find ways to deal with all this. Whether it's a belief in God or fate or karma, or even just through sheer force of will, they are able to push such thoughts out of their consciousness. None of these options are available to me, and I'm at a loss to understand exactly why. I worry that perhaps this is all a mistake, that maybe I'm not meant or built to be involved in such an intense affair. Just as a fuse will explode if fed too strong an electric current, my heart cannot handle this. I'll never be able to cope with anything less than the continuation of our present over an eternity. I can't bear the idea of anything changing, anything at all. I can't bear the thought of anything but the impossible.

The moonlight, unhampered by curtain or blind, shines in through the window and casts Kira's form in a pure and gentle glow, lending emphasis to her angelic constitution. Her left arm provides a pillow for her lovely head, which at the moment is facing me though her eyes are in shadow. She is asleep. She says she can sleep in no position other than this. I tell her that throughout the night she assumes many others. To this she just shrugs and says she wouldn't know about that.

Watching your loved one sleep is like communing with the physical manifestation of serenity. The way the shadows play on the angles of Kira's brow and jaw would make a perfect focal point for a painted portrait. I reach over and trace the outline of the lips which I have kissed and longed for, and will continue to do so always. I have been staring at her for an hour now, trying to commit this sight to memory, every last detail, so that I may perfectly recreate it someday in some form that might allow others to share such perfection.

What might she be dreaming of? She'd probably never in her wildest dreams be able to imagine the thoughts passing through my mind. I have never mentioned any of my irrational concerns to her. There is nothing she could say or do to change or improve my plight; it would only serve to upset her. I would kill myself a hundred different ways before I would ever do her any harm. I've never seen her cry, and I intend to do all I can to see that I never do. These thoughts further perpetuate my dilemma and nudge me closer and closer still to the edge of the precipice on which I'm balanced, and soon shall fall from. Into what, I cannot know.

I feel a stinging in my eyes, and before I know it, they are filling with fire that threatens to overflow. A single tear traces its heat down my cheek, clearing a path for a steady stream that leaves me embarrassed and scared. What is wrong with me? Here I am living a waking dream, everything I or anyone else could ever want is laid out for my taking; yet all I can think about is how it is all going to end someday. If Kira were to wake up right now, how would I explain away these tears?

That damn cliché keeps cycling around my head—is it better to have loved and lost than never to have loved at all? I used to think I knew the answer; that of course it wasn't, but Kira brought me to see the other side, that to experience true love, even for a minute, would be worth whatever the pain of losing it would be. Now I wonder if I might have been mistaken. Perhaps the moment of love would forge an intense happiness as never before imagined or conceived, but how could life be worth living after losing such a thing? Would not everything that followed simply be meaningless and pointless? Even the things that were once pleasurable would become bland and diluted.

Can you think of a statement more true than "ignorance is bliss"? When I'm reading about irreplaceable rain forests being cleared away and turned into furniture, or the entire population of a village being hacked to pieces for living on the wrong side of the fence, I think I would much prefer to live as a hermit in the mountains of B.C. Just me and the trees. To hell with the world of humanity and all its pleasure and pain.

But how much more rewarding would such a life be when shared with Kira? It would be paradise. I just can't help but worry that it might be the fool's kind.

~~~~~

I'm wakened suddenly by the foreign sound of Len growling. This is the first time I've ever heard him do this, and my adrenalin is instantly pumping. The situation is made all the stranger by the fact that along with this, I can hear a low humming sound, which might only be in my head. An electric sensation permeates the air, and every hair on my body is standing on end as though charged with static. The boat is very dark, and looking down the length of the cabin, I can see nothing more than the dim light glinting here and there off the various reflective surfaces.

"Len, what is it buddy?"

"Grrrrr...rrrr."

"Do you want me to turn the light on, is the dark making you scared, old boy?" I whisper, more to ease my own level of stress than his.

"That won't be necessary, sir. Unless it would put you and your dog more at ease."

What the hell was that? Unless Len has been using his down time to amazing purpose and learned how to imitate the human voice, someone else is on the boat with us. I'm paralyzed, only physically of course. My brain races, searching for possible explanations.

"I'm sorry. I did not mean to scare you." The disembodied, religiously calm voice is coming from the main quarters. The most disturbing aspect of it is its familiarity. I cannot place it definitively, but I know I've heard it before, perhaps long ago. I'm still unable to make a move, my voice now also paralyzed, and a few moments pass in silence, disturbed only by Len's continued growling.

"I do wish you would say something to me, and if not to me, then to the dog, so that he might be reassured."

This provides my mind with a route to take toward action, and at last I manage to mutter, "Len, Len boy, come here, buddy." With a whimper, he jumps onto my bed and takes up a seated position behind me, still hyper-alert. Are these words in my head? Is Len just sensing madness in me? Tell me I'm just dreaming, someone.

"Much obliged, sir," says the deep, eerie voice. I'm still at a loss for what to do, but I know I don't want to turn on any lights. The darkness keeps the reality at bay; it's still possible to believe I might be dreaming.

"No, you are not dreaming, my brother, though I am here to ask you about the reality you exist in." This obtuse statement does nothing to clear up my confusion, and a moment later, the voice adds, "Are you sure you want to do this?" The voice is not unfriendly, and in many respects is pleasant, almost fatherly in its tone.

"Do what?" I manage to blurt out, doing a poor job of matching his casual manner.

"I wish not to give it any more validity by airing the thought out loud, but rest assured I am well apprised of the situation."

For some reason I know not to doubt him, but why? Who is this man that has suddenly thrust himself into the confines of my eremitic existence? Just then the boat rocks a little from the shifting of weight somewhere, causing both Len and me to tense up further. My eyes are slowly adjusting to the darkness, and I strain to see anything out of the ordinary. I notice a blur of movement, which upon terminating reveals a patch of greyish-silver reflecting the faint moonlight coming through the portholes. "I do really wish you would share some words with me. That's why I am here, after all."

My eyes continue their struggle to identify familiar shapes, and suddenly I realize that what I'm seeing is indeed a human form, the silver reflection being the hair on the top of his head.

"What the hell do you want to talk about?" I announce sternly. This game has gone far enough.

"Are you *sure* you want to do this?" he says again, his voice as placid as it ever was.

"How about you answer some of my questions? It *is* my boat you're sitting in, uninvited." Only the silence responds, so I continue. "Like who the hell are you and how on earth did

you get onto my boat? We're at least a kilometre from shore!"
I'm yelling now, gaining courage with each word as my fear is
replaced with anger at this man's audacity.

"I do wish you would remain civil, it would really make
everything so much easier," he replies.

"That's not an answer!"

"Quite right, do forgive me," he says, pausing before adding,
"Well, sir, I am afraid there is not much of significance I can tell
you about myself, as I prefer always to talk of others. And at this
precise moment I would much prefer to talk about you. More to
the point, I would like to ask you again if you are sure you want
to do this."

His single-minded insistence on this line of questioning
causes the frustration to well up inside me. I'm overcome by
anger, surprised by its vitality. I want to do something to him, I
don't know what, but something inside won't let me. Suddenly
the air changes, and my anger subsides. I feel a calm resignation
and acceptance washing over me.

"Am I sure I want to do this? Assuming you *do* know what
I'm up to, then you must know that I'm sure. I've been sailing
south for a month and a half. Would I be doing that if I weren't
sure of what I was doing? I'm as sure as anyone ever can be."

"What do you mean by that, 'as sure as anyone ever can be'?
Do you mean anyone, or do you mean you?"

The calmness fades as quickly as it came, and again the rage
overpowers me. "I mean me, goddamn it! Yeah, yeah, no one
can ever be completely free of doubt. Is that what you want to
hear? People are always torn between poles, right? Whether
they face that fact or not, right? Well, my water-walking friend,
I don't fit into that category any longer, I've found a way to
overcome all that bullshit. It's not something I asked for! In a
heartbeat, I'd go back and change so many things if I could, but
it's too late now, nothing else can be done!" My heart is racing,
and I can feel sweat trickling down my back and along my

temples. Saying nothing, the man repositions himself so that he's now in the faintest trace of light, and I can clearly make out his shape. He is very thin, and his head is surrounded by shining hair pulled back from his forehead. At once I connect it with the voice and feel my breath escaping me as though I've been kicked in the chest. "It's, it's you."

"Yes," he says simply.

I sit speechless.

"I just need to know, please, search your depths and tell me honestly. Are you sure you want to do this?"

"Damn you!" I scream. "What the hell does it matter it to you?"

"I care about you, sir."

"What?" I shout, exasperated and at wit's end.

"You ask so many questions, you massage all the 0's and 1's, but I fear that you are missing the most important things, the things that should be so clear to you. The only questions you need to ask are of yourself," he says, emphatic now.

"You condescending bastard!" I yell, leaping to my feet and momentarily losing sight of my surroundings. "How can you say that? How can you doubt that I have asked myself such things a million times? How could I have done otherwise? I'm not some ten-year-old boy acting on a whim! I'm more sure of this than I've been of anything in my life. If it's absolutes you want, then you'd best find another dimension to go and harass!" I scream, fumbling around in the darkness for the light switch.

There's no reply, and locating the switch at last, I turn it on. The light blinds me, and I close my eyes to absorb the brightness. Turning to face him, I open my eyes and find, to my ultimate shock and frustration, there's no one there, no one at all. Looking around the cabin, I can find no traces of anyone. There really is nowhere to hide. The hum is gone as well, replaced by silence accentuated by the gentle lapping of the water. Turning back to Len, I see him on my bed, sleeping peacefully.

SCUTTLE

Tuesday, May 7th, Day 52: Champerico, Guatemala
Approaching Champerico this afternoon, the weather was
hot and humid with lazy and listless winds, but eventually we
leaked into the marina and eased up alongside the weather-
beaten dock. There were two large cargo ships anchored
offshore, and we had to be careful avoiding the traffic ferrying
back and forth between them. Champerico is the largest port
town on the west coast of Guatemala, though it actually has no
port to speak of. Ships must anchor offshore, and their cargo—
usually bananas or coffee—is brought to them via a steady
stream of smaller taxi vessels. There is a simple marina for
smaller boats such as ours, though it is right beside the loading
area of the taxi boats, and I worry that *The Count* may well end
up filled with fruit.

After securing *The Count* alongside the dock, I stepped
reluctantly onto the weather-beaten wooden planks, feeling
emotional, knowing that this would be the last time I would
skipper this worthy vessel. Len on the other hand, was more
stoic, only interested in finding a fresh place to relieve himself.
Moments later we were approached by a couple of sceptical
looking police officers asking us our business in Spanish. When I
showed them my passport and told them in Spanish that we were
tourists from Canada, their demeanour instantly changed.

After asking me many friendly questions about where we

had come from and the route and conditions, they guided me along the dock to a sagging old Jeep. All of us, including Len, got in and headed for the customs office. A short, bumpy ride later, we arrived at the office, a concrete square with dirty windows all along the front. A simple affair that would more accurately be described as a shack. We entered the musty smelling room, and the squeaky screen door sprang closed behind us, sealing us in. There was one desk in the middle of the room piled haphazardly with papers of various sizes and colours. The walls were strewn with various posters listing wanted criminals and import/export regulations, as well as anti-drug messages and the penalties for smuggling. No one else was in the room.

"We don't get many tourists landing here. Plenty of surfers, but not many sailors. That's why we only have this little building here," said one of the guards. Very tall, with dark olive skin and a capable air, he seemed to be the second-in-command. He had no nameplate on his chest, but the other had one that said "Miguel". Miguel, shorter and more muscular but just as dark, took the chair behind the desk and motioned silently for me to take the other in front. They exhibited no hard edges, so I wasn't too nervous. Of course, you never know, but since the peace agreement was signed in 1996, Guatemala has been very easy to get into and relatively safe. Like so many developing countries, they have become highly desirous of tourist dollars such as mine. Entry visas are generally available on the spot—a person needs only a valid passport. I must say, though, I didn't expect the guards to be quite so friendly.

"I'll tell you right off the bad news," said the seated guard. These words brought a chill over me, but it quickly warmed. "The dog will have to be put into quarantine until we can test him. This can take up to two weeks. How long will you be staying here?" I breathed a small sigh of relief.

"I thought as much when I brought him," I said. "But to be

honest, I'm hoping to find a good home for him here. I only got him for the trip. You know, to keep me company—steady the mind over the long days and nights. But I can't take him any further than this. I plan on spending a month or so travelling on land before I get back to the boat and carry on. He's a good dog, smart, good-natured—I really wish I could keep him, but I'm afraid I must try to find someone to take him off my hands." I felt distinct pangs of guilt as I considered Len and how great he'd been, but I'd already dealt with all that in my mind.

As I was speaking, I noticed the taller guard perk up at my mention of giving Len away. An excited expression stole over his face as he asked, "So you are just giving him away?"

"Yes, sir," I said, affecting my most obsequious tone. "As long as Len—that's his name—seems willing to go with the new owner. You know how animals have a sixth sense about people."

"Well, let's go see!" he said, dislodging himself from his position against the wall and gesturing for me to follow him out of the office.

I threw a look at the guard at the desk, and he motioned for me to go ahead, saying, "Just give me your passport, and I'll start on the forms." I handed it over and followed the other guard outside.

Len immediately rushed over to us and commenced sniffing the guard. Of course, I haven't seen Len around many people, but his complete lack of suspicion or hesitation spoke well of the guard. "So you really want to give him up, Señor?" he asked, crouching down and scratching Len under his mouth, apparently knowing his way around a dog.

"You really want him?"

"Do I want him? It's not very often you see a fine dog like this around these parts. All of the dogs here are street dogs, wild mutts scavenging around for any kind of food they can find. I would love to have myself a real dog. I could even make him a police dog," he replied, grinning ear to ear. I smiled

at the thought of my trusty first mate landing work in law
enforcement. I was very relieved to have found Len a new home
so easily and quickly. The bottom line was that from this point
on, Len would be much better off with him than with me.

As we entered the office once again, I was immediately met
with a question from Miguel. "You haven't got any stamps from
America or Mexico in your passport. Yet you say you sailed all
the way from Canada? Did you not stop at immigration in these
places?"

"No, of course not. I sailed all the way through. This is the
first dry land I've stepped on since Vancouver." He stared at me
for a moment as though weighing my words, then carried on in
a more casual tone.

"So you say you are going to travel around the area. What
are you going to do with your yacht?" I had never thought of
The Count as a yacht before, and the label seemed embarrassing,
almost euphemistic. "Surely you aren't going to leave it here the
whole time?" he added.

This was the hard part. In actuality I would not be returning
for the boat and could care less if I got money for it, but I had to
be careful not to arouse any suspicion. I would obviously need
it for the continuation of my trip. "Well, let me tell you my exact
plan. You can see from my ownership papers that I just bought
her for this trip. The fact of the matter is that I've just started two
years worth of travelling, and I've wanted to sail the west coast
all my life. My father had some ancestry here, and in the small
amount of time I had access to him, he always told me I must
come to Central America some day. And he said Guatemala is
the first place I should go. Ever since I can remember, it's been
my dream to sail from Vancouver to Guatemala. Finally it's safe
to come, so, here I am." The guards seemed to be following my
story with interest, so I felt comfortable continuing. "Now that
I've finally done it, the return trip is inconsequential really. So,
either I'll sell the boat and fly to my next destination, or I'll

sail it further south and sell it down there, Panama maybe. I'm afraid I have little use for it now, but of course I don't want to just give it away, as I did my dog." I laughed as I said this and was relieved when they joined in. "I was hoping that I might be able to store it for a month or so while I travel. I know your town is small, and I have little hope of getting a fair price for it if I were to sell it here."

"Well, to be sure, it's a fine boat," said the nameless guard. "There is only one person here who could afford a luxury like that, and you might have some luck with him. He seems happy to throw his money at any expensive thing he can get his hands on. He just may be the person to help you out." My heart leapt. I felt a tremor of apprehension at this. It was all going too smoothly, really, but sometimes in life you just have to trust the randomness of it all and let the leaves fall where they may.

"Whatever you can do, I am eternally grateful for," I said.

"Come back down tomorrow about the same time, and I'll let you know if he's interested."

We finished the paperwork, and I was free to go. I purposefully neglected to ask advice about where to stay as I didn't want anyone knowing where I was. Saying goodbye to Len—which was quite hard—I made my way back to *The Count* to secure her for the night. I could stay on her tonight, but now that I'm here, it no longer feels right. I must now get down to business, no sense prolonging the neutral luxury of the boat.

After gathering my stores, I stepped onto the dock and took one last look at my ship. Saying goodbye to *The Count* was no easier than saying goodbye to Len. She had truly served me well. She got me here against some healthy opponents, and neither of us are the worse for wear. I can go back and see either of my companions later, but I avoid saying goodbye unless it's truly going to be such.

Turning my back on *The Count of Monte Cristo*, I felt profoundly alone, abandoned. Here I am in Guatemala of all

places, all alone, and with the hardest part of my journey still
lying in wait. But I have strength and resolve such that I have
never felt before, and I will be strong. Leaving the dock and
the ocean behind, I headed down the road and toward town,
turning my back for good on everything I've ever known, and a
self soon to be long-forgotten.

Champerico is an ossified port town built on the coffee boom
of the late nineteenth century. From here, the coffee beans were
shipped to thirsty cities all over North and South America. It's
a town like so many in developing nations, looking as though
the maid quit fifty years ago and has never been replaced.
Everything appears to be crumbling, disintegrating. From
the walls of the houses to the dirt of the roads to the paint on
the walls, the transience of life is manifest in everything you
see. Nothing here looks even remotely new, perhaps only the
youngest of the children scampering around the streets, but
even they have a soiled, used quality to them, as though they
have seen more in their short lives than most ever will, and all
without a shower. Above all though, this place feels real, and
that is a great comfort to me right now. This is not exactly a
tourist town, though it is a beach town, and they're getting an
increasing number of tourists coming for the surfing, which is
why I intend to stay well away from the beach.
   The streets themselves are ribbons of dirt filling the space
between rows of crumbling concrete buildings and slouching
grass roofs, many selling day to day necessities, others housing
the occasional bar and specialty store. There are torn awnings
hanging over the front of each business, the proprietors
knowing that they have not a hope of selling their wares unless
they throw in complimentary relief from the glaring sun. The
heat today is very near intolerable, especially if you happen to
be sensitive to such things. I myself seem to grow less tolerant of

heat the older I get, humidity in particular. Being Canadian, my inclination is naturally toward cooler temperatures, and each drop of sweat that becomes one with the dirt below saps a little more strength from my body.

After a couple of hours wandering and condensing, I found the hotel in which I'm now writing this. It's perfect in that there are actually a few other tourists staying here as well. The room itself is your typical jail cell. The concrete mix was obviously a bit too heavy on the water, as it's cracking and crumbling everywhere, just like the rest of the town. A bed, sink, and mirror are included in the price. It is clean, however, and for this I'm thankful. The sheets on the bed smell like soap, which must be this place's claim to fame and the reason it's not completely empty as most of the other places in this town are.

And so here I sit, cross-legged on the bed, writing, as usual. I will go to sleep early tonight, though I worry that sleep might not come, inescapable heat and humidity have a habit of driving it away. As the darkness has set in and the daytime sounds have left the stage to those of the night, I'm presented with the cold, hard reality of my situation once again. How did I get here? Will I truly have the strength to see it through? Please let me have the strength.

I know I will have the strength.

I wake up with the sun because there is nothing on the east-facing window to block it out. Even this early in the morning it's as hot as coffee and sticky enough for the sheets to remain attached to me as I sit up on the squeaky bed. Despite the all night heat, I managed to sleep quite well due to the general fatigue from the weeks of sailing. After having a shower in the communal facilities down the hall, I feel worlds better. I force myself to do everything slowly, in a determined but ill-fated attempt to avoid sweating. The air itself seems to be applying the sweat to my body with a paintbrush, and within fifteen minutes I'm left wondering why I even bothered towelling off.

I spend the morning familiarizing myself with the layout of the small town, while at the same time trying my best to keep a low profile. The town is small, perhaps seven thousand people, most of them working in the fishing or shipping trades. Everyone looks poor, though no one seems to be unbearably so. This is most likely an illusion in a country where seventy per cent of the arable land is owned by three per cent of the people. The peace treaty went a long way to end the official corruption and abuse, but since then, other, more private interests, have taken their place.

I don't mean to belittle the effect of the changes wrought with the historic signing of that piece of paper—over twenty-nine years, more than two hundred thousand people were killed or disappeared in a vicious civil war that was in every way as grotesque and ugly as any that have occurred in this planet's bloody history. Until recently, Guatemala was one of the most infamous and notorious countries in the Western Hemisphere, if not the world. Entire villages were massacred and burned to the ground by the army in a conflict stemming from the usual human motivations—rich versus poor, native versus conquerors, us versus them. But all this changed on December 29, 1996, when the "government" and the Guatemalan National Revolutionary Unity Front—a guerrilla group of freedom fighters—signed the long-hoped-for peace accord. This was a watershed moment in Guatemalan history, officially ending at last the civil war. It offered the people their first real hope for peace in many years, but unfortunately, the problems it put an end to were replaced almost overnight by new ones.

The military leaders—despite the accountability clauses in the document—went free and became wealthy landowners. Making problems worse is the fact that a society that lives with violence for thirty years has a hard time letting it go. Violence is such a part of the way of life here that many people do not know how to cope in its absence. Levels of violent crime are intolerably high, and official justice is a metaphysical construct at best. The current court system and police force are unable to cope with the volume of crime and virtually all guilty go free. Lynching is becoming more and more prevalent as frustrated people begin to take the law into their own hands. Time may in fact heal all wounds, but the Guatemalan people, like so many others in this world, have been patient long enough.

"I'm afraid the man I mentioned yesterday is not interested in your yacht," says Miguel, adding, "he is already in possession of a suitable yacht."

This news suits me just fine. It means a bit more work on my part, but it's probably safer and more convenient this way. "Well, that's too bad, I suppose, but as I said yesterday, I didn't really expect to be able to sell it here." I pause a moment and then say, "Is there somewhere I can put it for safekeeping while I'm travelling?"

"Oh yes, certainly. I can't guarantee its safety one hundred per cent, but you can keep it docked where it is. We can keep an eye on it for you as well, but of course there will be a small charge." Of course. After making the arrangements and paying the fee, I provide them with an imaginary itinerary and am free to do as I please. But I have one last order of business to conduct with these gentlemen before I say goodbye to them for good. It's a definite risk to bring it up, but the other options are even more dangerous. I have thought about it long and hard, and my instinct tells me that these guys are my best bet. Besides, they seem to believe and trust me up to this point. I shall not let on too much, however. And, as always, money is the force-10 wind at my disposal.

"Well, gentlemen, thank you so much for your help and

hospitality, but there is one last favour I would like to ask of you before I leave you to your work. That is if you don't mind, of course."

"We're here to serve, sir," the nameless guard says to me, sounding formidably sincere. I smile at his use of the English word "sir".

"Well, actually it's advice I'm looking for. You must understand, I'm not really the kind of person to take risks, and I know I have taken a large one just coming here, despite what the travel brochures say." It's clear by their expressions that they're not about to lead me into any false notions. "So, I wish for your advice on whether or not I'd be better off in my travels if I were to carry a gun with me." I search their countenances for any sign of suspicion or disbelief. Finding none, I continue, "If you think I would be safer with one then, I wonder, could you tell me where I might find such a thing? Of course I'm willing to pay the appropriate price to all concerned."

As I expected, their eyes spark up at the mention of money. Then, as naturally and calmly as if he were a salesman by profession and not an immigration officer, Miguel pipes up. "Well, señor, I must instruct you that to carry a gun in this country is illegal. *But,* between you and me only, I would tell you that it would be a very good idea to have a gun if you plan to travel in my country. I tell you, if either of us were in your shoes, there is no way we would undertake the trip you speak of without one."

That is exactly the response I was hoping for, but again I feel the unease of a plan unfolding too perfectly. I also know that in reality it would be exceedingly idiotic of me to carry a gun while travelling around Guatemala. These guys just want to make money off me, and that's fine with me. I pretend to ponder what he has just told me.

"Do you know your way around a gun?" asks the other guard.

"Oh, sure, I was in the army for a couple of years," I lie.

"Canada has an army, you say?" Miguel asks, sounding shocked, and I can't quite decide if he's joking or not.

"Of course!" I reply, as though his comment were preposterous.

He considers for a moment then tells me, "I can get you exactly what you need."

I'm told to wait, and they both exit the building and pile into the time-ravaged Jeep. I watch their bodies jerk and sway like dummies as the truck bounces over the bumps and ruts in the road. I use the time to go see Len, who is tied up behind the office. I feel a definite pang of guilt as he jumps all over me, licking my face with his extremely moist tongue. "I'm sorry, old boy. I guess I should have told you to pack your summer coat." He'll shed soon enough, and he seems perfectly healthy, so I'm not too worried about him. "So I see these guys have decided to let you off the hook on the old quarantine business, eh? Don't worry, boy. I'm sure your new owner is going to take real good care of you, better than I can now anyway, I'm afraid." We play around together, until ten minutes later I see the Jeep come storming up the road and skid to a stop in the dirt in front of the office.

"Come inside," says Miguel, stepping off the Jeep and motioning for me to follow him. Entering the office, he again takes the seat behind the desk, and I adopt the other. Len's new dad remains outside. "Now, first of all, tell me again why you want this gun," he says very formally. I take it as a good sign that he seems to be treating this business somewhat seriously—I wouldn't want to buy a gun from someone acting otherwise. As I speak, he stares at me intently, as though trying to decide once and for all whether or not I'm presenting myself honestly.

"I just don't want to end up lynched or kidnapped without at least putting up some kind of fight," I tell him.

He narrows his eyes and looks at me a few moments longer, then turns his gaze out the window. Still looking out the window he says, "Okay then. I hope you're being honest with me. It would not be smart to lie." Turning back to face me, he leans into the table, placing his forearms on it and clasping his hands together with eyes staring into mine. "I mean what I say." I nod confidently, despite feeling the slightest bit nervous now. "I must warn you as well that if you get caught with this, you will be in very big trouble. The police will assume you're a drug dealer…or worse. Keep it hidden and hidden well, all the time. You don't look like a threat, so the police will not bother you too much. And of course, don't even dream of using it unless you truly have no choice. And this is the most important of all the things I will say: if it's found, you will under no circumstances, regardless of consequences, tell where you got this gun. You seem like a good guy, and I like you, but that my friend, would be the biggest mistake you could make. Do you understand?" This last phrase he says in English.

I am calm and steady. "I understand one hundred per cent," I give back, also in English. "Nothing will ever come back to you. Other than me, for my boat that is," I add, trying to lighten the tension. "You can even have the gun back then," I offer.

Another moment of silence passes, then he places a small handgun heavily on the table between us. His face loosens its grave expression. "Here it is, perfect for you—a genuine Colt. Of course you know the name. It's American-made and very reliable, small and light, and easily hidden. Well, there certainly are smaller guns available, but you wouldn't catch me trusting my life to any of them." I have had all but no experience with guns, and as I pick it up, I'm amazed by how solid and heavy it feels. Holding it in my hands, I feel a range of emotions wash over me; most notably, there is a feeling of arrival.

It looks to be of fine craftsmanship, like an expensive boat or car part. I don't want to stir his suspicions by making it too obvious that I'm enthralled by the gun, or that I've never even held one before, so I try my hardest to look as though I'm not afraid of it. Turning it over, keeping my finger well clear of the trigger, I pretend to give it a cursory inspection. "Colt Defender" is etched along the machined barrel, and the cold steel is a deep grey colour. It looks straight out of a movie, though about a thousand times more menacing in person. I feel afraid, but there is an unmistakeable feeling of strength and empowerment that comes from holding it in my hands.

"So, have you ever seen that model before?" he asks.

"No. Actually, I don't have much experience with handguns, only rifles really," I answer. He reaches over, and I relinquish it, but find myself mesmerized, unable to take my eyes off it.

"It's very simple really," he tells me. "This here is the safety, which you're going to keep on all the time, of course. And this is the magazine," he says, pressing a button near the trigger and ejecting it from the bottom of the handle about a centimetre. Pulling it out, he shows it to me and tells me, "It'll hold seven, and one in the chamber." He reaches under the table once again and produces a box of ammunition. Opening it, he removes some cartridges and shows me how to feed them into the magazine. It makes me think of the old Pez dispensers I used to have as a kid. I loved how neatly and precisely the little rectangular candies would load into the body. It seemed incredibly sophisticated for such a cheap toy. Finished loading it, he inserts the magazine back into the handle and locks it into place with the palm of his left hand.

"You load the first cartridge into the chamber by sliding the top of the gun towards you. And now you make sure that you have the safety on and never point it at anything that you don't want to put a big hole through."

He hands it to me again, and if it felt dangerous before, it feels positively alive with possibilities now. It's even heavier with the cartridges in it and commands a deadly air. Before it was just a piece of formed steel screwed and riveted together, now it has life, as though the insertion of the bullets was its conception. From potential to reality. Taking it back, he shows me how to remove the cartridge from the chamber and directs me to put it back in the magazine and load it again. The ammunition is gold coloured, with a lead tip and a chrome segment at the rear. I notice the small circle that compresses under the hammer, causing the gunpowder to explode and propel the bullet forward. The cartridges themselves seem even scarier than the gun.

After successfully performing my task, he takes the gun from me and places it between us on the table once again.

"So how much money are we talking here?" I ask.

"How much ammunition do you want?"

"I think the seven will do just fine."

"Are you sure about that? You don't want to run out?"

"I'm not planning on fighting a war," I say. "Hell, if I'm firing it at all, I'm probably dead anyway."

"Okay then," he says, and again turns to stare out the window. After some consideration, without looking at me, he tells me, "I think seven hundred and fifty dollars U.S. is more than fair."

I change my expression to one of surprise and let out a whistle. It doesn't matter to me how much it costs, but I can't let him know that. "Are you serious? I had no idea," I mutter.

"Look. señor, this is a quality gun, and you certainly are getting a good deal."

"Oh, I'm sure the price is fine, it's just…well I didn't expect it to be nearly so high. How about a rental price?" I offer.

"Hmmm, rental, huh? Are you sure you're coming back?"

"Well, if I don't, you can have my boat. How's that for a deal?"

"Hmmm, all right, six hundred dollars. But if you fire it, you must buy it," he says with an air of finality.

"All right, it's a deal," I say and reach across the table to shake hands with him. "I think I've got about that much on me now." I find the money and give it to him. His eyes glow as he takes the bundle of bills and begins to slowly count them.

"Well then, my friend, it's yours, and remember, be damn careful and don't show it to anyone, no one, not even trying to impress the chiquitas," he says, winking.

"I don't need a gun for that," I joke as he hands it to me.

"You put this in the bottom of that bag, and don't even look at it. Put it somewhere better as soon as you can."

"Oh, there's just one more thing," I say. "I need a vehicle too."

He's obviously more than happy to make money off me but jokes anyway, "Are you going to ask for a house next? We have work to do, you know."

"Oh, really?" I say.

LAND HO!

Namsos, Norway: My Past

I really knew she was the girl for me when she tried to tell me that there was a proper way to install a roll of toilet paper. One morning I had put a new roll in the dispenser, as usual unconcerned with what direction it would unwind in. When I went back later in the afternoon, I noticed that it was rolling off the front. I was certain that when I had installed it in the morning, it happened to be rolling off the back. Had someone actually turned it around? Who could possibly be anal enough?

My curiosity got the better of me, and I asked Kira if she had changed it. She was embarrassed and wouldn't admit to it at first, but gave in eventually. She explained that with the paper coming off the top, it was less likely to get caught in the "no man's land" between the roll and the wall. I teased and laughed at her, of course—she had actually changed the direction of the toilet roll to suit her taste. At first I thought it was so cute, but the more I thought about it, the more I realized that it told me a lot about who she was. It didn't matter how mundane the scenario was, it's that it mattered to her. She noticed that God is in the details and took the time to set them right.

~~~~~

His appearance is not what I'd expected, though truth be told, I'd

had a hard time imagining him at all. He's of average height—
maybe five ten—and quite skinny, but with a large round belly
that looks out of place on such a small frame, all the more so as
he walks with it jutting out in front of him as though perfectly
content to be led around by it. A mop of dark hair suffused
with grey clings to his head like an afterthought. A typically
Latin moustache adorns his upper lip but does nothing to
draw attention away from his large, bloated lower lip, ripe and
puffy and mottled with thin, blue veins, like a large uncooked
sausage. His dark eyes are set wide apart and deep in their
sockets, giving them an air of distance, as though they're trying
to shy away from the world and hide themselves within him, as
they should.

He sat alone all night, sharing only the constant
companionship of his drink. There was, however, a steady
stream of people approaching to engage him in pleasantries
and casual banter, always in an overly friendly and pitifully
obsequious manner. For most of these people, his demeanour
was the same, a forced pleasantness lacking any pretence of
sincerity. For some, however, he could not even manage that,
and it was all he could do to make eye contact. His glance found
its way to myself a few times, as it did the middle-aged French
couple sitting at the corner table with a couple of locals. Each
time his wandering eyes met mine, I forced a smile to my lips
and held his gaze long enough to internalize those eyes, those
hateful eyes, sullen and seeming to swirl like the dark drain hole
of a bathtub sucking up the universe whole.

I tried not to stare too much, but it was difficult not to. Here
before me was the man I had travelled all these miles over land
and sea to see. Now that I have seen him, it's all I can do to
remain calm and in control of my urges. And now, crouching
in the dark tangle of plants and trees across the road from his
home, I am a wild animal on the hunt. His house is not small,
but not as large as I had gathered it would be either. For an

ex-army colonel and current plantation owner, I had expected more stateliness. Perhaps all his money goes into bribes and payoffs now.

Turning onto the road, I direct myself back to my own, more meagre quarters. A thirty-minute walk later, I'm in my room, lying on the bed. I'm floating. My body is numb, and my senses do not want to work properly any longer. They don't like what I'm feeding them, or where I'm leading them. The room is spinning, and my stomach is nauseated. I must have sleep.

~~~~~

Free will, have we decided where we sit relative to that particular fence? For a topic that has such ramifications for how we live our lives and interact with each other, it amazes me it doesn't get more airtime. What if we do not have it, what if we're simply a product of our hardwiring and our upbringing? Perhaps self-awareness is only that, it gives us the illusion of free will, but not necessarily the thing itself. Do you believe that each and every one of us is a prime mover? Do you believe that we are not an effect, that each of us is a cause in and of ourselves? Is there not a paradox here whereby we live in a cause and effect universe, but we present each of ourselves as being an individual cause? What happened to the effect, where did it disappear?

The courts have found ways to decide whether a person is responsible or not. Like the age at which a person can drink or operate a car, they have drawn a line in the sand of the mind and said that all of us on this side are responsible, and all of you on that side are not. I don't mean to make it sound so arbitrary, but it is what it is. For practical reasons there must be a line, so there it sits.

Imagining that we don't have free will, how should we punish people for behaving contrary to the social contract that we all signed involuntarily through the very act of being born? My own answer would be that despite what we know about free will, laws must exist and punishment for acting contrary to those laws must continue to be meted out.

The real problem with a punishment, rather than prevention based law system, is that it's inevitably unequal in its application. We have all heard the saying that the only difference between guilt and innocence is a good lawyer. Well, you can simplify the idea by replacing the words "good lawyer", with the word "money". In any country in the world, if you have money you are far less likely to be found responsible for your crimes than someone without. This can come about through various means ranging from quality of lawyers and political leverage, to bribes and payoffs.

Whatever do we do? What can we do? I once read a book where a hypothetical scenario was offered for the most equitable way to design a set of laws for society: you choose five or ten willing people and lock them up in a room until they reach a consensus on a set of laws. That sounds difficult, but there is one crucial caveat: once they finally reach consensus, at that exact moment, they will all fall over dead. They would have been working with the knowledge that after dying, each will be reincarnated at random according to the current distribution of socio-economic and racial status. The idea is that they would have chosen a law system that would be equitable for all because in a sense, once they signed up for the task, they essentially became the ideal of an "everyman", as they had gained equal probability of becoming any one of us. It's the ultimate empathy scenario, you become everyone and all at once you understand how it feels to stand in everyone else's shoes. And ideally you begin to care. Or perhaps it's just self-interest, but whatever the motivation, the end result is the same—a system of laws meant to be equitable for all. Nothing less than a miracle. That's all we're looking for.

~~~~~

After watching his house for the last six nights, I feel comfortable with the situation. It couldn't be more perfect. The night I saw him at the bar seems to be an anomaly, as he has not been back since. A couple of times he's left for extended periods in his beige Range Rover, going who knows where—inspecting the plantation perhaps—but both times he returned before the sun went down. He has had only one visitor, and that was only for half an hour before supper yesterday, most likely business related. His schedule is not overly predictable during the day but at night it seems to be infinitely so. Most of the time he's inside the house doing nothing really: watching satellite TV or reading. Three days ago he came out with a rifle, and for one frightful moment I was certain he had spotted me, but he went into the yard, set up some wine bottles, and practised his shooting. I can say that his marksmanship is pretty good, though I would bet that it's suffered since his army days. Seeing him with his gun was, however, a strong reminder that I had best remember how dangerous he is. I'm not at all afraid, but I don't want to mess things up.

In the evening he usually makes himself supper around six p.m., which is about the same time he starts drinking. From then on he has a drink in hand continuously throughout the night. He starts off with red wine then moves on to the hard stuff, the exact type I have not been able to discern. At any rate, he's invariably drunk by ten and asleep by eleven. I'm able to observe all this, as the house is covered in windows, which are always open on account of the oppressive heat. A few times he has come out onto the porch and sat drinking outside. The bottom line is that he seems to be a solitary alcoholic, which could not be more perfect for me. There is however one sticky point that takes the form of an armed guard.

This guard lives in a small guesthouse in the backyard and

basically sleeps all day then sits watch on the front porch all night from ten p.m. I have never seen them exchange more than thirty seconds' worth of words. Throughout the night he passes his time by reading, pacing and sleeping. I can say that Señor Penadoros is definitely not getting his money's worth.

The location of the house itself is convenient, a thirty-minute walk from town on a small road that continues on past his house, to where I don't know. I've yet to see another person out here other than the one guest and the guard. The house is set about fifty metres off the road in a cleared area surrounded by forest. The front door is left wide open all night while the guard is on duty. There is a paved driveway describing a half circle in front of the house, and a large two-car garage off to the side where he usually keeps his truck. The guard's old half-ton sits outside, and I've never seen the other half of the garage open. I have yet to work out a definite plan, but I'm confident that it will all work out in the end. It has to.

MERMAID

Namsos, Norway: My Past

"Kira...please don't, don't cry, please..." How can I possibly be doing this to her? Both of us wonder. "Kira?" Her face cradled in her hands, she won't look at me. All I can see is her chin protruding between her small wrists.

"We'll just try it and see how it turns out," I say softly. "Please, say something," I plead.

"I can't say anything. What the hell can I say?" she stutters, and I wonder the same thing myself. Reaching for her wrists, I pull them toward me, and she resists at first, but eventually gives way to me, revealing herself, eyes still closed, haloed in red. Tears stream down her face and fall off, creating damp patches on her blue sweatshirt. A moment later she stands up and declares, "I can hear it in your voice—do you think I'm a fool? Tell me the fucking truth! You don't want to be with me!"

Now it's my turn to be silent.

"A job offer with the *Globe and Mail*? You haven't even been looking for a job! They must really need writers! What? Did a bunch of writers get killed in the field covering some economic summit or something?" Each phrase is interrupted as she sniffles and dries the tears from her face with her sleeve. "I'm not going to beg you to stay, but I want the truth, that's all."

I look at her for a moment and manage to answer pitifully, "It is the truth." Seeing her this way, knowing that I am the cause of her distress, I have never, not even once in my entire life, come close to feeling this dismal, this much hate for myself. I want to leap over to the drawer, grab the sharpest knife in there and pass the cold blade through my frozen heart.

"So that's it? You want to go back to Canada and take this job and leave me in Africa, is that it? And you want to stay in touch? Where did this *come* from?" she says, then looks up at me. "I can't believe this, you want to leave me. We were going to get married! You quit your job to follow me here. You turned your entire life upside down! You...you changed everything." These last words she whispers, staring at the floor. She hides her face behind her hands once again, rocking ever so slightly back and forth. I feel hot tears flow down my own cheeks and drip onto my own shirt. I kneel at her feet and once again pry her hands from her face, holding them in mine. She turns her head away from me. I squeeze her hands hard, wanting desperately to put her soul at ease but knowing that by my very own words, I have forever robbed myself of that ability. I try anyway.

"Kira, look at me. Kira, please." A moment later, her moist eyelashes part, and she is looking into my eyes, penetrating my soul.

"You say you know I'm lying, well tell me, am I lying when I say this—I love you more than anyone I have ever known, more than any idea, more than any blade of grass or mountain, more than my own self. You're the only thing in the world that matters to me. If you were to die right now, I would join you by my own hand. You *have* to believe me, Kira."

"Then *why*? I don't understand!"

"Because of all those things, Kira. Because of the truth of all those things, I have to do this." I'm not lying in all this, but I am avoiding the greatest truth.

"I can't live like that! You know that. I need definites," she implores. "Either I'm with you or I'm...without you."

The house is dead silent. Time no longer moves for us. We

are teetering on the edge of a world, and to let go of even a word will tip the balance in a manner we are not prepared to commit to. I am deathly afraid and uncertain, but at the very least I'm stubbornly determined.

"I have to do this," I whisper at last, plunging us into oblivion. And with that she is falling away. It's as though she's shrinking into herself. Lifelessness takes over her body, her face, her eyes. She removes herself from my hands and sits unmoving, as though turned to stone. An eternity passes.

"I think you had better go now," she says in an empty voice, the voice of a woman who's been pushed too far and can never come back. I feel haunted by the gravity of the words and immediately want to take it all back, but know that I never can, it can never be the same. Once you've pulled the trigger, you can never put the bullet back into the gun. Knowing it's useless to say anything else, I take only the time necessary to find my wallet and passport and leave her house with only the shirt on my back. It will be a long cold walk to the train station, but for both our sanities, I dare not stay a second longer. Walking down the drive, feeling the damp gusts of salty ocean air chill me to the bone, I am too afraid to look back, not even one glance. But there is no longer any reason to look forward either.

~~~~~

Have you ever really stared into a mirror, the way you sometimes fixate on a person's reflection in the window of a train? Dwell on those eyebrows, ponder the hard line of the jaw, philosophize about those emerging wrinkles. Penetrate your own eyes. Do you know that person you are staring at, or is it a stranger, a transient, a wanderer without a name? Do you feel comfortable staring yourself down? What a feeling to realize you are a stranger to yourself. You shrink from your own image, looking away from yourself. And it all.

~~~~~

It's a throng, an army, a swarm of entities, a formless, directionless machine of destruction. In the swirling, teeming mass, vague outlines—of fish, birds, squirrels, maybe that's a deer there, here is a skunk, and over there are the writhing forms of snakes. Filling in the interstices are countless, tiny, flapping wings of mosquitoes, horse and houseflies, dragonflies, black and fruit flies, moths and beetles and cockroaches. And amongst all these are microscopic fungi and bacteria and viruses and God knows what else. It's a teeming hurricane of life, or better yet, death.

These are the things I am responsible for killing in my years of life on this planet. All ceased their sentient existences on account of my carelessness, my malice. They swirl and gyrate down the city street toward me. The shrill sound of a million hacksaws cutting into steel piping resonates within my skull. The echo tears apart my brain and destroys my sanity. It's the sound of inherent evil, a hundred decibels of red-hot revenge. It sucks in my screams and spits them back at me. People on the street are running to get away but are caught and disappear behind expressions of tragedy and the dark mass.

I know why these people must die; it's my fault. This death cloud exists because I made it; it's my masterpiece. It's out to consume life and limb, dreams and destinies, love and desire, me. I killed so it kills, and it wants me. But it doesn't want just me—it wants all life, every last breath. As it bears down on me, I know it's pointless to resist. The closer it gets, the more I notice fine details on its surface, the tiny veins and hairs and a million single and compound eyes, all focused on me. They pull me in with the gravity of their combined stares. It's fifty metres away from me now, and a scalding heat scorches the skin of my face. I smell smoke and burning flesh as my clothing catches fire. The last thing I see fills me with such horror and morbid dread that my heart constricts in pained palpitations before I feel it explode inside me. My breathing stops as my vision drowns in crimson.

Awakening suddenly from my tortured sleep, I leap out of my bed and scramble over to the corner, holding my legs in my arms and burying my face in my knees. My skin feels like it's melting into the sweaty, searing air that surrounds me. My breathing is laboured and my heart rate surges. In my eyes still remains the afterimage of Kira's emaciated, jaundiced face, leering at me.

~~~~~

I'm soaked through to my skin, and it feels good. It helps me get even further inside of my animalistic, base nature where all reckoning ends. One plus one equals two and that's all I know; it's all I want to know. I'm a cat waiting to pounce. The pounding rain is a godsend, obscuring the sounds I make. Reaching again for the gun, I feel its chill and am comforted. My hands are beginning to cramp. I have been clutching this baseball bat for hours, as though it's my only hold on reality. Something solid.

Penadoros's bedroom light went out four hours ago, and if he is true to form, he will sleep straight through the night, the sound-sleep of a drunk. The guard has been dozing off and on for the last hour and a half. He usually awakens every fifteen minutes or so, looks around disinterestedly, and slumps back down into a consistent slumber, for another fifteen minutes. It's as though he long ago decided that this was all that was required of him, and he's very proficient at his limited task. As I crouch in the jungle at its nearest point to the clearing of the yard, it is another one of those awakenings that I'm waiting for.

Two minutes later, his body tenses, and he surprises himself awake once again. He doesn't even open his eyes fully this time. Raising his left hand to scratch his right cheek, he relieves the itch, and his body once again becomes still. Making sure everything is attached to me that needs to be, I move through the dense greenery until I'm directly alongside the house. I leave the wet embrace of the trees and sprint through the open until I'm consumed by the shadow of the house. My bare feet make only a minimum of noise that is easily masked by the beating rain.

This is the riskiest part of the whole plan. From here the guard is out of my sight. If he wakes up while I'm creeping up along the front of the house, he will surely see me and all is lost. This thought makes my already racing heart skip a beat. I hug the wall of the house and reach the front stairs having made no noise. Thank you, rain. Peeking up onto the porch, I see his idle body, still asleep. Scurrying over to the far side of the stairs I take a deep breath and place my right foot on the bottom step, weighting it slightly. Feeling no give, I step up completely, and there is no noise other than the rain hammering onto the house and vegetation. Next step same thing, then the same again. As I make my painfully slow way up the stairs, I'm staring into the guard's face the whole time. He is angled such that his head faces me directly, all it would take is for him to open his eyes a sliver and…

By the time I've crested the final stair, I'm burning up and feel as though I'm going to have a heart attack. How absurd that would be. He is but three feet from me now, and I need move no further. It seems a miracle that he cannot sense me standing so near, but not the slightest ripple disturbs this still pond. I plant my feet and raise the bat, holding it like I would if I were preparing to receive a pitch. Holding it at its furthest extension, I pause.

This is it, the absolute moment; the point that sometimes comes in a person's life when they are called to real action, where their entire life and existence alters; the world becomes a new one. On the other side of this, I will be changed forever, and there will be no way back. The line is drawn in the sand, and if I don't hurry, the wind may blow me over it before I have the chance to step over voluntarily. I thought this would all come mechanically, that my fight-or-flight impulse would take over, and I would simply be along for the ride. If anything though, my entire involuntary response system has decided to flee in fear. I must force through sheer willpower every muscle contraction, every breath.

Cramming one final gasp of humid air deep into my lungs, I leap the chasm. With a highly complex sound—like a slap and a thud smothering a crack—the kinetic force of my controlled swing is transferred from the bat to the guard's skull. I want to close my eyes but dare not take the chance. His head rolls foreward. I wait to see what happens. Nothing does. On his forhead where the bat made contact, there is a small breakage of the skin. A trickle of blood winds its way out, each drop hesitating a moment on his chin, then, unable to hold on any longer, falls to the darkness below. The sight of the blood comes as a shock, but the fact that it continues to flow is a good sign.

For the moment my body is still cooperating with my brain and continues to follow orders. I reach for his right arm to check his pulse, and a tremble passes through my body as I make contact with his skin. I imagine that his soul has just passed into mine. I worry that I will pass out, and as I fail to feel any trace of life under his skin, I think I truly will explode. I reposition my fingers a few times, hoping desperately that I have simply missed it. Finally I feel it, the echo of his determined heart, still forcing blood through his veins. The wave of relief that rushes over me is enough to make me sick, and leaning over the railing, in a series of painful retches, I proceed to empty my stomach.

I did not want to kill this innocent man, but I had to make sure that no mistakes were made. I had to hit him hard enough to make sure he'd be out for a good long time. I hope that he'll wake with nothing more than a bad headache. If I had failed to subdue this man, it would have all been over, everything. If I had killed him, it would have all been over as well, just in a different way.

Recovering quickly, I refuse to let myself dwell in the moment any longer. Taking the roll of duct tape from my bag, I carefully place a piece of tape over his mouth. Then I press another piece firmly over the cut to try and stem the blood. It isn't bleeding too hard, and there's no chance of him dying of blood loss, but better safe than sorry. Next, I bind his hands behind his back then secure his feet by taping his ankles and knees together. Once this is done, I lift him out of the chair, and pulling him along by his armpits, drag him down the stairs and into the backyard. Finding the nearest tree, I prop him up against it, then wrap the tape around his torso and the tree. Surveying the scene, I feel content that there's no way he's going anywhere. I relax a bit now as the most dangerous part is over, and from here it should be relatively smooth sailing. But there's no time to waste.

I pull the gun out of the bag and proceed back toward the house with a new confidence. The fact that at this crucial stage I'm not having any second thoughts or nagging doubts fills me with bravery and courage. I am doing the right thing. I quickly make my way back to the front of the house and up the stairs to the front door. I gently pull it open. It gives easily, and I move into the eerie silence of the house. Closing the door behind me and leaving the lights off, I make my way toward the staircase.

I can hear my heart vibrating the bones of my ribcage, and I fear it will betray my presence. The rain can still be heard but is muffled now, sounding as though it's happening in another world. Compared to outside, it's deadly silent in here, and the atmosphere is claustrophobic. I feel as though I'm walking through a mausoleum, the musty smell doing nothing to spoil this image. The air is so thick, I feel as though I am wading through water. I can feel the withered touch of ghosts clutching at me and trying to drag me under, weighing down my feet like concrete. I force myself to continue up the stairs. A few steps later, I'm once again focussed and composed, all systems checked and functioning at optimal capacity.

The plush carpet of the stairs feels like heaven on my feet, which have been standing around on roots and foliage for the last five hours. At the top of the staircase I can see the darkness of the door to his room at the end of the hall. Once I get through that door, it's all over. This is the last of the danger. Reaching the door, I lean my ear against it, first ensuring to take up the slack in the jam so as not to rattle it. To hear snoring would be a comfort, but I must settle for silence. Standing here I'm filled with images from movies where the door explodes in a shotgun blast, or the guard I left for dead miraculously appears from out of nowhere to spray me with bullets. After all, who really knows who was cast as the bad guy? Everyone thinks it's the other guy, but it has to be someone, why not me? The things you think about when standing on the threshold of your destiny.

Like a wrecking ball, a thought hits me: what if there is a lock on the door? Jesus, I didn't even think of that. Why wouldn't there be a lock on the door? If I were this guy, I would certainly have a lock on my bedroom door. I'm afraid to try the knob for fear that I will not like what I feel; as long as uncertainty exists, it remains possible that it's not locked. After a few moments in which I take another listen, I try the knob, and my short-tempered side tries desperately to convince me into a screaming fit. It's locked.

Stay calm, calm the fuck down! All my natural reactions in this situation—screaming, yelling, and kicking the wall—would be disastrous. I only narrowly manage to resist them. How the hell could I be so fucking stupid? Pulling my flashlight out of my shorts, I direct it at the doorknob and twist the head slowly. A trace of light comes out and reveals a brass ball with a small hole in the centre. Immediately the panicked madness is sucked out of my head and swirls into the black hole in the doorknob. I again want to scream out. Could it really be this simple?

Trying not to get too excited, I pull out my Swiss army knife and kiss the sky for the fact that the bone-coloured plastic toothpick is still in its proper place. I stick it into the hole, feeling for the protruding surface, and there it is. Clasping the knob with my left hand I press on the toothpick and rotate the knob, which does not resist this time. Pushing lightly on the door and feeling the beautiful lack of resistance, I shake my head and assume that I indeed must be the good guy.

Opening the door enough for my head to squeeze through, I peer in, and the faint light coming in through the windows illuminates the form of a body in the bed. One bare leg protrudes from the thin sheet that covers the rest of Señor Penadoros. It's all over. Stepping confidently now, I enter the room and take in the dim surroundings. I can see little more than the bed and the bedside table, upon which rests a lamp, an open book lying spreadeagled on its pages, and a small handgun. This sight checks my confidence somewhat, but I reason that the weapon you can see is much safer than the weapon you can't. I walk over to it, and keeping my eyes on the back of his sleeping head, pick up the gun and place it under his bed. My own gun in my right hand, I stand over him, still as a stone, a tableau of human culpability. There he is, laid out before me as though on a platter, such a sorrowfully vulnerable state. How did we humans ever get so far when we're all so ill-adapted to handle physical aggression in the absence of the tools we've invented? Of course, I'm thankful for this now, as I have a tool and he does not, a microcosm of society as a whole, except the one to one ratio is an unfair representation of the truth.

Surveying the full layout of his body, the position of each limb, I map out my attack. All measurements made, I steel my resolve and leap onto the bed. A second later I'm sitting on the side of his stomach between his hip and rib cage, his left arm pinned underneath me, his right trapped under his own body. Gun pressed firmly against his temple, I scream, "Don't move a fucking muscle, or I'll blow you're fucking head off! Don't fucking move!"

THE ODYSSEY

Toronto, Canada: My Past

It's been a boring day—the kind that asks you to tell it why it is exactly that you're doing what you are, instead of what you really wish. It's cold and brisk, late winter, and now that the bright sun has departed for places over the horizon, it feels ten times colder and reminds me of how much I hate winter in the city. The offices are quiet now; most of my co-workers have gone home for the day, or are out on stories. I don't mind working here most days of the week, but not today for some reason. I think I'll buy a bottle of wine to have with dinner tonight and maybe play my guitar awhile. It's been too long.

There's nothing interesting in these updates, just the usual car crashes and cuts in transfer payments to social programs, drug busts and calls to step down, mega mergers and missing persons. Working for a newspaper, spending the majority of your waking life dealing with the news, unable to ignore the external world and all its misery, forces you to come up with some interesting coping mechanisms. At least, that's what I hear. I myself have been unable to come up with any effective strategies of my own. I think someday I'll just remove myself from society for good, go live in the forest with no TV, no radio, no newspapers, and just leave the world to its own devices. I'll simply concern myself with the birds and the soil and the trees, nothing more and nothing less. I don't think I can handle a full

lifetime of being around so many human beings.
Suddenly, my life ends.

*Associated Press, 02/17 Juan Joaquim Penadoros, ex-Corporal
of the Guatemalan National Police, voluntarily retired after
signing of Peace Accord 12/31/96, has yet to be brought up on
charges for the rape and murder of a Norwegian aid worker last
year. The body of Kira Evi-May Andersson, 28, was found last
May in a ditch outside of Champerico, Guatemala. An autopsy
provided proof of rape. Despite eyewitness testimony, Penadoros
remains free, and Guatemalan police officials state they have
no plans to charge or arrest him. Residents have joined with
NGOs and the Norwegian government in calling for justice in
the case, but as yet the judicial system has been reluctant to act.
Sources say that such problems are endemic in post-peace accord
Guatemala, where high-ranking army and government officials
regularly use their wealth to influence criminal investigations.*
  Andrew Adams, AP

It can't be, there's no… Clenching the paper in my fist, I rush
to my cubicle and read it again. The name—Kira Andersson, Kira
Andersson, Kira… Kira, no, God no! I try desperately to turn
off my brain—just stop it! But something in my heart refuses to
allow me the benefit of ignorance or denial. I look again at the
date, and I understand clearly. I know it's her; there can be no
question. It's her, she's gone; I feel it. I've known all along. I'm
floating in space, watching the earth recede into the distance,
smaller and smaller, farther and farther. There is nothing left but
emptiness, nowhere left to go, nothing left to hope or dream. I
want to lash out, steal back time and deny physics, but I may as
well not even exist. I am no longer part of this world.

I run out of the office and push open the door to the stairs,
running three at a time down the twenty-two flights. I'm nearly
hyperventilating by the time I run through the lobby and the

rotating doors out onto Front Street and the awaiting cold winds. Where do I go? What do I do? I'm quite literally going insane, my mind is spiralling viciously out of control. All lines have been severed. Looking one last time at the crumpled paper still in my hand, I turn north and start to run again.

Somewhere over the Atlantic Ocean: My Past

The hot rays of the sun warm my face and provide bright illumination for the curvaceous plumes of cotton batten clouds thousands of feet below me, but I can find no beauty or divinity in the sight. I sit here in ignominy and finish the fourth Scotch the flight attendant has grudgingly provided me with. Since turning my back on Kira and her misery, my being is no longer capable of feeling; for the sake of survival my brain has decided to force that facility out of business. There are still some boxes to be taken away, but soon enough the space will be vacant and peace will reign supreme. A desirable state of affairs really, no news is good news and emptiness has its privileges.

~~~~~

Penadoros is securely tied to the last chair he will ever sit in. Thanks to the weeks of sailing, I can now tie the fisherman's bend with my eyes closed. No matter how he clenched his muscles while I tied him, he's not getting out of this.

The rain is still pouring, and thankfully the grey sun is still another four hours away—more than enough time. We're enclosed in the shelter of the garage, just the rapist and I. I feel a permanent nausea in my stomach, which only gets worse when I let my brain wander into the territory of imagining what this man did to Kira, the only good in my world.

~~~~~

Do we ever really know anyone? Is such a thing possible? Myself for example, no one would have guessed I was capable of doing what I'm doing here. How does a person go from being an everyday Joe to a killer? Perhaps it was in me all along, and I simply never acted on my urges. Perhaps. But I must say I would never have thought myself capable of these things either. We are our own greatest mystery. Perhaps you go through life thinking you would never be able to kill anyone, but how can you know for sure? Certain events occur, things happen, and you find that you're a new person, a derivative. I suppose this is our common bond, our human-ness—our transience.

~~~~~

I have not gagged him. I want him to be an active participant in what shall transpire from here on. He is not saying anything at all, but I can see real fear in his eyes. He probably thinks I'm crazy.

"Certain things, once they're done, can never be forgotten by the people they're done to." I take out the picture of Kira and I together in New York, holding it up to his face. He closes his eyes and turns away from the image as though it were a red-hot poker, trying to hide from his own shame. "That's right you worthless nothing, this was the only girl I ever loved, the only girl I will ever love. The only girl I could ever love." I'm unable to hold back the tears any longer. "I put her on a pedestal, she was my everything. Fuck, I even refused to be with her because I, I..." I punch his face. With everything I've got. I want to pull his jaw right out of his sickening head, but I don't want him to die yet, not by a mile. He hangs his head limp, and I can see blood trickling down from his exploded sausage lip. A moment later he spits on the floor, and I hear a clicking sound that I assume to be a tooth. I like the pain my hand has become.

"We have to stop things like you from happening. It's our duty as a species to stop these things from happening. It's the only way we can save ourselves. People can only forgive so much. If you had never existed, never done what you did, I might have been who I was instead of who I am, which is a monster. I know that, and you better know that, and you better know that I'm going to rid the world of you."

With that he turns his gaze to meet my eyes and looking at me for a moment, he opens his mouth as if to say something, but decides in the end to remain silent.

Moving over to him, I press the muzzle of the gun against his teeth until he opens his mouth, and I force the barrel into the fetid cavity, holding it there. Tears are streaming down his cheeks and he is mumbling something now. Each tear I see makes me even more furious, even more nauseated.

"Those tears should be for Kira!" I yell at him. "There are no tears anywhere for you. Even your mother in heaven has dry eyes! Your duty, the only thing you can contribute is your death. You've been corrupted and spoiled. I don't even blame you, you couldn't help it, you're only human. But I can't help this either—you drove me to it. If you can't see the logic at work here, then you deserve to die all the more."

Removing the gun from his mouth I ask him, "How many people have you killed?" No answer. I punch his face again, infuriated. "Tell me!"

"I…I don't know. Why are you doing this, please, stop!" I punch him again.

"Don't you ask me a goddamn thing! Now tell me! Dead man! How many people have you killed?" My emotions are on a rollercoaster ride. One moment I want to tear his heart out and burn it, the next minute I want to beg for mercy.

"I'm telling you, I don't know!" he yells. I have to struggle to understand him, as he is breathless and his words are smothering in the blood that drips from his mouth. Looking into his eyes once again, I want to cry out in anguish for us all as I realize the truth. He really does not know.

"How do you do it? How do you just kill a person, a brother, a sister, a mother…a person exactly like yourself, without even feeling it?" Again I receive no reply. "Tell me!" I shout again, needing to know how a monster operates, desperate to understand, desperate to keep my mind together. "Tell me, goddamn it!" I scream, hitting him again.

He whimpers, and stutters, "Oh, God, please stop, just stop."

I put the gun in his mouth again, enraged. "Is that what Kira said when you were raping her!" There are no words. I don't even want to kill him any more. I want to torture him for the rest of eternity and make him pay for what he did. If every one of his screams brought back even one single atom of Kira, I would punish and torture him until she was whole again, in my arms. I want to see this disaster of a man face his demons.

"Do you realize I sailed all the way here from Canada? Fifty days on the water just to do this to you. I gave up my job, my life, everything, just to be here with you, just to kill you and make you pay. You will pay for what you did. Do you have any idea how much beauty you took out of the world? You brought me here, you made me do it." His eyes are closed now, and he is not moving. "Open your eyes!" I slap him but get no response. "Open your eyes, you goddamn fuck, OPEN THEM!" He does. "Now look at me. Look at me!"

Once he does so, I take Kira's letter out of my pocket, the one she left me in the New York hotel room, and proceed to read it to him, translating as I go. The voice of the dead. While I read, he cries a steady stream of tears. "And then here she is, this work of art, in your country trying to help your brothers and sisters, the ones you and the rest of you fucked over, and you violate her in the most evil and vile manner conceivable, stealing her dignity and then her life! You, You!" I hit him across the face with the gun this time, as my hand is too sore to use any longer, and I feel the give in his jaw as it separates from his skull. He still makes no sound, only crying and whimpering, and at this moment, I know beyond a shadow of a doubt that he did it. *He did it.*

As I stare into his eyes, those evil, guilty eyes, my own vision blurs, and the surrounding flesh and bone reconfigures itself and soon Penadoros is gone. In his place is the silver-haired man.

"Go away!" I scream in desperate, frantic horror. "You have no right! This is mine! Mine!"

"Are you sure you want to do this? It's not too late to stop," he says in his infernally calm voice that makes me want to turn the gun on myself.

"I told you. Jesus! Yes, all right, here I am, a gun in my fucking swollen hand, answering your question—YES I AM FUCKING SURE I WANT TO KILL THIS MAN, I WANT TO DESTROY HIM, I WANT HIM ERASED FROM THE SURFACE OF THIS PLANET, I WANT TO SEE HIS BODY TORN TO SHREDS BY A PACK OF FUCKING WOLVES!" I almost black out from the exertion of yelling so hard.

"All I can say is that I think what—"

"Get the fuck out! You have no right to keep doing this to me."

"But you know that by doing this you are no better than he is."

"I never said I was better than *anyone!*"

"All right, do what you must, but know and remember that I will always love you—"

"Yeah fucking yeah—"

"—son."

This last word cuts into me like a straight razor—not the meaning, but the delivery. The tone, the timbre, the intonation is so familiar from years ago, so many years ago. And now that I reflect, I notice other things as well, a cascade of associations. But looking at him again, I see he is gone and Penadoros is back.

He is looking at me with an expression of mortal fear in his eyes, as though he is looking at a madman.

Perhaps sensing it is his last hope, he begins to plead with me through his broken jaw. "Listen to me, please you must listen to me…please, I did not do it, I did not do it!" He has the nerve to slur these mendacious words at me. Such a useless, see-through, desperate plea, condescending. I can take no more.

"Say goodbye. This is it, you cheap man, you worthless, rotten, cheap man! I despise you." I take my rigging knife from my back pocket and feel around his chest and ribs for the right place. "I see right through you. Don't say another word." His desperate pleading is all mumbles and tears now as he bucks and squirms, but he can go nowhere. Locating the proper point I place the tip of the blade there, pushing it in enough to break the skin and keep the place marked.

"Remember what you did to her as you feel this knife in your heart. Remember how you violated her and what you destroyed." He lets out an otherworldly death scream as I push forward on the knife with all my strength, surprised at how effortlessly it slices into his body. As it sinks fully into him, the handle obstructed by his ribs, I can feel a slight tremor transmitted through the hilt as his heart, which it has just cut into, empties of blood and performs its last panicked contractions. Every muscle in his body is rigid, the veins in his neck strain against the quivering skin that contains them, as they rush the last few drops of blood to his dying brain.

His eyes register a combination of emotions so uncommonly seen that I am at a loss to catalogue them. It's as though his life is indeed passing before his eyes, and he is reliving all at once the joy and pain and suffering of his human experience. Though my face is only inches away from his and I'm looking straight into his terrified eyes, he is not looking at me, but through me, as though his vision has already made the jump to the next dimension. Soon the trembling of his body subsides, but his eyes remain wide open. I hope that as a final punishment he is forced to relive his act over and over, realizing the evil now, but unable even to blink, for an eternity.

EPILOGUE

It's been a peaceful flight, both externally and internally. Even though I know Kira would be appalled at me, I'm content knowing that I stayed true to my love for her. It all seems like a dream now—what happened to her, and what I have done. But more than that, our time together seems like another lifetime, like a metaphysical conception of perfection, seemingly unreachable. But I know I was there. Maybe it was another lifetime. Maybe the instant familiarity we felt is because we're two halves of one soul, destined to live out an endless cycle of life and death and truth. A nice thought. It reminds me of a night that might have been long ago.

I had been out drinking with some friends and was in a daze, feeling extremely tired and weary. In my room I put on some music and sat at my desk, staring at a poster hanging on the wall in front of me. My eyes delved into it, a photograph of some unnamed mountain in some unknown range, unknown only because I could not tear my eyes or mind away from the image to seek the information I had never sought before. It was a jagged peak bathed in a pink morning glow, with perfect white clouds endearing themselves to it like cats rubbing against your bare legs. For some reason I could not dissociate my own being from the image in the photo. I became one with it, I became that mountain, wholly and completely, I became a realization of nature. I took up my position in that fantastically beautiful place on top of the world. Above it all at last, I was transported, I touched heaven, the pink encompassed me, warming me. I glowed. I shone. I bathed in radiance. I was illumination. To the core of my being, I was warmth and love and compassion. I could see it all. It all came together. Every plane of thought met and merged on that peak upon which I stood. And I was transformed into oneness with the earth, as though I had been struck by the combined electricity of six billion thoughts and melded whole into the rock. I hope that's what the end is like.

~~~~~

I didn't realize it—I mean, I didn't exactly have a timeline or schedule set up, but by some twist of fate my date of arrival here is May seventeenth. You may not know it, but this is the day on which Norway celebrates the signing of its constitution in 1814. Everyone is dressed in traditional costume, primary colours assault my eyes from every direction and red, blue, and white flags wave from every hand. It makes me feel happy. It's so easy to picture Kira here, amongst these people celebrating joyously. And I imagine that she is in fact here and maybe, just maybe, she has noticed my dark hair among all the light and has come to walk with me.

Perhaps she has been with me the whole way, through the narrow streets of the small town and out through the countryside to this small cemetery behind this ancient stone church overlooking the ocean. And perhaps she is standing beside me now as I read her gravestone. The words are in Norwegian, but if I had ever harboured any doubt, the name carved in stone, Kira Evi-May Andersson, is the period on the end of two lives.

"Kira, if you can hear me, you know what a leap of faith it is for me to be trying to talk to you right now. But that's what you mean to me. I…I'm so sorry…for everything. I want you to know that I love you... I just, I couldn't bear the thought of hurting you, hurting us...I know. Excuses...I was afraid, simply, deathly, afraid. Afraid of the pain that I thought must inevitably accompany such perfect happiness. I never intended...I know you know I loved you. LOVE you. How could you not? I'm so proud of you, you are my life, you know. It was all about you, before I ever even met you, ever since I was young, it was always about you."

My eyes wet, I fall on my knees and onto my chest, arms outstretched, hugging the cold grass, trying to give it shape, a form that I can hold, consume, become. "You know I could never live with myself after this. I don't deserve to live. I will see you soon. God, I hope so, please let it be. I can't wait any longer. You are my everything. I love you, Kira. I love you. I love you. I love..."

British Columbia, Canada: My Past

"Excuse me, Mr. Mailman, sir. Could we please have your spare elastics?"

"Well, I don't know, son, these are expensive pieces of equipment, you know."

"Oh, I know. And we really appreciate your generosity. Really, we do."

"Well...all right, here you go then," he says, handing us nine elastics.

"Thank you so much, sir. We'll see you again tomorrow, eh?" I say over my shoulder as we mount our bikes and head toward the bush.

Reaching the tree, we take the nine elastics and carefully attach them to our contraption. This is a flying machine we're making, and someday it will work. Right now though, even with today's elastics, it won't even hold my weight. I feel sorry for Joel, he's bigger than me and will have to wait even longer, but his turn will come. It's frustrating having to wait, but we'll keep adding to it, adding the pieces until it will hold us. Then we'll add even more, until we can really use it to fly. I know it sounds hard to believe, but eventually we'll overcome gravity and be airborne, just like the birds, weightless and free. Free to grab the highest branches, free to grab the air and the clouds, free to grab life.

~~~~~

...and now I leave to hopefully say hello once more. To you who have found this testament, know that there is always a choice.

Acknowledgements

Thanks to all my friends, family and teachers who helped make this book what it is. Specifically, thanks to Kirsti Tasala, Katherine, Susan and Pauline Rodriguez, Holly Sharpe, Scott Allan, Robin Erickson, Kevin McParland, Len Wallis, Ted Richardson, Theo Risoe, Greg Genco, Saiko Fujibayashi, Miyako Ide, Shizuyo Kaneko, Atsuko Kuwahara, and Dr. Richard Berg. Thanks also to my publisher, Sylvia McConnell, and my editor, Allister Thompson, without whom this book would not be in your hands, and certainly not in such fine form.

And finally, thanks to all those who have ever stood up for justice and decency—without you there would be no inspiration.

jp Rodriguez grew up in Thunder Bay, Ontario. He studied in Thunder Bay, Vancouver and Toronto, eventually ending up with a teaching degree. He spent five years in Tokyo, and that experience greatly influenced him and his work.

After two years in London and a lot of travelling, he returned to Thunder Bay to study social work. He currently works in that field.

He has written and published many short stories. *The Space Between* is his first novel.